This Book Belongs
To William L. (?) Morse.

BY NOEL BEHN
THE KREMLIN LETTER

THE
SHADOWBOXER

NOEL BEHN

SIMON AND SCHUSTER · NEW YORK

TO LEE

CONTENTS

United States to Quit World War II in 90 Days

Exposure of Secret Anglo-Russian Treachery Reason for Withdrawal

Special to GPG

WASHINGTON, —— 1944—President Roosevelt announced today that the United States can no longer tolerate the illegal Russo-English mandate of unconditional surrender imposed upon the innocent people of Germany and that under the right circumstances his government was to withdraw its military forces from the European theater of war as early as 90 days from today.

The President states that this historic move was prompted by information just received exposing a secret Anglo-Russian pact to deliberately obscure and withhold the true facts concerning the outbreak and continuation of hostilities with the Third Reich as a subterfuge to lure and keep the United States in the war.

The President proclaimed that from this day forward he and his government were anxious and willing to enter into meaningful peace negotiations with any National Socialist or Wehrmacht officials other than Hitler, Goering, Bormann, Goebbels, Himmler, von Ribbentrop and Keitel.

Mr. Roosevelt expressed confidence that such negotiators would organize themselves along democratic representational government lines. He further announced the formation of a blue-ribbon panel and a secret survey to assure that the right of German citizens would be protected by the selection of approved representatives.

Washington rumors indicate such talk secretly began in Sweden late yesterday.

—Lead story from the *German Popular Gazette*, printed 2 January 1944, for release 1 May 1944

PROLOGUE

The Intruder

THE INTRUDER eased back into the shadows, his filth-crusted prison uniform melting into the dark. Tower II's search beam swung down, swept along the gray wooden façade of the windowless barracks, rose and disappeared into the midnight drizzle. He glanced around the side of the building. The patrol was crossing the roll-call yard. He tapped twice against the wall, then once more. Three tiers of boarding were pushed forward near the rooftop. Unseen arms lowered Martin Vetter through the opening. His scrawny form hung suspended for a moment. On the fourth tap he was dropped to the ground.

The intruder jerked Vetter to his feet, pushed him back against the building and again peered out into the yard. The guards were gone. Vetter's teeth began to chatter. The intruder slapped him sharply, then pulled him toward the corner.

Tower V's searchlight scanned the row of barracks opposite. Darkness was restored. The intruder pointed to the brick kitchen buildings at the far end of the roll-call field and shoved Vetter forward. The tattered figure ran frantically over the frozen mud, reached the cooks' billet and ducked behind it.

The intruder whistled silently to himself, his body spread-eagled against the wall, and waited. The Tower II light arced down and sped past. He dashed into the open, his bony legs pumping desperately as he zigzagged in a running crouch. His unshod toe caught a pothole. He stumbled sidewise, flailed his arms, partially regained balance, spun, staggered and pitched face down into an ice-flaked puddle. He jammed the side of his hand into his mouth and bit down until his breathing became regular. The hand withdrew. He wiped the mud from his eyes and blinked. The building was fifteen yards away. He lifted his head. The Tower V light was streaking toward him. Swallowing hard, he lay motionless. The glaring beam missed him by inches. He rose and scrambled forward on all fours.

Vetter sat huddled beside the locked garbage stall. The intruder motioned him to the chimney, felt along the base, found the right spot, pushed his fingers into the warm clay and began digging until he exhumed a pair of dirt-laden pliers.

The two men crawled along the rear of the second cooks' billet. The smell of soup and meat was distinct; the laughter from within, unnerving. The intruder pointed. Vetter was shivering, his head remained lowered. His companion jabbed him in the ribs and again indicated a direction. Vetter gazed up at the string of shielded light bulbs illuminating the west fence thirty yards beyond. He stared numbly at the thick, close lines of barbed wire rising twelve feet high on concrete columns which arched inward at the top. His eyes trailed down the barrier to the left, to the guard tower standing high above the junction of the west and north fences, to Tower II. A black-helmeted SS guard leaned casually against the Spandau machine gun mounted on the outside platform. Another guard could be seen standing in the booth behind. A third operated the revolving search-light on the roof deck. Vetter tried not to look to his right, to Tower I at the southwest corner of the enclosure, but he did. The structure was distant, but three guards were visible.

Martin Vetter had not cried for eight years, not since the last day of interrogation, not since he had been led from the city hall, paraded into the square, stripped of his mayoral robes and chain and proclaimed a traitor—not since he had entered a camp. Now tears flooded his eyes again.

"Let me go back," he whimpered.

The intruder continued staring out at the woods beyond the fence.

"Let me go back. I can't do it. It's impossible. The wires are electrified. We'll never—"

One hand clamped over Vetter's mouth, the other behind his neck, the intruder drew Vetter's head close to his lips. "Listen, comrade," he whispered, "Kuprov himself is out there. He's in the trees, waiting. So are the others from the old Kerensky Circle. They haven't forgotten you, comrade. They've come all the way from the Soviet, from Mother Russia, just to help *you*. Think about that, comrade, think about it. We can't let Kuprov down, can we?"

14

The drizzle turned to rain. The cooks' laughter grew louder, more drunken. Vetter lay clutching his scrawny arms to his chest. He tried to control the trembling, fought to restrain the chattering teeth; struggled to regain confidence. He mustn't disappoint Kuprov, he told himself. Kuprov was an important man now. A soldier. A general who had won many victories. Kuprov had taken the time to seek him out, to contact him, to arrange the escape.

No. He could not let Kuprov down. But why couldn't they have given him more time? Why couldn't the escape have taken place a week from tonight, as the messages had first stated? Vetter began trembling more violently than ever.

The cooks broke into raucous song.

Of course he was still important, Vetter repeated to himself. Why else would Kuprov leave the battlefield? Why else would Kuprov take the risk of coming halfway across Germany? Martin Vetter was still important. What other German Communist had ever won a Bavarian election with such a majority? What other German Communist had such a following that the National Socialists had waited three full years before arresting him? These were not facts to be forgotten, he told himself. He must still have a following somewhere.

His companion motioned. The two men crawled forward and stopped beside the locked iron potato shed. The singing was still audible behind them.

Vetter began to wonder what it would be like in Russia, whether he would be sent to Moscow. Then he saw the lights flicker. Along the south fence, the string of light bulbs dimmed, blazed bright, dimmed again and went out. The north and west lines plunged into darkness. Vetter looked to his right, to his left, over his shoulder. The guard towers were also dark. He started to rise. The intruder pulled him down.

Shouts could be heard. A match flared briefly in Tower II. The wick was lit. The flame grew stronger. Soon all the tower houses were illuminated by kerosene lanterns. Vetter tried to rush forward. Again he was restrained.

His trembling returned. Perspiration beaded his face. The fence bulbs glowed a faint orange, then lit up as brightly as before. Vetter knew the emergency electrical system was operative—they had missed their chance. He did not know if he was relieved or disappointed.

Vetter saw the flash before he heard the explosion. His head jerked to the side in time to see the guardhouse on Tower II rise slowly a full two feet from the platform and shatter into flame. A second explosion spun his head to the right. Tower I was ablaze and collapsing. More noise came from the direction of the south fence. Two additional explosions were followed by three in quick succession. The line of electric bulbs flickered. A moment later the entire camp went dark. Flames were the only source of light. Hand sirens began to sound. The cooks had stopped their singing.

The intruder pulled Vetter to his feet. They raced through the rain, leaped into the "death strip" ditch, scrambled up the fifteen-yard incline and dove to the foot of the fence. More explosions could be heard on the opposite side of the compound.

The intruder snipped the barbed wire and bent the strands back. Vetter scurried through the opening, turned and waited.

"I won't be joining you, comrade," the intruder said quietly.

"But—"

"You'll see a light coming from the woods in a moment. Head straight for it. You'll find white rags tied to the trees. Follow them. They'll mark your way to the truck."

"You *have* to come. I can't make it alone."

"I would like to, comrade, believe me I would like to—but I can't. Kuprov's orders. He's waiting for you in the truck. Look, there's the signal. Hurry."

Vetter stared at his companion. He could see the guard patrols in the background. He turned slowly to the forest and gazed across the void. A light flashed twice. He began running.

Vetter fell against a tree with a white rag tied to a lower limb and fought for breath. He glanced back at the camp. Five guard towers were aflame. He stumbled into the woods. The rags were distinct, the path easily followed. He pushed through a thicket. A truck stood waiting. He dashed toward it. It began to move. He jumped onto the

16

runningboard and scrambled into the cab. He had never before seen the man behind the wheel.

"Where is Kuprov?" Vetter demanded. "Why isn't Kuprov here? Kuprov was—" He did not have to look down to know a knife was pressing against his ribs.

"Keep it quiet and mind your manners," Erik Spangler said gently, "and everything will be all right."

The exterior guard was alerted within seconds of the explosions. Patrols fanned out and took prearranged emergency positions. The truck was spotted bouncing wildly along a hill crest. Machine guns and light artillery were ready. The barrage was accurate. The vehicle disintegrated in the glare of exploding gasoline.

PART ONE

The

Webber Proposition

I

WASHINGTON, D.C.,——1944—U. S. Senate investigators today stated that British claims of German bombing damage to London and other major cities had been greatly exaggerated.

The investigators found that most English cities, including London, were generally unharmed and that what little damage there was had been limited strictly to strategic military targets.

The investigators lauded the skill and humanity of Luftwaffe personnel in sparing innocent civilians—especially in light of the Royal Air Force's policy of saturation bombing of German cities.

—Article from the *German Popular Gazette,* printed 17 January 1944, for release no sooner than 25 April 1944

CHRONOLOGY OF EVENTS
(C.O.E.)
(Revised 15 January 1944)

Date	Investigator	Location	Event
8 Feb 1942	WVHA	Ebansee CC	Believed to have freed prisoner A. Goulston.
17 Feb 1942	WVHA	Flossenburg CC	Believed to have freed prisoner S. Briggle.

Date	Investigator	Location	Event
26 Feb 1942	WVHA	Neuengamme CC	Believed to have freed prisoner L. Harmon. (Note: Goulston, Briggle, Harmon all Catholic priests. This is only incidence of occupational pattern among escaped prisoners.)
14 Mar 1942	TK	Papenburg CC	Believed to have freed prisoner D. Goodman.
27 Mar 1942	TK	Natviller CC	Believed to have freed prisoner R. Kamlot.
7 Apr 1942	TK	Romainville CC	Believed to have freed prisoner F. Nicole.
11 Apr 1942	TK	Gusen CC	Believed to have freed prisoner R. Steenberg.
23 Apr 1942	TK-WVHA	Mauthausen CC	Believed to have freed prisoner D. Rissner.
23 Apr 1942	Gestapo	Mauthausen CC	Believed to have murdered Mauthausen guard A. Foshko. (Note: Foshko on exterior patrol at time of Rissner's escape. Foshko was strangled with a belt. First recorded death associated with SPANGLER.)
8 Jun 1942	Gestapo	Ebansee CC	Believed to have freed prisoner J. Brandaman.
17 Jun 1942	Gestapo	Bergen-Belsen CC	Believed to have freed prisoner H. Lipsitz.
5 Oct 1942	Gestapo	Prinz-Albrecht-Strasse P	Believed to have murdered prisoner H. Tramont. (Note: Tramont first and only person captured who could give positive physical description of SPANGLER. Tramont part of SPANGLER apparatus. Tramont's neck

Date	Investigator	Location	Event
			snapped backward before desired information could be extracted.)
6 Oct 1942	Gestapo	Gestapo Command, Berlin	Believed to have murdered Gestapo agent R. G. Benke. (Note: Benke main interrogator of prisoner Tramont. Benke found dead in own office. Vicious and prolonged beating had been inflicted. Death incurred by neck being snapped forward.)
26 Dec 1942	Gestapo	Ebansee CC	Believed to have freed prisoner L. Scarrone.
23 Mar 1943	Gestapo	Dachau CC	Believed to have freed prisoner P. Witt.
5 Apr 1943	Gestapo-KRIPO	Buchenwald CC	Believed to have murdered prisoner P. Rosen. (Note: First incident of SPANGLER killing CC prisoner. Rosen found 1.8 miles from Buchenwald with neck snapped backward.)
5 Apr 1943	KRIPO	Buchenwald CC	Believed to have murdered Buchenwald guards S. Kasten and P. V. Zeisler. (Note: Kasten and Zeisler found near Rosen's body. Both had necks snapped forward.)
26 Aug 1943	KRIPO	Sachsenhausen CC	Believed to have freed prisoner L. Melnik.
12 Oct 1943	KRIPO	Compiègne CC	Believed to have murdered prisoner S. Kahn. (Note: Kahn, an SS informant, was found three miles from Compiègne CC

Date	Investigator	Location	Event
			with neck snapped backward.)
12 Oct 1943	KRIPO	Compiègne CC	Believed to have murdered KRIPO security officer M. Rakin. (Note: Rakin had set up SPANGLER trap using Kahn. Rakin found in office with neck snapped forward.)
17 Nov 1943	KRIPO-SD	Breendonck CC	Believed to have freed prisoner M. Marmur.
20 Nov 1943	KRIPO-SD	Theresienstadt CC	Believed to have murdered prisoner I. Mandelbaum.
20 Nov 1943	KRIPO-SD	Theresienstadt CC	Believed to have murdered KRIPO-SD Colonel M. V. Korda. (Note: Korda set SPANGLER trap, using Mandelbaum. Mandelbaum found in barracks with neck snapped backward. Korda also disemboweled.)
9 Jan 1944	SD-AUSLAND	Gusen CC	Believed to have freed prisoner M. Vetter.

SS Standartenfuehrer Helmuth Webber, SD-Ausland, turned back to the first page of the Chronology of Events, began jotting down the dates of the events and rearranging them in columns. Webber flipped closed the worn cover of the three-inch-thick "Spangler Dossier," pushed it aside and glanced at his aide.

"We will be bringing the prisoner with us," he announced.

"Yes, Herr Standartenfuehrer."

"And make certain he's well treated."

"Yes, Herr Standartenfuehrer."

Webber waited for the door to close before glancing down at the columns again. His smile was hesitant; the first snicker, perfunctory.

Helmuth Webber was a dour, intractable man, a German far removed from frivolity. Now his laughter grew so intense he had to grip the edge of the Biedemeier table for stability. He was near convulsion when von Schleiben's steward entered the compartment. The confused attendant waited a full forty seconds before Webber gained control.

"Herr Standartenfuehrer," the steward finally managed to say, "your bath is ready."

"My what?" the colonel asked breathlessly.

"Your bath, Herr Standartenfuehrer. It's drawn."

Again laughter erupted. Webber rose weakly. "Why the devil not?" he rasped, slapping the startled attendant on the back. "Why shouldn't we all take a bath?" He followed the red-liveried steward through the private railroad car.

Von Schleiben's "Chariot" was legendary throughout the Reich. Everyone knew it had been a personal gift from Hermann Goering, who, as everyone also knew, had requisitioned it from a nameless French financier. But could a Frenchman's taste meet the standards of von Schleiben? The risk of comparison had been avoided deftly. Heinrich Himmler led the way. His SS had provided the funds for reconversion, while Himmler himself had donated the mahogany-paneled conference room with its blue velvet chairs, thick blue carpeting, Viennese chandeliers and priceless Biedemeier table. KRIPO, the State Criminal Police, and SIPO, the Reich's Security Police, had banded together and contributed the communications room. The all-metal galley had been provided by ABWEHR, German Military Intelligence.

It was the Gestapo which made the most expansive and calculated gesture for the comfort and favor of SS Obergruppenfuehrer von Schleiben—the salon.

All six Gestapo sections gave, and gave generously. One result was a bedroom reverberating in reds. The carved walnut four-poster boasted burgundy silk sheets, magenta cashmere blankets and a claret satin canopy. The walls were upholstered in scarlet velvet, which blended perfectly with the five-ply carpet.

It was with the bathroom that the Gestapo had hoped to outdo itself—and outshine its competitors. Carrara marble, ivory white with slight bleedings of pink, covered wall, ceiling and floor. The sunken rose-marble tub was adorned with golden spouts, golden drain top and five solid-gold faucets. Two of the handles controlled bath water, two the shower, and the fifth steam. With the flick of von Schleiben's wrist the marble room could be converted into a steam bath.

WVHA, the camp security group, had reached into its meager coffers and managed to have the exterior of the Chariot sprayed a rich vermilion.

The reason for all this concern and expense was a much-discussed secret: as director of the Council for Extreme Security, Hugo Thomas von Schleiben was one of the most powerful men in the Third Reich's maze of police and intelligence networks. Every major organization was only too eager to contribute to the general's private transportation.

It surprised no one and delighted all that the Chariot became von Schleiben's most prized and guarded possession. No one but the general himself and the maintenance staff had ever set foot, let alone ridden, in the vermilion railroad car.

Now, for the first time without von Schleiben aboard, the Chariot had been dispatched to the Belgian border for just one purpose: to transport Helmuth Webber, a mere colonel, back to Munich. The trip was classified Reich top secret.

The washcloth steamed. Webber held it tight to his face. He preferred Berlin water. You could always wash better in it. It improved your skin. Lather spread. Von Schleiben's gold straight razor, a gift from Heinrich Mueller of the Frontier Police, deftly sliced away the two-day stubble. He replaced the monocle over his left eye. The triptych mirrors were wiped clear of steam. Webber examined the three-quarter profile of aquiline nose, sunken cheek, arched forehead and thin lips.

"You know, dear fellow," he confided to his triple image, "it was there all the time. Just waiting there, right in front of them—but *we* were the only ones to see it. *We* were the only ones to make sense of it."

26

Helmuth Webber was a member of SD-Ausland, one of Germany's most elite and effective foreign-intelligence services. Seldom, if ever, did SD-Ausland demean itself with problems of a domestic nature, such as concentration-camp security.

Escapes from concentration camps were a different matter. Even though the basic jurisdiction for such events fell to WVHA or, in more critical instances, to the Gestapo, there was always the possibility that some Allied operation had penetrated the Reich's borders and had brought out not only prisoners, but information as well. Information concerning camp activities was a rather sensitive issue among Reich officials. Thus, SD-Ausland had always kept a watchful, though semiofficial, eye on these situations. As the incidence of assisted escapes began to accelerate, SD-Ausland had become more directly involved.

Webber slid into the hot water. The wall table was lowered over him, and a tray bearing gold dishes and a bottle of Dom Perignon champagne was set down. The covers were lifted. Malossol caviar. A *vol-au-vent*. Real butter. He began eating.

```
. . . ensuing confusion caused by explosions and subsequent
blackout (second power failure), prisoner Vetter escaped from
the compound through a hole cut in de-electrified west fence
and fled to wooded area half kilometer beyond.  Escape took
place at approximately 0100 hours 9 January 1944.
    (NOTE: Vetter is believed to have had one or more accomplices
    to this point. Investigation now in progress.)
On reaching tree line Vetter followed series of cloth markers
which led him to truck believed to be driven by SPANGLER.
    Tire tracks reveal truck followed a northwesterly route
across open field, turned due west along goat path and con-
tinued on path until reaching stream.  Truck followed along
stream bank in southerly direction for 2.2 kilometers, crossed
at shallow point, turned due east, skirted wheat field and
started parallel along hillside.
    At this juncture Exterior Guard Patrol (EGP) VII spotted
vehicle and radio-reported its position.  EGPs IV and XI moved
into area and deployed.  Patrols commenced firing, overturn-
ing and destroying truck.
```

Webber was a patient and meticulous researcher. His initial approach to the camp escape situation was simply to review every conceivable bit of information available. The Spangler file had been of no particular interest on first reading. Webber had noted, however, that no physical identification of Spangler had ever been made— even after the Gestapo had reported him dead.

What had attracted Webber from the outset was the Rag Man situation. Assassins were his hobby, but one who went to the trouble of freeing camp prisoners only to murder them later was even more intriguing. He had asked von Schleiben for jurisdiction over the case. It had been granted, in spite of Gestapo's objections. Now, less than two months later, he had stumbled upon the solution, had found the key.

Webber restrained a smile as he visualized the faces of other officers—especially Platt of Gestapo—when he announced his findings at the emergency Council meeting. He could see Platt blanch, then turn red, when he learned that not only were Spangler and Rag Man one and the same, but so were Tan Man, Willy Tanner and Eric Tannen. How would Platt react to that? What would he do when he realized that five men they had been trying to identify and capture for over two years were really one—that the five tails the Gestapo had been chasing all belonged to a single dog? Platt would be stupefied, immobile. And what about the final bit of information? What about the ultimate solution? Would Platt hemorrhage or simply have a coronary?

Webber poured himself another glass of champagne and reconsidered. Why bother with Platt and his Gestapo rabble in the first place? Why bother with any of the agencies at the Council and their petty rivalries? After all, Webber assured himself, I have solved a major case, haven't I? Put it together with remarkable brilliance? Even offered a final solution? What do I need with any of them?

He pondered. Why not release the revised Spangler Dossier immediately? Von Schleiben wouldn't object. Then when the meeting begins, Webber chuckled, toasting himself, I'll let loose with the real fireworks.

Webber dried his hands, placed the Spangler Dossier on the table and adjusted his monocle. He thumbed quickly to the final pages, found the last two reports and began reading.

28

. . . Fuel-tank explosion and ensuing fire prevented guards from approaching vehicle for fifteen minutes. Examination of smoldering remains revealed no persons inside. Vehicle had presumably been unoccupied for most of its journey around wheat field. Steering wheel was found to have been fixed in place by wires, and a charred piece of wood stuck to dashboard is believed to have been used to wedge the throttle. Badly burned clothing found in back of vehicle is believed to be discarded prison uniform of Vetter.

On discovery that vehicle was unoccupied, EGPs sealed off area and instituted intense search. No trace of SPANGLER or Vetter could be found.

General consensus of KRIPO and Gestapo officials is that SPANGLER and Vetter left vehicle at or near stream and set truck off in an easterly direction while they continued on along or in stream in a southerly direction until reaching a heavily wooded area. There is no evidence to substantiate this theory other than the logistics of the situation.

Webber turned a page.

RSHA NO.   AC–14 78–0042 (Summary, SIPO-SD Report
           AC–14 3321–Z, 15 January 1944)
OBJECTIVE: SPANGLER, Erik
ALIASES: TANNEN, Eric
           TANNER, Willy
           TAN MAN
           RAG MAN
RECEIVED: 16 January 1944
FROM: SIPO-SD

On 13 January 1944, at request of Gestapo-L5, SIPO-SD technicians initiated investigation of 9 January 1944 explosions at Concentration Camp Gusen.

Laboratory analysis indicates chemicals used were similar to, if not identical with, LUFTWAFFE Research Center's experimental liquid explosive TDL.

(NOTE: On 18 December 1943, Luftwaffe Research Center reported small quantity of TDL and of TDS—experimental solid-state explosive—lost in transit.)

Technicians believe TDL-like substance was added to kerosene tanks of emergency lanterns used in guard towers during first power failure. This assumption is reinforced by laboratory analysis of wick fragments taken from wreckage. Tests show that usual lantern wicking had been replaced by slow-burning cord fusing which possessed thickness and texture similar to original wicks'. Lighting of these fuses is be-

lieved to have acted as twenty- to thirty-seconds-delay deto-
nator to explosive in fuel tank below.

Investigation revealed camp protocol requires guard-tower
emergency equipment, including lanterns, to be serviced or
alternated in ten-day cycles. Camp records show that all lanterns in destroyed or damaged towers had been replaced on
6 January 1944, three days prior to explosions. Tower IX, the
only structure not to have suffered an explosion, had neg-
lected to exchange its lanterns of 6 January 1944. During
blackouts it lit its aid lantern with no adverse effects.

Examination of maintenance shops which service lanterns
within Concentration Camp Gusen reveals that facilities are
supervised by two Totenkopf guards, but operated by some 150
prisoners on rotating shifts. The particular area in which
lanterns are tended is under no special security and is quite
accessible to personnel other than those assigned to the maintenance shops.

The cause of the first power failure prior to explosions has
not yet been determined.

Investigators disagree with Gestapo reports AC–14 77–418,
establishing time of escape at 0100 hours, 9 January 1944.
Re-interview of guards reveals a tendency to expand explosion
times and general chaos. All technical evidence indicates
electrical system back in operation by 0500 hours 9 January
1944. SIPO-SD analysts believe escape occurred sometime between 2345 and 2355 hours, 8 January 1944.

Webber relaxed. He dried himself, wrapped his rosy body in a
toweling bathrobe and made his way to the bedroom, carrying the
dossier with him. Donning a pair of flaming-red silk pajamas, he
climbed into bed.

A hidden victrola was playing Debussy. He lifted his briefcase onto his lap, snapped open the cover and brought out two folders. To
the right was his plan of capture, the Webber Proposition. To the left
was the evidence he had amassed to argue his case. Both would have
to be presented to the Council the next afternoon. He was tired. A
decision would have to be made. The evidence file was the thinnest.
He put the Webber Proposition back into the case and lowered it to
the floor. He opened the manila envelope and looked down at the
crossword puzzle. The solitary pink shaded night light over his head
was insufficient. He scanned the room in vain for other lamps.

Annoyed, he searched around him for light switches. He finally found a panel on the night table and slid it back. A line of six un-marked buttons lay revealed. He pushed the first.

Debussy stopped. Four amber pin spots beamed down as the night light faded. Two Renoir nudes were illuminated on his right as a Vivaldi record began to play. Webber heard a rustling noise. He looked directly overhead. A horizontal curtain drew back, exposing a full-length mirror attached to the inside of the bed canopy.

He pressed the next button. The room went black. The Vivaldi ended. A moment later it was replaced by war whoops and thundering hooves. Galloping Indians flashed on a screen facing the bed. The camera cut to close-ups of their painted, bloodthirsty faces, then to straining horses' heads, then to a long shot of a stagecoach trailing dust over the Arizona plains, stark in black and white. The savages were drawing closer. Gary Cooper climbed up beside the stage driver, raised his rifle and fired back over his shoulder. A redskin bit the dust. Then another and another. Calmly Gary Cooper reloaded his Winchester and once more began his deadly fire.

The sound went off, but the movie continued. It wasn't, however, the same movie. This one was in color. Three breech-clothed Mongolian-looking savages were tying a girl to a post within a tepee. The girl was obviously a white woman, a blond Brunhilde type with braided hair, her features not unlike Jean Arthur's.

The savages left. The girl struggled at the post. Three more savages entered the tent. They were larger, fiercer, better painted and more Mongolian-looking than their predecessors. One of them whispered something in her ear. She shied away in mortification. Rebuffed, the savage lifted his loincloth and exposed himself. A close-up caught the full terror of her shriek. An even tighter frame magnified the cause of her distress. The camera moved back to catch the full impact of the Indian, now pointing his erect penis in her direction.

It was the second savage's turn to whisper. The girl's eyes opened wide and glazed. She shook her head violently. His hand reached across and ripped open her blouse. The camera moved in close on her more than ample bosom.

The third and most awesome native moved forward. Obviously

the leader of the trio, he did not demean himself with whispers. Legs firmly planted, he pounded on his chest as his wet determined lips shouted their silent demands. The maiden twisted and squirmed in a series of agonized noes. The chief stepped firmly forward and jammed his right hand up her buckskin skirt. The camera darted to her face as the eyeballs rolled to white. She fainted. There was, however, an enigmatic curl to her unconscious lips. A curl slightly upward. The chief stepped back in disgust. Thumped his chest and pointed. Two stark-naked Indian maids, their skin glistening with oil, darted forward and revived the less defiant white woman.

The captive's arms were lashed to a board behind her neck, and she was led out past an assortment of drum beaters, assorted bonfires and random dancers. Again the chief pointed. Even the Indian maidens balked momentarily, then dragged her into the largest of large tents.

The interior was more a circus ring than an Indian sanctum. In the center was a wooden railing about two feet wide and four feet from the ground. The white woman blinked as the chief's face moved into the frame. Nose to nose, he made his final demand. Lips quivered, eyeballs darted from side to side. She spit in his face.

The chief stepped back, gave a placid, knowing native glance and clapped his hands. The two Indian girls dashed from the tent and returned with three more maidens as naked as themselves. With them was a largish pony.

The white woman was led to the rail in the center of the ring. Her head stiffened in defiance as her clothes were ripped off and her hands untied from the board. She was forced to lean over the railing and her outstretched hands were manacled to iron rings in the dirt. A perfectionist, the chief gave another order. A pillow was inserted between the rail and the maiden's stomach, forcing her naked buttocks higher in the air. Two braves grabbed her legs and forced them open; the camera moved as close to the thighs as its optics would allow. The unmistakable fingers of the chief slid up into the victim and began rotating. A cut to the girl's tearful face revealed a certain excitement. Once more the chief shouted his conditions. The upside-down head shook sideways in somewhat regretful defiance.

The chief clapped twice. The pony was trotted around the ring by the naked Indian maids, then brought to a spot where the upsidedown Brunhilde could see the animal clearly. The Indian girls reached down for its genitals and began exciting them manually and orally. The prisoner's eyes opened wider than ever before, in horror and interest.

Webber pushed another button. The movie switched off, and drapes drew across the screen. Two reading spotlights shot down. Webber began examining the crossword puzzles. He started to make notes in the margin until his concentration ebbed. He closed the file and dropped it on the floor. He would arise earlier, he told himself, as he studied the buttons on the night table. He selected the middle one. He had picked correctly. The lights went off and he settled down to sleep. For the first time he was aware of the wheels clicking on the rails below. He lay in the darkness, wondering just where the train was at the moment. He knew Germany could not be too many hours away. But was not all Europe German now? His hand reached out and pushed the bottom button.

The Indian girls were fitting the pony's massive organ into the spread-eagled Brunhilde. A close-up caught every intricacy of the insertion. The camera panned to the anguish and pain on the pretty blond face. The camera trucked back as the Indian maidens pushed the pony back and forth to establish the rhythm. It was a very smart pony. Within seconds he had the idea and was enthusiastically on his own. The camera moved back to the captive's face. She bit her lip. The animal's appetite increased. Her face went from tears to a reluctant smile. The pony's fornication grew more frantic. The girl began to respond. Her buttocks raised high and pressed back, quicker and quicker, in time to the pony. Her face tensed with expectation. Her breathing quickened, her eyes closed, her lips opened, her nipples rose: she screamed. Her climax was obvious and monumental. Then came a second. Then a third.

The chief laughed and gave an order. She was cut loose and dragged to him. Her eroticism could no longer be controlled. She knelt before him and nodded. He repeated his demand. She lifted his loincloth and stared under it. Her mouth opened and took in the offering. Her teeth clamped down. The chief screeched in pain. Then she rushed to the pony, embraced it and reached her hand down for its member.

The action was back to black and white. The sound of beating horses' hooves could still be heard. Gary Cooper hadn't missed yet. The reel ran out. White flashes skitted back and forth. Another movie began. A lion roared. M-G-M's *Little Women* began.

Webber pressed the middle button. Once more the room was in darkness. He settled down between the silk sheets and squirmed to get comfortable. His eyes closed. He wondered what such a pretty girl could see in a pony. Then Webber was asleep.

2

U. S. Fact-finding Panel Clears Goering, Himmler of Nazi Affiliation. Pro-Jewish Attitudes Cited.

—Headline from *German Popular Gazette*,
printed 18 January 1944, for release 9 April 1944

THE HELMETED Bomb Detection Squad began its search with the walls of the fourteenth-century guildhall, then poked behind each burgundy velvet blackout curtain. Everything was inspected: wrought-iron chandeliers and torch stanchions, ventilation ducts, carved-stone fireplace, log supply, mounted spears and crossbows, tapestries, suits of armor. An hour and twelve minutes later the senior search officer pronounced the room "secure."

The doors were unlocked. A dozen white-gloved SS guards marched smartly through the room and deployed. Two more guards moved out onto the pulpit balcony. The combined SD-Ausland and Kripo cryptanalysis team entered and began setting up easels and display charts on the inquiry platform. Six secretaries occupied the benches under the tapestries. The Council stenographer settled in behind her portable desk. Webber and his four aides arranged themselves at the inquiry desks. He snapped open his briefcase and brought out the material. The newly issued 875-page Spangler Dossier was placed to his left, the 32-page orange-covered Webber Proposition, the SD-Ausland–Kripo plan to capture Erik Spangler, was set to his right. Two fat files of presentation material were stacked neatly in front of him. The four permanent members of the Council for Extreme Security entered and took their places at the massive oak conference table. They were followed by six "special" representatives.

The corner door opened. The officers snapped to their feet and froze at attention. It was only the provost. He entered carrying two red velvet goosedown pillows, which he placed on the unoccupied elevated throne chair at the head of the conference table.

Webber took his seat and surveyed the ten Council members. His attention focused momentarily on Platt of Gestapo and then quickly shifted to the Abwehr representative, Otto Zieff.

Under ordinary circumstances Webber's first concern at any Council meeting would be Abwehr. In the past military intelligence had been the traditional foe of all SS and civil police activities. The rivalry between Abwehr chief, Admiral Canaris, and Himmler had been bitter and persistent. Less than two weeks before, on February 14, Himmler had won. Canaris had been forced to resign. The most powerful of Abwehr units had gone under the command of General Walter Schellenberg—the same man who headed SD-Ausland.

Webber had expected Abwehr to become subservient to SD-Ausland; it hadn't. Webber had expected Abwehr to send Comart as today's representative at Council; it hadn't. Why was Zieff here instead of Comart? Would Zieff also try to discredit Webber's presentation? Did Abwehr suddenly want the Spangler case under its jurisdiction? Platt was predictable—he would fall into Webber's predetermined traps. Zieff was a far different matter. You could never tell what he was up to.

Again the corner door opened. Again the officers sprang rigidly to their feet. Ten seconds elapsed. Then another fifteen. The five-foot-

36

four-inch frame of General von Schleiben emerged. His black uniform was flawless, his boots gleamed with an unnatural shine. He crossed the parquet in quick, choppy steps, drove a fist into the goosedown pillows and climbed onto the throne chair.

"Officers," the provost proclaimed, "may now be seated."

Von Schleiben stretched forward, lifted the silver decanter and poured himself a glass of water. He took no notice of the assemblage as he sipped. He began to sniff.

"Air! Fresh air! Why isn't there fresh air?" he demanded.

"But, Herr Obergruppenfuehrer—" the provost began.

"It is a cold, crisp day outside," von Schleiben let it be known. "Little birds are singing. Why must I suffocate?"

The ventilators were switched off, the burgundy curtains drawn back, the Gothic window frames pushed open. Von Schleiben gazed out at a vista of freshly gutted Munich buildings, still smoldering in the bright morning sunlight. The fragrance of smoke and charred wood filtered into the room. The windows were hastily closed and the drapes pulled together. Von Schleiben's fingers snapped.

"Let it be agreed and understood, at forfeiture of life," the provost droned, "that all matters discussed within the confines of this room are now, and shall remain in perpetuity, Reich's Top Secret. Heil Hitler."

"Heil Hitler," the officers replied in chorus.

"Agenda," ordered von Schleiben.

"Presentation of the Webber Proposition," the provost began. "Introduction of—"

"Objection," Platt shouted as he stood.

"Sit down," von Schleiben said without looking up.

"But, Obergruppenfuehrer . . . I—I must object—"

"Then you will object sitting down," von Schleiben snapped, studying his agenda notes. "Have I ordered you to stand?"

"No, Obergruppenfuehrer."

"Then you will sit."

"Certainly, Obergruppenfuehrer," Platt agreed, taking his seat.

"State your objection—briefly."

"Obergruppenfuehrer, Gestapo officially protests the discussion of

37

the Webber Proposition until the revised Spangler Dossier can be authenticated. Herr Webber's plan to capture Spangler appears to be entirely predicated on the dossier's—the SD-Ausland dossier's—contention that not only is Spangler alive, but he is the Rag Man and three other persons as well. What proof is there? On what is this assumption based?"

"The initial assumption," Webber replied, strolling toward the conference table, "is based upon the most elementary deduction, dear Platt. SD-Ausland simply took every recorded incident of assisted escape from concentration camps and compared them all for similarities—something no other organization apparently bothered to do. We immediately isolated twenty men who had never been identified. A comparison of murder techniques and other operandi soon brought the list down to what we have now. It really wasn't that difficult."

"Deduction is theory," Platt shot back. "Where is the proof? Where is tangible evidence?"

Webber slid a notebook across the table to Platt. "This was found in a raid made on a Frankfurt apartment two days after the Vetter escape at Gusen. In it you will see a complete list of all prisoners appearing on the Chronology of Events in the Spangler Dossier—the revised Spangler Dossier.

"Also found in the same apartment were chemical equipment and traces of the experimental explosive TDL—the same TDL that was used in the lanterns at Gusen the night of Vetter's escape."

Platt blanched, then turned red as he studied the list of names. "Obergruppenfuehrer," he finally stammered, "why wasn't Gestapo advised of this discovery?"

"There wasn't time to advise anyone except Obergruppenfuehrer von Schleiben," Webber answered before the General could reply. "We had to prepare our capture plan as well as revise the dossier. But a full report of the event will be sent to you as soon as it is ready."

An aide whispered into Platt's ear. "Obergruppenfuehrer," the Gestapo representative said, "I suggest this meeting be postponed until this notebook and the raid which produced it can be verified.

38

Where did SD-Ausland get the information about this so-called apartment? How do we know that this notebook and its list are authentic? What if they are a plant? Obergruppenfuehrer, this Council cannot consider such a reckless and costly adventure as the Webber Proposition on the evidence of one notebook."

"I quite agree," Webber interjected. "We came across that list a week after we had compiled the revised Spangler Dossier. It only confirmed what we already had *deduced*—that the Gestapo and several other agencies here had been looking for one man under five different names."

"Then prove it!" Platt shouted. "Prove it before we go a step further."

"If you let me present my findings I'm sure everything will fall into place."

"That is not acceptable," Platt yelled, holding up the dossier. "Before anything is considered you must firmly establish that these eight-hundred-odd pages pertain to one man and one man alone."

Webber paused and then smiled at Platt. "SD-Ausland is certainly able and willing to do just that. But since it is our contention that Erik Spangler will attempt his next escape on January 26, seven days from now, we ask only one thing: that the Gestapo accept full responsibility if adequate preparations are not made because of delay at this Council."

"The twenty-sixth?" Platt questioned, turning to his aides. All shook their heads. "Where does it say anything about the intended escape taking place on the twenty-sixth?"

"It doesn't," Webber replied. "My proposition simply states that Spangler will be coming to Concentration Camp Oranienburg to free Hilka Tolan. Now we know that the escape attempt will take place on the twenty-sixth. If this Council allows me to present my material as planned, we will have time enough to capture him. If the Gestapo prefers that I interrupt my presentation to meet their demands, then I feel they must take full responsibility if Spangler is not captured. Well, Herr Platt?"

Platt glowered at Webber. His face grew a deep crimson. A vein in his forehead began to pulsate visibly.

"Standartenfuehrer," Otto Zieff of the Abwehr began, looking at his notes, "am I to understand that SD-Ausland contends that this Erik Spangler is planning an escape on the twenty-sixth of this month?"

"That is our contention."

"On the assumption that the revised Spangler Dossier does represent the case history of one man, not five, I don't seem to find any recorded instance where advance information of this nature was known."

"There is no instance. The date of a Spangler escape has never before been known in advance. *If* I am able to make my presentation, the process by which the date was determined will be clearly illustrated."

"I see," Zieff said, checking his notes once again. "On my reading through your revised dossier one item seems to have eluded me. Never has there been a report of Spangler having freed a female prisoner."

"To my knowledge he never has," Webber stated.

"And what of political prisoners? I seem to find only one instance where he has ever freed a political prisoner."

"He has freed only one political prisoner, Martin Vetter."

"But still SD-Ausland definitely maintains that on the twenty-sixth of this month Spangler will be coming to Oranienburg to effect the escape of Hilka Tolan, a *female political* prisoner?"

"We so maintain," Webber answered confidently.

"Can SD-Ausland substantiate this claim?" asked Zieff.

"We can if I am allowed to make my original presentation."

Von Schleiben folded his arms and leaned back in his chair. "Is your presentation prepared for this session or is more time required?"

"I am prepared at this session, Herr Obergruppenfuehrer."

"Proceed."

Webber walked to the display table, where a tattered newspaper-wrapped package was resting. "An exhibit like this," he explained, "was discovered hidden under the cooks' barracks at Oranienburg less than ten days ago." Webber opened the package and spread the

40

contents—two beets, a turnip, half a bar of ersatz soap and an eroded razor blade—at intervals along the table top. He picked up a wooden pointer and bounced it slowly back and forth among the items. It finally came to rest on the crumpled newspaper wrapping.

He nodded to the cryptologists. An eight-by-four-foot display card was unveiled.

Webber's pointer rapped against the card. "This completed crossword puzzle," he announced, "was found on the newspaper page. It contains a secret message."

Platt of Gestapo motioned for the floor. "By any chance, Herr Standartenfuehrer, is the key for extracting this secret message to be found in the date of the edition, May 25, 1939?"

"It is," Webber conceded.

"Could it conceivably be possible," Platt continued, "that you begin the deciphering by taking May, the fifth month of the year, and looking at either five down or five across?"

"Yes, that is how you begin."

"Bravo!" shouted Platt. "Bravo for Standartenfuehrer Webber and all those brilliantly deductive minds at SD-Ausland! In the months they have been assigned to the Spangler case, they have finally discovered—all by their ingenious selves—what four other agencies have known for better than two years: that crossword puzzles are one of the favorite methods used by camp prisoners for sending covert communications to one another. Bravo again. I suggest we all pause, here and now, to applaud Herr Webber and—"

"Enough," warned von Schleiben.

"Excuse me, Herr Obergruppenfuehrer," Platt gleefully beseeched, "but the idea that we have all rushed to an emergency session only to find that SD-Ausland's momentous discovery is a puzzle-message is too ridiculous to believe. Messages like this have been intercepted and deciphered by the dozens, and never have they had any relationship whatsoever with Spangler's activities."

"Messages like this have most definitely been discovered in the past," Webber agreed, "but they have always been random interceptions. One message here, another there. Never has a series been taken. That is why no sense could be made of them. SD-Ausland has intercepted three in the last ten days, therefore we have continuity—and we know what they mean."

"Wonderful, wonderful," Platt said laughingly. "And would Herr Webber like to tell this Council if this trio of messages have any mark or name on them which would establish that they came from Spangler?"

"The Gestapo is quite right," Webber answered politely. "These secret messages have no establishing name or mark in either message text. We would never have known they had come from Spangler if we hadn't been extremely lucky in finding something at Concentration Camp Gusen."

Webber motioned. The second display card was unveiled.

Koln
9 January

Most considerate Commandant,
Please forgive me for troubling you again about
my son Martin Vetter, who is one of your prisoners,
but as you know from my previous letters I am
gravely ill. The doctors now say the road to
recovery is off beyond all medical hope. I must
prepare to die. Please tell Martin the truck keys are
in the house of his Uncle Alfred. Please tell Martin
Alfred promised he won't drive it, only guard it.
Martin should call Alfred on his release and get it
back. Please, I beg you, might I telephone Martin?
I am ready for death, but hearing his voice would mean
so much.

May God bless you and yours.
Ilse Vetter

c/o Harovatin
38 Hohenzollernring
Koln.

The ankle locks were chained to the brackets imbedded in the pulpit-balcony floor, the wrist irons to the rungs protruding from the wooden railing. The white-gloved guards stepped back. The Council gazed up at the first witness.

"Name?" asked Webber.

"Prisoner L224537."

"Speak louder."

42

"Prisoner L224537," the intruder repeated in a somewhat stronger monotone.

"Prisoner from where?"

"Concentration Camp Gusen."

"Before serving at Gusen had you also been a prisoner at both Bergen-Belsen and Dachau?"

"Yes."

"Are you a member of a secret prisoner society at Gusen?"

"Yes."

"Was the society known as the Weeping Nuns?"

"Yes."

"Were they involved in the Vetter escape?"

"Yes."

"Have you ever seen this letter before?" Webber asked, pointing to the second easel.

"Yes."

"Does it contain a secret message?"

"Yes."

"From whom?"

"The Spangler Group."

"Extract the secret message for us."

". . . Ready . . . telephone call . . . guard house . . . truck off road . . ."

"How was this message deciphered?"

3

THE WAITING LINE for the Prague Industrial Free Clinic began forming in the street at 5 A.M. By dawn it stretched four and a half blocks, and newcomers were sent on their way. Rain started falling at six-thirty. At eight the first four dozen patients were allowed entry to the guarded outer lobby. SS processing was the first stage. Curfew permits, work identification cards, passports, food ration books, work leave-of-absence permits and transportation passes were all inspected, recorded and temporarily confiscated. The group was reassembled and shuttled on to the Medical Processing Section with their clinic permits.

"Name?" asked the Czech volunteer nurse.

"Grebic, Anatol."

"Middle name?"

"No middle name."

The woman looked up into the wide, flat face of deep-set black eyes, thick nose and bushy red mustache. "Every Czech has a middle name."

"This one doesn't."

"No insolence or you'll be sent to the end of the line."

"Forgive me, but I was born without a middle name."

The woman returned to the application form. "Factory?"

"Kulitz Works."

"Position?"

"Foreman, hand-grenade inspection, Division Two."

"Type of permit?"

"Dental."

"Priority?"

"Blue."

"What doctor are you to see?"

"Sadarski."

Sadarski set the alarm clock for nine minutes and began pumping the foot pedal. The drill burrowed into the second molar. He leaned closer to Grebic's ear. "Word has just been received over the Goliath Line," the dentist said softly in Russian. "The Germans believe that Vetter was intercepted by a man named Erik Spangler. This Spangler has been raiding their concentration camps for some time under various aliases, but he's never taken out a political prisoner before."

Sadarski stood up and glanced down the long row of dentists working on their patients. No one was watching. He leaned forward and resumed the drilling. "The Germans had known very little about this Spangler until the Vetter escape. The tighter security around political prisoners seems to have provided their first tangible information. A secret meeting of the Council for Extreme Security was called yesterday to consider it. The session took place in Munich. Von Schleiben presided. Carrol was provost. The four permanent members in attendance were Platt for Gestapo, Zieff for Abwehr, and Frankel and Lenz for Sipo-SD and Kripo respectively. Six alternate delegates were also present—Waffen-SS, Totenkopf, Frontier Police, Alpine Detachment, Luftwaffe Supply and the subcommandant of Oranienburg.

"The evidence on Spangler was presented by an SD-Ausland colonel named Webber—"

The patient pushed the drill away. "What is SD-Ausland doing on a camp case? The camps are under Gestapo jurisdiction."

The drill was replaced by a chisel. "Too many new camps are being built. Too many guards are being called to the front. Escapes are increasing. It is too much for the Gestapo alone. SD-Ausland went on the Spangler case two months ago. Webber was operations chief."

The chisel was set aside, the cavity examined by the mirror explorer. The drill went back into action. "Webber presented the council with a letter addressed to the commandant of Gusen. It was received several days before Vetter's escape. It was supposed to have been written by Vetter's mother, asking permission for something or other. Letters like this are never seen by the commandant, nor are they ever answered. They are read by prisoner secretaries and then burned. Two of these prisoner secretaries were members of the Weeping Nuns, a Catholic secret society at Gusen. The Weeping Nuns were Spangler's contact. The two secretaries and a third Weeping Nun, the man who led Vetter to the fence, were captured shortly after the escape. They appeared as witnesses at the council meeting. They confirmed the SD-Ausland claim that the letter from Vetter's mother contained a secret message. They demonstrated how the message text was extracted from the letter text. Then they—"

Grebic again pulled the hand from his mouth. "How was it done?"

"The key was in the return address on the back of the envelope, in the numeral part of the address," the dentist answered as he drilled. "If the address was 28 Ringstrasse, then the message was made up of the second word in the first line of the letter, the eighth word in the second line, the second word in the third line, the eighth word in the fourth line and so on. If the address began with an even number, then you started with the first line of the letter and worked down. If the address began with an odd number, then you began with the last full line, the bottom line, and worked up. Apparently the letter-to-the-commandant method of communication was used only by Spangler. The two Weeping Nun secretaries identified incoming Spangler mail by the names over the return address. 'Tannen,' 'Heyman,' 'Warwick' and 'Harovatin' meant the letter contained a secret message from Spangler."

The drill was replaced by the chisel. "Testimony at the council stated that the Weeping Nuns found out we were planning to free Vetter—"

46

The dentist's hand was again pulled away. "Were any names given?"

"Yes, comrade. Both 'Kerensky Circle' and 'Kuprov' were mentioned." The mirror explorer and pick began probing the open mouth. "It was the Weeping Nuns who learned we were coming for Vetter. They contacted Spangler, and the intercept was arranged. The witnesses claimed that Spangler, or what they called the Spangler Group, was one of the three outside organizations they had contact with. They had never seen Spangler or any of his organization. They knew nothing about his operation other than that he contacted them through letter-messages. They claimed that Spangler was their only outside contact specializing in escapes. They said that three weeks prior to Vetter's escape they received word from Spangler that he was interested in political prisoners. It was because of this that the Weeping Nuns notified him about our intention to bring out Vetter. The Weeping Nuns killed our man inside Gusen, replaced him with one of their own and convinced Vetter you were waiting for him beyond the fence. The Weeping Nuns claimed they had no part in the explosions of the guard towers. The witnesses stated they had no idea how it had been arranged."

The dentist switched back to the drill. "SD-Ausland was trying to use the Gusen letter to cross-identify a series of secret messages they had intercepted at Oranienburg in the last week and a half. Three messages were found. All were contained in newspaper crossword puzzles like the ones being sold on the camp black market. The puzzles were found in a drop at three-day intervals. SD-Ausland photographed each and returned them to their original hiding place. The messages were in simple cipher and read 'Miss Aïda,' 'Long for Aïda' and 'Alert Aïda.' SD-Ausland cryptologists interpreted these to mean 'Am interested in Aïda,' 'Prepare Aïda' and 'Alert Aïda.' All three messages were smuggled into Political Detention and delivered to Friedrich Tolan's daughter, Hilka. SD-Ausland is certain that Hilka Tolan is Aïda and that Spangler is coming for her."

The patient jerked the drill away. "Is Tolan still alive?"

"I have no idea, comrade," said Sadarski, pushing the bit back into the cavity. "I can only pass on to you what Goliath relayed to

47

me." He pumped on the foot pedal, and the drilling resumed. "The problem with the Aïda messages is that no date for escape was given. Neither was there any identification in the messages' text to prove who they came from. This is why a comparison was used.

"The three Weeping Nun witnesses testified that the unique characteristic of Spangler's letter-messages to Gusen was that no dates for escape were ever provided. Secret messages usually came in series. After the prisoner was selected and the escape plan was given, the second-to-last message would establish either a final signal or a secondary and final signal. The last message would be the 'ready' warning. From that point on, the Weeping Nuns would have to have the prisoner ready for transport at any time. They would have to wait for the final signals, but they never knew when they would come. In some cases they waited up to two weeks.

"In Vetter's situation two ready signals were employed. The first was a telephone call to the guardhouse stating that an incoming delivery truck had crashed nearby. A Weeping Nun prisoner who kept the guardhouse telephone logbook alerted his associates. Vetter was taken to the west fence to wait for the final signal, the second of two power failures."

Sadarski glanced over at the alarm clock. Three and a half minutes were left. "SD-Ausland was trying to establish that the Oranienburg and Gusen messages were similar in three respects: the date for escape was never given, a final-ready signal system was used, and the sender was never identified in the message text. Since the Gusen letter-message was known to have come from Spangler, they concluded that the crossword-puzzle messages had also come from him."

Sadarski swung the drill to the side. The chisel began its final scraping. "Two of the Weeping Nun witnesses did know of other organizations working on the no-date, no-identification, final-ready system. One witness remembered a group called the Rag Man who used this pattern in their communication with a secret prisoner society at Dachau. The messages had been conveyed in crossword puzzles. The second Weeping Nun claimed she remembered the crossword puzzle bearing no-date, no-identification, final-alert messages

48

employed by the Tan Man when she was imprisoned at Mauthausen."

Sadarski made a final probe of the cavtiy. "SD-Ausland produced three more witnesses and five depositions. Both testimony and statements came from former Weeping Nuns now at other camps. All verified that the crossword-puzzle-type messages were the trademark of either the Tan Man or the Rag Man. According to the revised German dossier on Spangler, both Rag Man and Tan Man are among his known aliases."

The chisel was used for one final ridge. "According to Goliath, the SD-Ausland seems to have convinced the council that Spangler is coming after Hilka Tolan, but they are meeting resistance from the Gestapo. The Gestapo apparently cannot risk the humiliation of another organization solving in two months what they failed with for over a year. The Gestapo is trying everything they can to block the Council's approval of the SD-Ausland capture plan—the Webber Proposition."

"Will they be able to?"

"It depends on this morning's meeting. If SD-Ausland can establish what day Spangler will be coming for the Tolan girl, then no, there's nothing the Gestapo can do but join in on the trap."

Sadarski began mixing the silver-amalgam filling. The alarm clock rang. "I am afraid there is not enough time left to close up the tooth," he said.

"Leave it as it is."

"It will be very painful, especially in this cold. You have a long way to travel before you reach our lines."

"Then pull it."

Sadarski sighed, picked up his forceps and extracted the molar. A moment later the buzzer sounded. All the dentists stopped work.

"Get word to Goliath," the patient said, spitting blood. "Say that I want an immediate meeting. Go by Situation Three. Also, get me a copy of that dossier."

Comrade General Kuprov rose to his feet, fell in line with the fifteen other patients and marched from the room.

49

4

THE COUNCIL looked up to the pulpit-balcony. The witness's striped uniform had been fashioned into a replica of the SS tunic and breeches. He stood unmanacled. An aura of shabby self-importance lingered.

"Name?" demanded Webber.

"Prisoner SP-M 32113, Herr Standartenfuehrer."

"Prisoner from where?"

"Concentration Camp Breendonck, now on special assignment to SD-Ausland, Standartenfuehrer."

"The prisoner," von Schleiben interjected, "will refrain from using the word 'Standartenfuehrer.' "

"List your occupations prior to arrest," Webber continued.

"Doctor of brain surgery, psychoanalyst, criminologist, professor, author, lect—"

"Were you a full professor?"

"Oh, quite assuredly, Herr Stand— Excuse me. Yes, a full professor."

"Where have you taught?"

"The University of Vienna, the University of Heidelberg, Princeton University—that is in the United States of America, Standartenfuehrer—Oxford Univ—"

"What subjects did you teach?"

"Criminology, Stand— criminology. Most particularly the area of criminal pathology and, to a lesser degree . . ."

50

Platt stared intently at the witness.

"Have you written books on the subject of criminal pathology?" Webber continued.

"Precisely eleven, Standartenfuehrer. Eleven volumes, of which five—"

"Then you could be considered an expert in the field of criminal pathology?"

"There was a time—"

"Prior to arrest, what was your name?"

"Excuse me, Herr Stan—"

"What was your name before you were arrested?"

". . . My name?"

"Yes, your name."

"Oh . . . of course. I was—I am Professor Franz Josef Tebet—"

"This is an outrage," Platt shouted, jumping to his feet. "Obergruppenfuehrer, Herr Webber has intentionally deceived and insulted this body by confronting it not only with a degenerate, but with a notorious and unconscionable charlatan as well. Even his fellow Jews have disavowed his mad rantings. If the facts be known—"

"If the facts be known," Webber countered, "Herr Platt was once a student of this so-called heretic, a student who twice failed the examinations."

"That is a lie, an abject lie. I demand—"

Von Schleiben's fist crashed onto the table. "Sit down."

"But—"

"Down."

Platt hesitated, flushed, then slowly lowered himself into his chair.

"If you have a request," von Schleiben announced with benevolence, "it will be made in ordinary tones, not at the top of your lungs."

"I request the removal of the charlatan, Obergruppenfuehrer," muttered Platt.

"Request noted. Webber, continue, but be warned: the introduction of alien and degenerate philosophy will not be tolerated."

"Of course, Obergruppenfuehrer." Webber turned back to Tebet.

"Have you read the dossier and other material relating to Erik Spangler?"

"I have read it most thoroughly, Herr Standartenfuehrer," Tebet replied, wiping the perspiration from his forehead.

"From the material presented you, is it possible to determine the date or dates on which Spangler will attempt to free Hilka Tolan?"

"Most definitely, Herr Standartenfuehrer."

"What are those dates?"

"The twenty-sixth of this month. It is possible he might appear on the eighth or the seventeenth of next month, but I would think such a delay is most improbable."

"Which material on Spangler led you to this conclusion?"

"The Chronology of Events."

"The three-page Chronology of Events in the Spangler Dossier?"

"Yes, Standartenfuehrer."

"The dossier contains over eight hundred pages," Webber commented in feigned amazement, "yet you contend that only three pages were required to establish the date of escape?"

Platt began to rise, but von Schleiben motioned him down. "Herr Webber," he counseled sternly, "whatever point you are trying to make with this witness, get on with it."

"Certainly, Herr Obergruppenfuehrer."

Webber motioned. Typewritten pages were distributed.

Von Schleiben stared down at the sheet.

EXHIBIT V

8 Feb 1942, Ebansee	6 Oct 1942	
17 Feb 1942	26 Dec 1942, Ebansee	
26 Feb 1942	23 Mar 1943	
14 Mar 1942	5 Apr 1943	
27 Mar 1942		
7 Apr 1942	5 Apr 1943	
11 Apr 1942	26 Aug 1943	
23 Apr 1942	12 Oct 1943	
23 Apr 1942	12 Oct 1943	
8 Jun 1942, Ebansee	17 Nov 1943	
17 Jun 1942	20 Nov 1943	
5 Oct 1942	20 Nov 1943	
	9 Jan 1944	

"Explain!" Webber commanded.

Tebet cleared his throat. "You see in front of you—"

"Louder!"

"You see in front of you," the prisoner repeated more audibly, "the list of dates extracted from the Chronology of Events in Spangler's dossier."

Tebet paused for reproaches. None came. "The word 'Ebansee' beside three of the dates shows the only times Spangler returned to a concentration camp more than once. Those dates which are underlined indicate when a murder was committed. There are two important factors to note: first, the numerical dates of Spangler's first three escapes—the eighth, the seventeenth and the twenty-sixth; and, second, the numerical dates immediately following a murder."

Webber motioned. A second sheet of paper was distributed.

EXHIBIT VI

A	B	C	D	E	F
8 Feb (E)	8 Jun (E)	26 Dec (E)	26 Aug	17 Nov	9 Jan
17 Feb	17 Jun	23 Mar	12 Oct	20 Nov	
26 Feb	5 Oct	5 Apr	12 Oct	20 Nov	
14 Mar	6 Oct	5 Apr			
27 Mar					
7 Mar					
11 Apr					
23 Apr					
23 Apr					

"In Exhibit Six, the days have been divided so that the dates following a murder are more clearly evident. We see at once that each column, with the exception of the last, F, starts with either eight, seventeen or twenty-six—the same pattern established with Spangler's first three escapes in Column A."

Tebet hesitated. Von Schleiben was staring at him curiously. Platt was busy making notes. "As for Column F, the ninth of January, it ostensibly indicates that day on which Vetter was first reported to have been freed by Spangler. It has subsequently been established, however, that Vetter left the compound slightly before midnight on January eighth. Thus we see that the eight–seventeen–twenty-six combination holds throughout. One can conclude, without hesitation, that once Spangler commits a murder his next escape will take place on either the eighth, the seventeenth or the twenty-sixth day of a month."

"But no murder has been committed," Platt yelled triumphantly. "Vetter was not killed, simply freed. Therefore, by your very own logic, Spangler could come for the Tolan woman on any date. Any date at all! So, Herr Professor of Criminal Pathology, how do you explain this contradiction?"

"Must Herr Platt shout at the witness?" Webber asked von Schleiben.

"Let the degenerate answer and I'll whisper. Let him explain the fact that his prediction is based on a murder that never took place!"

"You will stop shouting and you will sit down," von Schleiben warned Platt. "And you, Herr Webber, will instruct the witness to answer the question. How does he explain a prediction based on a murder that never occurred?"

Webber nodded to the balcony.

Tebet's thin, dry tongue tried to moisten the cracked lips. "My prediction is simply deduced from the patterns of behavior found in the Chronology of Events. The eight–seventeen–twenty-six sequence shows us Spangler's *safe* numerals—those days on which he *will not* commit a murder. Actually, his key *safe* number is eight. I'm certain all of you have noticed that the one and the seven of seventeen add up to eight, as do the two and the six of twenty-six. To be specific, we should say that Spangler shows us he is incapable of committing murder on the numeral eight or any numbers that total eight.

"Since it is the Council's contention that Spangler will be coming for the Tolan woman, that the Tolan woman is important to him *alive,* it would seem apparent he would not want to hurt her in the process of escape. To insure such protection, Spangler will elect a day when his impulse—or ability—to murder is either negligible or nonexistent. He will attempt to release her on a *safe* day, on an eight day—either the eighth itself, the seventeenth or the twenty-sixth. He freed Vetter on the eighth of this month; the last of the intercepted messages to the Tolan woman came on the seventeenth of this month; that leaves him the twenty-sixth. It is my conclusion he will come for her next week on the twenty-sixth."

Platt's motion to be heard was ignored by von Schleiben. "I take it, then," the General said to Tebet, "you have little doubt that this revised Spangler Dossier records the activities of one man—not five, as had previously been assumed?"

"In my humble judgment, Obergruppenfuehrer, the revised dossier depicts the mental and emotional processes of a unique, assimilated personality," Tebet replied. "A personality which could scarcely belong to more than one individual."

Von Schleiben leaned forward, set his elbows firmly on the table and laced his stubby fingers under his chin. "Point out some of these mental and emotional 'processes' for us."

"The eight–seventeen–twenty-six pattern is the end result of just such a situation, Obergruppenfuehrer. To better understand the dynamics, we must go back to the beginning of the dossier's Chronology of Events and trace the time lapses *following* a murder.

"We see that Spangler frees eight prisoners before killing his first victim, an exterior guard at Mauthausen. All eight escapes occur within a three-month time span. The longest term of inactivity during this period is sixteen days. Yet after murdering the guard he does not reappear to free another prisoner for over *forty* days. After his double murders of October fifth and sixth he remains inactive for more than *eighty* days. Subsequent to the murders in April he does not return to the camps for better than *one hundred and twenty* days. Then, curiously, he kills again on October twelfth, but is back at the camps within a month.

"This forty–eighty–one-hundred-twenty–day time lapse following murders is a common response syndrome in the evolution of certain types of pyschopathic assassins. We can now safely assume that the exterior guard at Mauthausen was the first man Spangler has ever killed. We are also certain that this initial slaying was unintentional not premeditated. The guard most likely stumbled upon Spangler and the prisoner Rissner when they were in the process of escaping. Spangler strangles the guard with his belt. Spangler then plunges into a *forty*-day period of trauma and self-evaluation.

"That the murder was motivated by self-preservation seldom enters the slayer's mind in such cases. Instead he becomes obssessed with the beast that rages within him. Now that the beast has come out, will he take over for all time or can he be checked—can he be pushed back into his cage? Defenses must be sought out and developed. Thus Spangler begins his search for controls during the *forty*-day recovery period.

"Man's reliance on superstition or mysticism in time of crisis is age-old. Spangler, we see, believes that either geographic locations or numerical dates may be the antidote for his dark urges. At the end of the *forty* days he returns to Gusen, on June eighth, and frees his next prisoner without murdering. He returns to the same camp on the same numerical day as his first recorded escape in February.

"Spangler now tests numerical dates against location. His next escape occurs on June seventeenth, the same-number day as his second recorded escape assist in February at Flossenburg, but instead of going to Flossenburg he picks Bergen-Belsen. Once again he does not murder.

"Numbers appear to have a more controlling effect than geography. Even so, the Chronology shows that Spangler reaches a far more drastic conclusion at this point: stay away from concentration camps altogether and the impulse to kill will stop, the beast will be neutralized. That such an attempt was made can be seen in the period immediately subsequent to the June-seventeenth escape—Spangler was inactive for over four months. This too is a common syndrome among first murderers. They move to different cities or countries, often change names or occupations, sometimes even religions, to appease their phobia.

"Up to this point Spangler was hardly the pathological assassin he considered himself to be. He was simply a man who had killed another man accidentally and was exaggerating the event. All things being equal, Spangler would never have killed again. But an incident now occurs which is the *turning point* in his mental and emotional processes (it is always the second murder that shapes the assassin, never the first): Spangler gets word that the Gestapo has captured an intimate friend and underground associate, the man Tramont.

56

Spangler fights all temptation, but finally breaks his resolve. He penetrates the Gestapo prison and manages to get into Tramont's cell. He finds that Tramont has been beaten too badly to escape, that he is in great agony and close to death. It is quite likely that Tramont pleads with Spangler to put him out of his misery. Spangler kills him—"

"Preposterous!" Platt shouted, again jumping to his feet. "Spangler murdered Tramont to silence him."

"Then you admit it was Spangler who killed him, and not the Rag Man?" Webber demanded.

"I admit nothing, but I will not allow this charlatan to say it was a *mercy* killing. Tramont could identify him—the Rag Man. All we needed was a day or two more. That's why Tramont was murdered."

"If the slaying had been premeditated, Standartenfuehrer," Tebet offered cautiously, "wouldn't a weapon have been brought and employed? A knife? A wire? A rope? Why would Spangler use his hands if he had planned—"

"We don't know it was Spangler," Platt erupted, as he spun toward von Schleiben. "Obergruppenfuehrer, I protest this Jew's wild, unsubstantiated claims!"

"Sit down," von Schleiben warned.

"But—"

"If you persist in playing the dunce, you will be treated like the dunce. One more outburst and you will be sent to the corner. Now sit down."

"Certainly, Obergruppenfuehrer."

"Let the prisoner continue—without interruption," the General commanded.

Tebet tugged at his collar button. "Tramont—Tramont is murdered, and the next night Ben . . . Menk . . . Obergruppenfuehrer, is it possible that I might have a dossier to refresh my memory?"

"Get him a dossier."

Webber looked to his aides, who shook their heads. "All copies are classified and assigned, Obergruppenfuehrer. There are no extras."

"Platt," called von Schleiben, "give him yours."

"Mine, Obergruppenfuehrer?"

"Yours."

Platt's dossier was passed up to the pulpit-balcony. Tebet leafed to the Chronology of Events. His finger trailed down the desired page. "The next night Spangler waits in the office of Benke, the Gestapo officer who was Tramont's main interrogator. Benke is murdered and then savagely beaten. This is Spangler's first premeditated slaying; also the first mutilation of a corpse. The acuteness of his emotional response is reflected by the fact that more than *eighty* days elapsed before his next escape attempt.

"Which murder is he responding to," von Schleiben interjected, "Tramont's or Benke's—or both?"

"I would think Tramont's death would have the greatest effect, Obergruppenfuehrer. It is the murder of someone he knows, someone he is very close to. It is quite possible that Spangler has few friends. I think Spangler felt not only the guilt of murdering a friend —even at the friend's request—but the added guilt of having involved him in underground activities in the first place. The extent of his emotions toward Tramont is seen in the rage with which he murders and mutilates Benke."

"And after these double killings," von Schleiben asked, "Spangler waits his eighty-odd days and then returns to test his number and location theories?"

"I would say so, Obergruppenfuehrer. We see that he frees two—"

"What other patterns?" von Schleiben interjected.

"Obergruppenfuehrer?"

"What other patterns in the dossier make you think we are dealing with one man?"

"His methodology of assassination, Obergruppenfuehrer. Tramont and the prisoners were killed by having their necks snapped *backward*—a quick, easy way to inflict death. Gestapo, SS guards and Kripo had their necks snapped *forward,* a longer, more painful way to die. This second method also tells us of Spangler's extreme strength. Few men are powerful enough to snap the human neck forward."

"Will he always kill by one of these two methods?"

"I would think so, Obergruppenfuehrer. He may do other things to the corpse afterward, but the killing must be done with his own hands in one of the two ways already described. Might I have a glass of water?"

Von Schleiben's fingers drummed on the table top. "Do you think Spangler is coming for the Tolan woman?" he finally asked.

"It is my opinion that he will, Obergruppenfuehrer."

"Why?"

"There are two possible explanations, Herr Obergruppenfuehrer. First, Spangler has joined forces with an organization which is interested in both Vetter and the Tolan girl. Spangler probably began his underground career working with a small religious resistance group, the group for which he freed his first three prisoners, the three priests. From that point forward he operated independently or with a few close associates at most. From that point forward his primary motivation was an all-consuming obsession with concentration camps. That is why, with the exception of Ebansee, he never raided the same camp twice. That is why, except for the three priests, he has never freed prisoners with similar occupations.

"The one thing the dossier shows us quite clearly is that never once has Spangler brought out a political prisoner. Now not only does he free Vetter, but he lets it be known he will come after Hilka Tolan, both of them convicted of political crimes. I therefore conclude that Spangler still is not interested in political prisoners—but someone else is."

"You said there were two possible explanations for Spangler's coming for the girl. What is the second?"

"It is more speculation than deduction, Herr Obergruppen-fuehrer."

"I will be the judge of that. Proceed."

"It is conceivable that Spangler is intentionally telling you when and where and whom he is after."

"Are you saying that Spangler is assisting in his own capture?"

"It is possible he has always been doing so, Herr Obergruppen-fuehrer."

"Explain."

"Spangler's dominant characteristic is his intelligence, quite an amazing intelligence. It is displayed everywhere we look. We see his ability to enter and leave concentration camps at will, to penetrate Gestapo headquarters, to deal with explosives, to devise communications. Another proof of this intelligence is the fact that not only has Spangler not been *caught* after all these years, he hasn't even been *identified.*"

"Doesn't it seem odd that after all this time you should suddenly be inundated with information? Doesn't it appear somewhat coincidental that with the capture of one prisoner at Gusen you are able to solve Spangler's communications systems, cross-reference them to link Spangler with several of his aliases, find messages indicating the pending escape of Hilka Tolan? Doesn't it seem curious that Spangler should attempt to contact Hilka Tolan through the open concentration-camp smuggling circuits—circuits he knows are watched by security guards? And what of that mysterious phone call in Frankfurt? Who was that unknown informant who led you to the apartment where you found the black book verifying the names in the dossier?"

Von Schleiben scowled and pinched his neck. "If we follow your logic," he finally began, "Spangler must have anticipated our locating you so that the dates could be established."

"If you will excuse me, Herr Obergruppenfuehrer, might it not be possible that you have reversed the order of events? Might it not be conceivable that Spangler had expected your men to uncover his various aliases and to interpret the Chronology long before now? Couldn't it be possible that when this *didn't* occur, he helped by allowing his messages to be intercepted and by planting the list in Frankfurt?"

"Why would he go to such lengths to have himself caught?"

"Perhaps to make it more exciting, Herr Obergruppenfuehrer. Perhaps to end it all. When intellect dominates psychopathic urges we are never sure of the ultimate motivation. Neither is Spangler. Perhaps that is what he is searching for."

"What other dominant characteristics are evident to you?"

"Loyalty to friends, Herr Obergruppenfuehrer. I doubt if Spangler is close to many people, but when he is, he is savagely loyal. We see this when he penetrates a Gestapo prison in an attempt to save Tramont."

"What else?"

Tebet gripped the railing and leaned slightly forward. "The Chronology indicates something quite intriguing, Herr Obergruppenfuehrer. As we have seen before, the seventeenth and the twenty-sixth of the eight–seventeen–twenty-six pattern add up to eight. Eight is Spangler's dominant *safe* number. But eight also has another possible interpretation. If we take the figure 8 rather than the number eight, we find it is composed of two zeros placed one on top of the other. The double zero set in this order was once the symbol of a medieval cult of Satan worshipers. Add to this the fact that the first three prisoners Spangler ever freed were Catholic priests, and we have a most intriguing situation: Spangler the black ritualist coming to save three priests on the traditional days of Satan worship and blood sacrifice. Throughout the Chronology we see that the eights, the devil days meant for death, are the only days on which Spangler will not kill."

"What do you interpret this to mean?"

"I am not certain, Herr Obergruppenfuehrer. Perhaps he has confused salvation with destruction." Tebet replied with a trace of glee.

5

VON SCHLEIBEN was exasperated. To begin with, there was no one to whom he could report the theft except himself. As director of the Council for Extreme Security, the Reichssicherheitshauptamt, better known as R. S. H. A., he was as much the German police force as anyone in Germany. Not that the loss was important. It was only a clothing locker, but it had been built to the General's personal specifications in Finland less than half a year before. It was made of a lightweight burnished metal and had the uncommon dimensions of two and three-quarter meters in length, a meter in width and one and a quarter meters in height. Three brass clasps, two combination locks and four leather straps secured the exterior. The lining consisted of triple layers of thick burgundy velvet. The locker was sprayed a deep vermilion. It was also waterpoof.

A far graver point of irritation was the attention the Spangler case was receiving. Even though the Council sessions were under strictest security, word was out that a supercriminal existed, had operated for years without being identified. If the Tolan girl were freed, the entire political detention system would have to be revised. Prisoners would be shuttled around like chess pieces. If the Tolan girl were freed, von Schleiben would suffer great embarrassment—or worse.

Another issue of concern was Zieff, the Abwehr representative. Zieff was too quiet, too noncommittal. He was up to something. Von Schleiben knew that military intelligence had been covertly watching the camps—but why? What were they after? What did they know?

Hadn't the change of command from Canaris to Schellenberg made any difference?

Von Schleiben had never liked Munich. He had always felt it was a city of thieves. Now one of them had confirmed his suspicions, had had the audacity, not to mention the skill, to elude the SS guards, penetrate the General's private railroad car and make off with his vermilion locker.

Von Schleiben searched his compartment one last time, reluctantly notified the provost of his loss, climbed into the limousine and began his trip back to the Council session.

Debate was cut short. The issue was clearly defined. The vote would be either for or against the Webber Proposition, the detailed forty-four-page SD-Ausland–Kripo blueprint to capture Erik Spangler at Oranienburg. The combined operation would require men and material from every organization represented on the Council.

"SS?" the provost called out.

"SS for," the delegate responded.

"Sipo?"

"For."

"Kripo?"

"For the Webber Proposition," the Kripo representative said enthusiastically.

"Totenkopf?"

"For."

"Gestapo?"

". . . For."

"Abwehr?"

"The Abwehr," Zieff began quietly, "requests permission to be released from all activities of the Council in matters concerning the alleged Erik Spangler."

"No agency can withdraw from this body," von Schleiben thundered.

"We do not ask withdrawal, our request is for temporary release, Herr Obergruppenfuehrer."

"On whose authority?"

63

"By direct command of Obergruppenfuehrer Schellenberg."

"Schellenberg heads SD-Ausland as well as Abwehr," von Schleiben barked. "How can he let one of his groups undertake an operation and order the other not to participate?"

"Obergruppenfuehrer Schellenberg will most certainly provide the details."

"Schellenberg is not here. You are. I demand the specifications."

"It is beyond my authority to discuss it."

"Your authority has just been extended—by my order."

Zieff gazed calmly at the General. "We believe, Herr Obergruppenfuehrer, that a security leak exists within this body."

Von Schleiben eased back into his chair. His hands tented under his chin. "Would it be too much to ask who the traitor is, and to whom his information is going?"

"We believe the information is traveling east, to the Russians."

"And the traitor—are we privy to this fact?"

"All that we can say is that we believe it is one of two organizations."

"Two organizations represented in this room, I suppose?"

"Yes."

"And can I assume that were I to inquire which organizations are suspect, you would plead security?"

"You are correct in your assumption, Obergruppenfuehrer."

"Request for temporary release granted," von Schleiben said. He watched Zieff rise and leave the room. "The Webber Proposition," the General ordained, "is accepted and approved. Implementation will proceed at the conclusion of this meeting. Provost, what other matters are on the agenda?"

"Intelligence concerning reception of high-frequency radio test signals believed to be coming from a new Anglo-American espionage communications center somewhere in northern England. A proposal just received for exchange of captured agents. Detection of Egyptian instal—"

"Begin with the exchange proposal," was von Schleiben's mandate.

6

THE PLATOONS of Totenkopf elite tiptoed through the darkness. An order was whispered. The steel-helmeted guards stopped. Bayonets were attached. The wait began. The sleet tapered off. A second whispered order was passed along. Rifles were raised to hip level. The stop watch moved to 05, 04, 02 . . . Floodlights sparked on. Barbed-wire gates were pulled open. The platoons ran double-time into the compound and ringed the roll-call area. The lights in barracks S15 through S21 went on. Padlocks were opened. Kapos burst through the doors. Prisoners were roused, pulled, tugged, kicked.

The perimeter of poised weapons began filling with dazed shivering inmates. No overclothing had been allowed. No personal effects other than crude eating cups and spoons had been permitted.

Selection began. Eight hundred of the fifteen hundred prisoners were picked. They formed into ranks of four.

Webber and his aides meandered through the ragged contingent. Faces were studied, clothes examined, notes taken. Then the officers returned to their armada of cars and drove off.

The sleet began again. A Totenkopf captain raised his arm. The column began marching out of Kreisberg.

Steam gathered force. Drive shafts locked. Engine wheels skidded and sparked along the siding rails. Passenger wagons banged into

65

one another. The train came to a stop. The regiments debarked, checked their battle equipment and clambered onto waiting trucks. By 0900 hours they had reached Zone B. Deployment began.

At 0926 hours a seven-man detachment approached the farmhouse.

"How many volunteer laborers do you have?" a captain demanded.

"Five," answered the nervous farmer.

"How many bonded laborers?"

"Twelve."

"Are there other employees?"

"The cook, only the cook."

"How many in your family?"

"Three, just three. My daughter, my wife and myself. The cook is a third cousin, though. I suppose you could count her. She's paid, you know. Our son is in the Army. He is a hero. He has two medals. I have them upstairs. I can show them to you. He has been wounded three times. Wait, I'll get the medals."

"By order of the Gauleiter, this farm and all on it are hereby placed in a state of quarantine."

"What—what does that mean?"

"Neither you, your family nor your laborers are permitted to leave your living quarters unless notified."

"But—but what have I done?"

"In addition, you will quarter six of my men. Compensation will be paid."

"The farmwork? The animals? The fields? What will happen to them if we can't go out?"

"My men will allow what they feel is necessary. Do you own a telephone?"

"Yes. It's in the kitchen."

"It will be disconnected."

"But why? What have I done?"

"As to supplies, foodstuffs and other essentials, you will provide lists and money. We will see that they are purchased."

"How long will this go on?"

"Heil Hitler!"

By dusk eighty per cent of Zone B was secure. By midnight the job was complete. Radio communication was established with Zones A, C and D. The first phase of the Webber Proposition had been accomplished on schedule.

7

THE SIGNAL ROCKET arched high into the subzero night and burst into a shower of steel-blue phosphorescence. The artillery duel stopped. A yellow aerial flare was launched, reached the prescribed altitude and ignited. It was answered by a green missile. The forty-minute cease-fire was in effect.

The exchange prisoners, a quartet of captured Soviet espionage agents, were lifted out of the slit trench and stood on their feet. The leg irons were removed and blindfolds applied. The ropes binding their hands behind their backs were tightened. The lead line looped around their necks at four-pace intervals was tugged.

A lieutenant, bundled up in his greatcoat, guided the captives up past steaming 88s, littered shell casings, exhausted gun crews, shattered trees and ice-crusted machine-gun nests to the observation post where von Schleiben and his aides waited. The exchange prisoners were laid face down in the frozen mud.

The spotter raised his arm in the direction of the opposite ridge. Von Schleiben focused his Zeiss field glasses on the shadowy forms of retreating Russian soldiers staggering and stumbling back up over the crest. Traces of shell smoke hovered indecisively overhead, caught a descending crosswind, slid down the long slope and settled atop the blanket of thick warm undulating ground fog.

Von Schleiben handed his pistol to the spotter and grasped a white flag in his hand. Cautiously he started down the steep hillside, cold in the fur-lined, red-lapeled greatcoat of an infantry general.

An odor became evident, persisted, grew stronger. He descended into the thinning fog cover, breathing through his mouth. He emerged below and froze to a stop. Perspiration rose on his brow and turned to ice.

As far as von Schleiben's gaze would carry, no earth could be seen. No earth, no mud, no grass, no shrub, no tree, no crater. Nothing. Only bodies. Bodies which were the remnants of thirty-one unsuccessful Russian assaults in forty-eight hours. Body on top of body, layer upon layer of whole and partial and twisted and mangled and dismembered and torn soldiers, starting at von Schleiben's feet and stretching out along the valley floor, rising up the opposite slope and disappearing into the overcast. Most were dead and frozen in postures of agonizing and fearful mortality. A few still lived, groaning and near death.

"Schleebund—over here, Schleebund."

Von Schleiben turned slowly to his right. Kuprov leaned, cross-legged and open-jacketed, against a wall of frozen dead. His gloveless hands held a smoking cigarette. He wore the uniform of a Russian private.

Von Schleiben picked his way across the carnage.

"Good to see you, Schleebund, always good to see you. I miss the happy times we have together. Have you heard any funny jokes lately? What has them laughing at Berchtesgaden these days besides you in an infantry uniform?" Kuprov said. He nodded toward a mound of tangled ice-covered bodies. "Sit down and tell me a funny joke, Schleebund. Sit down and we'll have a chuckle or two together."

"I prefer to stand."

"Is something the matter with your voice? Do you have a cold, Schleebund?"

The German tried breathing through his nose. "Nothing is the matter," he replied, half gagging from the stench. "I don't have a cold."

"Good, Schleebund, very good. I wouldn't want anything to happen to an old comrade like you. Who would tell me jokes? Did you bring the cigarettes?"

Von Schleiben thrust a gloved hand into his greatcoat pocket, brought out a pack of Lucky Strikes and tossed them to the Russian espionage chief.

"American? Hurray for you, Schleebund. You are a reliable man. I'll think of both you and the Americans when I smoke these. Now what about that funny joke?"

"I have none."

"Then I suppose we should get the preliminaries out of the way, eh? What prisoners did you bring me?"

Von Schleiben reached into his cuff, withdrew an envelope and handed it to Kuprov.

"Only four?" the Russian said, reading the page. "You have only four men of mine?"

"The Army shot the others before I could get to them."

"Ah, Schleebund, such is war. Or should I say such is spying?" Kuprov laughed briefly at his own joke. "And how many Germans do you want in return?"

"Twelve. It will have to be three to one."

"Pretty high, isn't it?" Kuprov smiled as he passed von Schleiben the Russian list of captured Reich's agents. "You sound as if Germany were still winning."

"The Oberkommando is against *any* exchange. They finally agreed to a three-to-one ratio."

"Then three to one they shall have. We must show the Oberkommando what a clever negotiator you are, mustn't we? Which men on that paper do you want?"

Von Schleiben read down the columns. "Walters, Dietz, . . . Wagner, . . . Mazer. The balance are not important."

Kuprov nodded. "Then Walters, Dietz, Wagner and Mazer will be shot, and I'll give you whoever I damn well please. And tell the Army that since we are capturing ten Germans to every one Russian they take, in the future I'll shoot ten captured agents for every one of my men executed. After all, Schleebund, to the victor goes a certain privilege in ratio. Your teeth are chattering, Schleebund. Jump up and down, it helps the circulation."

70

"I'm not cold."

"Then perhaps it's the meeting place I've chosen that makes you tremble?" Kuprov looked sadly around him. "I know what pains you took in selecting our last rendezvous point. I was only trying to reciprocate, only trying to make you comfortable, Schleebund. I wanted you to feel at ease, at home, as if you had never left Germany. I have failed."

"Neither the temperature or location bothers me. I am perfectly well."

A hand brushed weakly against von Schleiben's boot. He jumped back and stared down. The Russian soldier he had been standing on was not quite dead.

"Of course you're perfectly well, Schleebund," Kuprov agreed. "Just because you are a midget I keep thinking that you have the endurance of a midget. I forget that you are a giant, a gladiator—a Goliath. Interesting isn't it, Goliath, how deceiving appearances can be? On looking at you, who would realize what you really are, eh? Well, enough of that. Tell me about this Spangler situation."

"Didn't you get my message?"

"Of course I received your message, Schleebund. It cost me a tooth. I also read that endless dossier you sent on. Both failed to say what happened to Vetter after he was taken from Gusen."

"We won't know that until after Spangler is captured."

"But I don't want him captured."

"What?"

"Schleebund, who is this Spangler working for?"

"We're not certain he's affiliated with anyone. He may be just another of those madmen who appear during wars and cause trouble."

"No, Schleebund, no. The cold must be numbing your mind. This Spangler person may have been independent in the past, but now he is connected. What organization or what country, Schleebund, is suddenly interested in both Vetter, a German Communist leader, and Hilka Tolan, the daughter of a disgraced right-wing German politician?"

"I don't know."

"But now we can find out, eh, Schleebund? Let this Spangler bring out the Tolan girl and he will lead you to the answer."

"That's impossible."

"Schleebund, an odd collection of German exiles has suddenly begun disappearing from various parts of the world. First it was former newspapermen, writers, intellectuals and technicians. Next actors and historians. Now it appears to be the politicians' turn. Thomas Hutch has just vanished from Rio de Janeiro."

"Hutch the Socialist?"

"Socialist, forger, extortionist or whatever. So you see, Schleebund, something is up. Perhaps our friend Spangler will lead us to the source."

"No. It is quite impossible to let him escape—whatever the reason."

"Schleebund, Schleebund, Schleebund. Possibility or impossibility have nothing to do with it. I order you not to capture him. He must be followed."

"The order is disregarded."

"If it is, the Fuehrer will learn that one of his highest-ranking police officials is a traitor."

"Don't be naïve, General Kuprov. Part of my job is to stay in touch with enemy agents of comparable rank. Everyone knows I am meeting you here for a prisoner exchange. Every meeting we have ever had has been known of—and recorded. If all points of discussion were not included in my reports, who is going to know the difference—and who is going to believe you? The fact of the matter is, my revolutionary friend, it is assumed in high places *you* are on the verge of defecting to the Reich, not that *I* have begun cooperating with the East."

Kuprov smiled faintly. "Schleebund, I want this Spangler followed —not captured."

"Spangler's adventures with political inmates could mean an entire revamping of our detention system. It could also result in my removal as chairman of the council. If you value my future services I would suggest avoiding such a replacement. The best possible insurance for my holding this mutually beneficial position in the Reich's police affairs is the capture of Herr Spangler."

"And what if he eludes your trap?"

"Then I will either have to place the blame on someone else, come up with a new plan or resign. There is always the probability, on the other hand, that I will be imprisoned—or shot. If this is the case, then I shall have to choose between prison, death or Russia. At present, they seem equally unappealing."

Kuprov considered. "All in all, Schleebund, I think it would be better if he were not captured."

"All in all, Kuprov, I must refuse you. Is there anything else?"

Again the Russian thought. "Until this Spangler thing is settled— one way or another—I think it good we bring as many German Communists out of the camps as possible."

"Political prisoners cannot be touched at this time."

"It sounds as if you're raising the stakes. Is that what you're doing? All right, I'll pay you twice the price for each."

"They cannot be touched. If Spangler is taken, that may change."

Kuprov shrugged, pushed off from the wall of dead and started toward his own lines. He stopped and turned back. "Schleebund," he called, "there was something interesting I forgot to tell you. One of my men infiltrated a Catholic resistance organization in the east of France. He knew this man Tramont. You remember Tramont, the one your dossier says Spangler killed in a Gestapo prison. My man says this Tramont was a mountaineer, a good trapper and hunter and all that, but he didn't know of his being connected with any underground or group. Tramont would go on long hunting trips, though. My man says that Tramont lived in a cabin with a son. After Tramont disappeared for good there were rumors that someone came and took the son. No one knew who it was or much cared at the time. We're following up on it now. If I get something I'll send it to you."

"Thank you."

"No, Schleebund, it is I who should do the thanking. Thank you for the cigarettes and the jokes. You had some funny jokes for me to-night after all, eh?"

73

8

Two BLACK buses with yellow stripes wound up the snow-choked mountain road, crunched onto the forest trail, skirted the ice-covered lake, shifted into low gear, climbed the sharp rise and pulled in front of the drift-covered frame buildings of the summer *Kinder-kamp*. Gestapo men piled out of the first bus. All were lean and bony. Each had a three-day growth of beard. Gestapo Auxiliary women debarked from the second bus. They too were thin.

The fifty men and women crossed the frozen recreation field, entered a chilly dormitory, hung up their uniform overcoats and filled the two rows of facing chairs. Orderlies draped coarse sheets about their shoulders. Barbers clipped away their hair and shaved the skulls clean.

Clerks waited at the far end of the room to receive watches, rings and other valuables. Receipts were logged. Clothing cupboards were assigned. In the men's were torn striped trousers and jackets; in the women's, cotton prison dresses.

The women lined the north wall, the men the south. An order was given. All began to undress.

The bald men and women stood naked, embarrassed and shivering on the frigid slat flooring as orderlies moved among them, distributing tattered undergarments and flat-handled, short-bladed pig

74

knives. They each taped a knife to the inside of the thigh, then pulled on the unwashed, faded uniform.

The new "prisoners" moved along to the leather-coated team of corporals. A variety of footwear was distributed. Some received ragged shoes or worn boots, others cardboard slippers. Six were given only uneven strips of burlap with which to bind their feet.

The "prisoners" assembled on the paradeground. Ten men and ten women were given axes and led to the woods, where they began felling trees. The remainder received rough-handled shovels and began digging up the frozen earth as the third and fourth buses arrived.

The new contingent of twenty-six men and twenty-three women were shaved, processed and sent out to join the others with either ax or shovel. The fifth and sixth buses arrived an hour apart. Twenty-one more women and eighteen men joined the labor battalion.

Work ceased at ten that evening. One hundred and twenty-eight new "prisoners" trudged into one unheated simulated barracks, were fed a thin soup scattered with occasional bits of old potatoes and were allowed to sleep two to an unmattressed wooden bunk for a full four hours. Men and women could not share the same bed.

At three in the morning they were mustered in the recreation area in a snowstorm. Instructions began in concentration-camp procedure. Roll call was practiced a dozen times. Food-line procedure took even more rehearsal. Marching received slightly less attention. Other details followed. Two more buses arrived. Thirty-seven more women joined the contingent.

There was no breakfast or lunch. Digging and chopping began at six in the morning and lasted until nine at night. Twenty-three men dropped out from exhaustion or exposure. The casualties for women totaled fifty-five. Twelve men and fifteen women were placed in a special barracks to recuperate, to be given another chance. The remaining fifty-seven were put into ambulances and sent on to Munich.

The third day's schedule was the same as the second. By nightfall the ranks had thinned to thirty-six men and thirty-one women.

No one was wakened until nine on the fourth morning. The sixty-seven survivors gathered in the heated dining hall for a meal of Wurstel with mustard, Bortchen, beer and coffee. Most could not eat. Cigarettes were passed out as orderlies climbed onto a small stage at the end of the room and set up three easels. Large diagrams and photographs were placed on them.

The "prisoners" stood to attention. Webber entered, crossed the room, mounted the platform, took up a long wooden pointer and stepped beside the first easel. The audience was ordered seated.

"This is Oranienburg." The pointer rapped against the large diagram divided by thick green lines. "Sometime between midnight, the twenty-fifth of February, and midnight of the twenty-sixth, an escape attempt is expected." The pointer moved to the yellow shaded area. "This sector of Oranienburg is called 'Privileged Detention.'" Webber stepped to the center easel, to an enlargement of Special Detention. "In these barracks are housed important prisoners—political, religious, former National Socialists, Wehrmacht officers and so on. This is where the trouble will come."

Webber moved to the last easel. "This is a diagram of the two barracks within Special Detention that house female prisoners. These two barracks are cut off from the rest of Special Detention by electrified fencing. The gates into the women's sector are open during the day, closed at night. Whether the gates are opened or closed, no male is ever allowed inside."

He motioned. Overlays were placed on the existing chart. "Your mission is to serve as sentinels, as a human alarm system, in case any unauthorized person either leaves or enters the women's compound during the twenty-sixth of the month. Eight of you women will work in the women's compound as gardeners. Two more will be assigned as attendants in the barracks themselves."

Webber returned to the center easel. "Word has gone out through Oranienburg that it has been selected as a model camp, that it will soon be inspected and photographed. The prisoners know that such an impending inspection means a great deal of extra labor in the cleaning-up process. They anticipate new projects and long hours. They will not be disappointed. One of the new projects will be a sewage line, or at least the ditch for a sewage line."

Webber's crayon slashed a mark to the south of Privileged Detention. "This is the path of the ditch. Digging will go on day and night. Some of you will be on every shift.

"Another 'show project' will be a new shower house." The crayon circled an area to the north of Privileged Detention. "Many of you will be on each of those twelve-hour shifts. Other projects will be under way in various parts of the camp, but they are not our concern. They simply make it look as if everyone is involved."

The pointer ran east and west between the ditch and shower-house projects. "What we have done," Webber announced, "is create a corridor through which the escape will probably take place. Some of you will be in each of the barracks along this corridor. Since we do not know how the escape is to be engineered, we must look for two things: unauthorized persons entering Privileged Detention, in particular the women's sector, and anyone leaving Privileged Detention. Since Privileged Detention is a quarantine sector, no one is allowed to leave or enter it, with the exception of the eight women prisoners who work in the female barracks. Since those eight women will be from this room, anyone else is our suspect.

"As I said before, your function is that of a warning system." He began marking black crosses on the overlay. "These will be the relay stations. They will be manned by two of you day and night. Some will be working on barracks roofs, others filling potholes in the street areas. If anyone is seen entering the Privileged area you notify the nearest relay station. They in turn will notify the patrol stations." An arc of orange X's were marked on the overlay.

Webber stepped to the front of the stage. The pointer began beating against his boot. "The reason for this strategy is quite simple. *We do not know what our man looks like.* We do not know if he will come into the camp for the prisoner Hilka Tolan or whether she will be led out to meet him. Therefore we must observe both the entrance route and the escape route without interfering. Once she has been led out of the camp we will know the person with her is our man. Your job is the most important: to notify the others when contact is first made.

"Our man must be captured with the Tolan woman outside the camp—that is the only way we can identify him. Therefore, under no conditions will you attempt to intercept anybody entering or leaving Privileged Detention without authorization. Even if you are attacked you will do nothing."

"But, Standartenfuehrer," one of Webber's aides interrupted, "everyone has been given a knife."

"On whose authority?" shouted the colonel. "The knives will be confiscated immediately. Even if the suspect has his hands on your necks, you will do nothing. *Nothing!* Is that understood?"

Assignments were given, and the various groups split up for their special instruction. At noon another hot meal was served. Vitamin and nutrition shots were given.

The "new prisoners" were issued battered cups and spoons and instructed in how to tie them to their clothing. The march began at 1400 hours. They tramped through the knee-high forest snow and descended onto a frozen mud path. By 1830 hours they had passed through the "outer ring" of dug-in, camouflaged Alpine Troops. At 1900 hours they were met by the Death's Head Totenkopf guard from Oranienburg and led between the hidden white-uniformed Waffen-SS paratroopers with white-sprayed submachine guns who composed the "outer center ring." At 1920, with nine battalions of troops behind them, the "prisoners" reached a well-concealed road observation point overlooking the Autobahn.

The line of prisoners from Kreisberg stretched a quarter of a mile —a quarter of a mile of stooped, silent figures trudging through the fresh snow, clutching their arms around themselves. Not one head was unbowed, not one glance wasted to right or left—just a soundless procession of half-frozen men in rags. Not a soul noticed or cared when the Gestapo's "new prisoners" fell in at the end of the line and joined the trek to Oranienburg.

9

THE FISHING BOAT passed Belle-Île, circled the German patrol lines, slid into the fog bank and slowed its engine.

The Peppermint Priest buttoned his slicker tightly over the black cassock and tugged down the brim of his storm hat. A revolver was offered. He shook his head and climbed on deck. He sat on the gunwale and squinted out over the midnight water. The haze was thining; a *pointilliste* outline of waterfront buildings began to materialize.

The boat drifted between the lines of piling and bumped to a stop. The Priest stepped over the side and swung himself out onto the moss-covered rungs. He reached the top of the ladder. The hatch was closed. He gave three long taps, followed by two short. He signaled again. The hatch squeaked open. He stared directly up the plump pantless female thighs. Orange-lacquered fingers reached down. He was lifted into the kitchen.

The face was doll-painted, the age elusive. The woman could have been forty, perhaps fifty; possibly older. She stood back, examined the sea-sprayed visitor and pressed a warning finger against her Clara Bow lips. A solitary button below the midriff strained to keep the white linen gown together. She motioned him to follow. Music was audible from a scratched victrola record.

The staircase creaked with every footstep. The narrow hall was red-papered and gas-lit. They passed five doors; she pushed open the sixth. The Peppermint Priest entered. The door closed behind him. A lock clicked. He was alone.

A solitary glazed candelabra on the long wooden table provided the sole illumination. Silver trays of fruits and nuts lay waiting. Six bottles of iced Dom Perignon stood neatly in line.

Thick, rich blue carpeting covered the floor. The walls were covered in a lighter blue, the curtains were still lighter. The canopied brass bed was covered in blue satin and trimmed in gold. On the wall opposite the bed hung a large gold-tinted rococo picture frame enclosing an oil painting of Marshal Pétain. At least the head was Pétain's. The body belonged to a satyr. The organs, both male and female, were grossly exaggerated. The golden hooves stood in a pool of blood.

The Priest hung his slicker and cap on the coatrack, slipped off his shoes and socks and placed them on the blue-tiled corner stove. He felt his cassock. It was damp. He decided to keep it on. He reached beneath, brought out an oilskin package and tossed it on the bed.

He moved to the French doors leading to an adjoining room and tried the brass handles. They were locked from the other side. His ear went to the louvers. The two French voices were female. The man spoke German. Talk erupted into laughter. Silence followed.

The Priest returned to the stove and warmed his hands. The chill persisted. He raised his cassock high and stepped closer to the warm tile.

The shrieks startled him. Cassock up, he spun around. The louvered doors lay open. Two girls stared gleefully through. Both were young, sixteen at the most. Both were pretty. Their hair swept tightly back behind their ears. The faces bore no trace of makeup. Each was dressed in a thin virginal white linen sheath, held together by a single button below the waist.

The cassock dropped. The girls scurried from the room. One reached back in and pulled the doors closed. Excited chatter was heard from the other side. Then whispers. Then silence.

The doors opened again. Von Schleiben, clad only in an open

80

admiral's tunic, stood in the doorway with the girls peeking over his shoulders.

"It's been a long time, hasn't it, Father?" the German reminisced. "I've missed our little tête-à-têtes."

"Have you, Wilhelm?" the man replied with a turn of the head. "How very odd. I haven't missed you in the least."

"You are refreshing, Peppermint. Revitalizing. You look in good health."

"From all I can see, so do you. A naval uniform suits you. Are we only playing sailor this week or is the fleet actually waiting in the bathtub?"

Von Schleiben crossed the room, boosted himself onto the table and let his legs swing free. The girls remained leaning in the doorway. "I am by the sea. I dress for the occasion. By that token you should be wearing stars and stripes. Rumor has it, Father, that you have become extremely close to the Americans."

"They're extremely generous with their donations."

"Donations? Ah, yes, now I recall." Von Schleiben snapped his fingers and pointed. The girls left the room pulling the doors closed. "That was your phrase, wasn't it? Donations for—now, what was the name of that organization?"

"International Refugee Assistance Program. IRAP."

"Of course. Now, why would I forget a splendid group like that?"

"Perhaps because we're nonprofit."

"Innuendo, Peppermint? Are you forgetting how many refugees I helped you bring out of Europe? How much assistance and *information* I provided your volunteers? Didn't I singlehandedly get that entire Belgian family you wanted off the Continent? No, Father, when it came to you, I was most charitable."

"It was never your charity I questioned, it was the additional expenses."

"Smuggling has a rather high overhead."

"And profit margin."

"A man must live, Father. He must think to his future. Tell me, do you think the Americans would be interested in my services?"

"You would have to ask the Americans."

"I value your opinion in such matters, Peppermint. I know you share many confidences. As an old friend, what is your opinion? Would they be interested?"

"I should think that would depend on what you have to offer."

"You saw what I could do in the past, before my promotions. You know my present position within the Reich. You know what I could do for them now."

"And how much money will it cost?"

"Money is immaterial."

"You being generous? Come, now, Wilhelm, I wasn't born yesterday. You'd sell your grandmother to an ape if there was half a mark in it."

"My dear Peppermint, is it any secret that Germany will lose the war? I must prepare for the future. The Casablanca accord somewhat complicates matters. My affiliation with concentration camps makes the situation even bleaker. I am already dealing with the Russians. Now, quite simply, I would like to see if I can better my lot."

"You play the louse with astonishing conviction. Have you been practicing?"

"No more than the rest of mankind."

The Peppermint Priest scratched behind his ear and smiled a sad smile. "All right, Wilhelm, I will make contact for you, but I must know *exactly* what merchandise you can provide—and what you expect in return."

"The Americans can have access to all secret information under my jurisdiction."

"Information is too general a term. You will have to speak in specifics."

Von Schleiben paused. "Perhaps they would be interested to learn that we are listening in on the transatlantic-cable conversations between Roosevelt and Churchill."

"They already know that."

"There is a plan afoot to assassinate Pétain if the Allies attempt to rescue him."

"They are fully aware of the SD commando detachment waiting in the south of France. I myself passed the information on."

"I could offer an outline of Kuprov's operation. He has infiltrated German hospitals with low-grade agents, usually wounded or deformed men, who serve as orderlies or menials. The demand for this type of labor is so great that almost no security clearance is required. Once the agents have penetrated the hospitals they report back on the number of wounded soldiers and officers brought in as well as the units they come from. With this sampling the Russians are able to make projections establishing the total casualties of each German division. Needless to say, this information also gives the Russians a rather accurate picture of the Army's order-of-battle deployment."

"I think the British might be greatly interested in this."

"No. I want the Americans."

"Then provide something they will find appealing."

Von Schleiben paused in obvious concentration.

"Perhaps," he began confidentially, "the Americans would like to know what I have collected on G. P. G."

"G. P. G.?"

"Have you ever heard of it?"

"No—not that I can remember."

"How odd, dear Peppermint. How very peculiar—since G. P. G. is precisely the American operation you are now employed by. Ah, yes," continued von Schleiben, "your International Assistance group did good work It brought many a refugee out of wartorn Europe and provided for them. It constantly attempted to help even more. In the name of humanity it made contact with various churches, charities, governments, espionage services, resistance groups—anyone who could help. You even dealt with me. But none of this is unusual for a refugee organization, is it?

"The degree of your legitimacy always eluded me, Peppermint. Now I realize that you were a front from the very beginning. American intelligence elements organized you long before that country's entry into the war. You were the perfect listening post on friend and foe alike—but I have a strong suspicion that your main concern was the concentration camps. You were the organization where all camp escapees were cared for—and *interrogated*. Almost all your early

83

contacts had some relationship to the camps. That's how you came across Erik Spangler. You *do* recall Spangler?"

"Spangler?"

"You used him on many occasions then, remember, Father? I think I even provided you with information that was subsequently passed on to him."

"The name sounds vaguely familiar—but I deal with so many people. Please, don't interrupt your fairy tale. The suspense is killing me."

"My pleasure, Peppermint," von Schleiben replied with a half salute. "After America entered the war, you went under the direct jurisdiction of the O. S. S.—even though your main contact appeared to be the British MI-6. Then approximately eight months ago the O. S. S. was out of the picture and you were instructed to function independently. It was during this period that your main interest shifted from concentration camps and began to rest on establishing stronger relationships with clandestine resistance groups within Germany, as well as on the worldwide search for exile German writers, technicians and other assorted professions. The motives behind these orders were unknown to you at the beginning, but as your operation grew in manpower, money and equipment you became a much more dominant factor in the project. For all I know, Peppermint, you may be one of the main planners."

"Am I allowed to know in what?"

"G. P. G."

"Those curious initials again, Wilhelm?"

"Very curious and *very* secret, Father. G. P. G. is so secret that the British know nothing of it—nor are they supposed to. In fact, even the United States military is kept in the dark. All that certain privileged generals and admirals have been told is that orders marked 'G. P. G.' must receive maximum priority and dispatch—and minimum questioning. It all sounds very important, wouldn't you say, Peppermint?"

"And mysterious, Wilhelm."

"Oh, G. P. G. has its more human side. Take, for example, Lady

Cecelia. The center of G. P. G.'s clandestine activities is a country estate on the eastern coast of Britain with the highly Anglo-romanticized name of Westerly. Westerly covers approximately forty-five square miles of land and was rented seven weeks ago from its owner, Lady Cecelia.

"Lady Cecelia is a charming lunatic. First of all, she refused to move from the grounds, so she was installed in the gatehouse near the main entrance. Secondly, she is maniacally inquisitive. When she discovered she had been isolated from her lands by a barbed-wire fence, she took to sitting on her rooftop with opera glasses. When this wasn't enough for her curiosity she took to crawling over or under the fencing.

"With true American ingenuity the fence was electrified, which led to a mass slaughter of the magpies who came to roost on the wires. Lady Cecelia is a wildlife fanatic, so she rushed to the defense of her feathered friends. Large signs were erectd near the main gate calling her tenants murderers. The daily death toll was painted in three-foot-high letters.

"The sophism of American gentility emerged, and behold, the fence was de-electrified. For perimeter protection a second fence, four feet higher, was erected three yards inside the first. The area within the two fences was seeded with electronic listening devices. If so much as a twig should drop on this hallowed strip, arc lights flash on, sirens wail, hordes of half-crazed watchdogs are released and mobile as well as foot patrols rush to the suspicious point. And this is exactly what happened—twigs began dropping. Sometimes branches and often acorns, but mainly twigs. Once they hit the ground, the estate lit up like the Burning Bush." Von Schleiben paused and uncorked a bottle of champagne.

"Astounding, Wilhelm. This information will bring a record price from almost any comic-book publisher."

"Here's to comic books." Von Schleiben lifted his silver goblet. "Our second installment can cover the American exotic machinations *within* their double-fenced sanctuary.

"First the outer fence goes up. The following day the convoys bring machinery and four hundred men up the winding path. In twenty-four hours the gardens are torn out and completely replaced with new landscaping. Capability Brown gives way to Versailles.

"Now the Americans take to working only at night. The main house and the connecting South Hall and Great North Hall are completely refurbished. Heating and air-conditioning units are installed. Intricate electrical security systems are installed. The three buildings are sectioned off into four isolated sections. Each section has its own electrical system and secondary alarm system. Each section has its own kitchens, dining rooms and living facilities. Double passes and identification cards are needed to move from one section to the next. The passes and identification cards change daily. There is one section that no one, so far, has been allowed into. That is the Great North Hall. Work is still going on inside, but, even so, no one from the other three sections has ever passed the guard gates.

"Below the hill, to the rear of the main buildings, camouflage netting has been raised. Underneath are fifty Quonset huts and thirty-two wood frame buildings. An emergency power plant was concealed underneath an ornamental swimming pool. A secret airstrip has been built deep in the woods. The ruins of the abbey above the forest preserve now conceal a steel radio tower twenty meters high that rises at night and retracts at dawn.

"The most interesting fact about all of this construction was the time span in which it was accomplished. Everything I have told you about was completed within twelve days of the Americans' putting up the first fence."

"And was that all the building that was done?" the Priest inquired.

"Oh, no, there was one last little project. Since Lady Cecelia persisted in observing all movement through the main gate, the Americans have just completed an eighteen-mile double-lane concrete highway leading out of the rear of Westerly. The first convoy up this new highway arrived by night and was under the strictest security. It consisted of eighteen tarpaulin-draped trailer trucks carrying printing presses—the type you publish large newspapers with." The last of the Dom Perignon trickled into von Schleiben's glass. He reached for another bottle and began to untwist the metal cap seal.

"And what is the meaning of those initials G. P. G?" asked the Priest.

"Its cover name is General Preparations Group, but its actual meaning is German Propaganda Group. Well, good Father, what do you think? Will the Americans be interested in what I have just related?"

"Why should they be interested in what they already know?"

"So that their British and Russian allies don't find out, for one thing."

"Wilhelm, blackmail is hardly the cornerstone on which to build a lasting relationship."

"What if I revealed my source of information concerning G. P. G. at Westerly?"

"That, Wilhelm, would certainly be interpreted as a token of good faith by the Americans."

"What if I went further and told you where to find this informant?"

Peppermint nodded. "I would say that we then have the beginning of a most appealing package."

"The informant is Rudi Hecht, one of my undercover agents. He is going under the name of Harvey Leigh and is presently employed as personal secretary to Lady Cecelia. Shall I remove him or will you?"

"If there are no objections, Wilhelm, I prefer looking after those arrangements in my own fashion."

The cork popped off the champagne bottle. "And now, good Father, why don't I make the offering to G. P. G. even more appealing? Why don't I give them exactly what they are after?"

"What is it you think they are after so exactly?"

"German political prisoners. Important political prisoners, not leftovers like Vetter or Hilka Tolan."

"If G. P. G. is a propaganda operation, as you said, what would they want with political prisoners?"

"If we are to enact business, I prefer not speculating on the answer to that question, Peppermint. Would G. P. G. be interested in major political prisoners?"

"I didn't think any were still alive."

"No, Father, no, no, no. You most definitely do think some are still alive, but you don't know which ones, or where they are being kept. That is why you brought out Vetter and are planning to free Hilka Tolan. You reason that if the girl can be freed successfully, our security measures will have to be drastically tightened. You anticipate that the most important political prisoners will be transferred to more protected areas. If this transfer occurs, you might be able to see just whom we are holding and where we are sending them.

"It is a desperate scheme, Peppermint. It reveals how badly you need political prisoners of importance. Why whistle a brash and soundless song? Let me supply G. P. G. with men of the caliber they desire."

"The Americans would want to know names."

"Ernst Hauller, Friedrich Tolan, Thomas Brome, Ludwig von Rausch, Hugo Bengl."

"They are all alive?"

"Alive, well and ready for shipment. G. P. G. can have its pick of one. Well, Father, are you interested?"

The Peppermint Priest considered. "There might be interest in Brome and von Rausch," he quietly admitted.

"I myself would have thought Bengl or Tolan would have more value. Each still has his own type of following in Germany, but perhaps I have read the situation wrong."

"And what," Peppermint asked uneasily, "do you want in return?"

"Complete immunity from any war trials that may result from an Allied victory. The guarantee of political asylum in the United States if I find I must flee Germany before hostilities cease. If the Allies do win—and only their own ineptitude could prevent this—I will also need immediate American citizenship. It will also be necessary for the United States government to allow me to transfer my money to their country without protest or examination."

"Is that all?"

Von Schleiben swished the champagne about in his glass. "Oh— perhaps the G. P. G. plan to bring out Hilka Tolan should be dropped. In fact, it must be dropped."

"What else?"

"Erik Spangler's life."

"Spangler again? I told you before, the name is only vaguely familiar."

"From your expression, Father, I would say you go back much further with Spangler than I first suspected. Was he with you in the beginning, when you first started documenting the camps?"

"You must have him confused with someone else. I cannot place the name."

"Yes, he was most definitely with you at the start. They are always the hardest to lose. I have never admired loyalty, Peppermint, not in our profession. Even so, I'll ease your burden. Have G. P. G. show me what he looks like. Let them provide photographs or a clear description. Have them tell me where he is. I will see to the rest—and you won't have been involved."

"And if the Americans refuse?"

"How *can* they refuse? I have what they need."

"They may still refuse."

Von Schleiben shook his head in disgust. "Should they refuse, then the Russians will be told that G. P. G. took Vetter—and why. Not only that, the Russians will further be informed that your real interest lies in the five political prisoners I offered earlier. It will be strongly suggested that if by chance the Russians got to any of the five before G. P. G. did, they would not only disrupt American plans, but also put themselves into excellent bargaining position for the return of Vetter."

Von Schleiben smiled contentedly. "Yes, Peppermint, that is exactly what I'll do if the Americans prove obdurate. I will make a real competition of it—to pay you back for undermining my position

89

with both the Council and Kuprov by sending Spangler to intercept Vetter. I will have those five precious political prisoners moved to new and more secure detention. Then I will sit back and watch the footrace between you and the Russians. It will be grand sport observing which honorable *ally* detects the first prisoner. It will be even more amusing to see if they can free him. Yes, that will be the most amusing way to spend the spring, dear Peppermint—because I have no intention of letting anyone get even near those men. But don't be dejected—at least you have five chances to fail."

"Is that all?"

"More or less. There is one final item I feel should be included."

"What?"

"Since you are back to using Spangler, I must assume that Jean-Claude is also involved. Get Jean-Claude out of Europe or the Bubels will have a new playmate. If you are not familiar with the term *Bubel* I suggest you ask Spangler for a definition.

"So there you have it, Father, plain and simple. I suggest the Americans give it their most serious consideration, for my sake as well as theirs. I really wouldn't want to end up in Russia or South America."

"When do you need your answer?"

"If no one comes after the Tolan girl, I will have my answer."

The Peppermint Priest stepped across the room and began putting on his slicker.

"Going, Father?"

"You wouldn't want me to miss the tide, would you?"

"But, Peppermint, who knows what eyes are watching? The façade must be complete. You must assist me. Every part must fit. Not a suspicion must be aroused."

Von Schleiben pulled open the louvered doors. The girls stood expectantly in the doorway. "Whores talk, Father. We must make everything look natural—or at least unnatural. I have promised my energetic young darlings something special; something they have always wanted. That is why they think you are here. We have been talking, Peppermint. I have been convincing you. I am known not to fail. I am known not to disappoint my darlings. They are waiting,

90

Father. They are waiting for a cleric of their own. It might prove embarrassing if you left without fulfilling their expectations. Then, of course, there is my own curiosity—I have never been sure if you really are a priest. Perhaps their findings will answer my question."

Von Schleiben leaned back against the table and watched the young women enter the room. The two whores stood facing the Peppermint Priest. They smiled enigmatically as their gowns fell open.

The boat floated free of the pilings and started its engine. The Peppermint Priest scrambled down the ladder, pushed into the tiny cabin, stripped off his cassock and took his neatly pressed uniform from the hanger. He had finished dressing and was adjusting his Ben Franklin glasses when the wireless operator stuck his head through the hatch.

"Contact G. P. G. Two, Purple Line," the former priest ordered. "Tell them the Lone Ranger must be delayed. He must not ride. Whatever happens, the Lone Ranger must stay off his horse. Tell them I think I can lay my hands on an Orator."

The petty officer returned half an hour later. "Major Julian, sir," he said unhappily, "Purple Line has just replied."

"And?"

"They received our message and got it through to the Lone Ranger—and, well . . ."

"What is it?"

"The Lone Ranger told them to fuck off."

10

AT DUSK the twelve "isolation" rooms on Floor One, B Barracks, were unlocked and the twelve women escorted out. They formed ranks, marched across Oranienburg and filed into the arrivals building. Each was given new shoes and a new prison dress for the inspection. Each was assigned the number of an office where her physical examination would take place.

Hilka Tolan entered door 11K. The room was dark except for spotlights glaring down on a crude wooden platform. She was ordered to stand at center stage. Three women lined up to her left, four to her right. All were in civilian dress. All had short-cropped haircuts like hers. All were the same height. All slightly resembled her— they were tall, blond, slightly reminiscent of Jean Arthur.

The woman to her immediate right was too fat. The woman second from her left was too thin. Both were dismissed.

Hilka and the five remaining women were ordered to undress. All six bodies bore appendix scars. Hilka was ushered to the left of the stage. In turn each of five companions was placed at her side. The first one's knees were slightly knocked. She was eliminated. The third one did not possess Hilka's high tight breasts. The fourth lacked her flat stomach, thin thighs and long graceful legs.

The second and the fifth were the final choices. They moved back center stage, and Hilka stepped between them.

The cosmeticians and the makeup people moved in. Brush and paint and powder and putty were applied. Within an hour, three beautiful blue-eyed, thin-lipped, oval-faced, ivory-skinned women were on display.

Hilka and the woman to the right stepped forward. The comparison took ten minutes. The woman to the right stood aside, and the woman to the left lined up. The second comparison was slightly shorter. Cosmeticians instituted further adjustments. Another comparison took place. The woman to the right was chosen to impersonate Hilka Tolan.

The lights went out. Hilka was dressed in an SS-Totenkopf greatcoat that fit perfectly and a death's-head several sizes too large. Her mouth was taped. She was pushed out the back door, down the outside steps and into the rear seat of a waiting Mercedes-Benz. Webber slid in beside her. His right wrist was handcuffed to her left. He adjusted his monocle with his free hand and gave an order. The staff car sped out of Oranienburg.

I I

THE GESTAPO'S informant's tip had been correct. The stolen Documents Division truck was found concealed near an orchard less than fifteen miles from Berlin. At least fifty newly printed and validated Reich passports were missing. So were uncountable numbers of other official permits.

The loss of the documents was not the only discovery. The truck contained a cache of recently missing goods. Included in the loot were uniforms taken from a Wehrmacht officers' club and many pieces of clothing stolen from three of the better Berlin shops. Two cases of ammunition and a crate of Lugers were also uncovered.

The most curious discovery was found in the front seat of the truck cab. There could be little doubt that it was the clothing locker stolen from von Schleiben in Munich. The General was contacted by phone, and the details of the discovery were painstakingly recounted to him.

A special car raced the locker back to Berlin despite the air raid.

12

THE BLUE-GRAY elevator cage descended to the fifth level of the underground bunker. Eight delegates to the Council for Extreme Security stepped out, moved quickly through the concrete tunnels and entered the conference room. Von Schleiben was waiting calmly at the head of the table. The time was 2230 hours, 20 February 1944.

"Where is Webber?" the General asked impatiently.

"Seeing to the Tolan woman's new detention, Herr Obergruppenfuehrer," Platt assured. "He'll be here any moment." The room shuddered slightly from the bomb explosions above.

"I see."

Webber had still not arrived by 2400 hours. Platt made a phone call.

"It is a very heavy raid, Herr Obergruppenfuehrer," he said to the General, hanging up the receiver. "He has probably taken refuge. Perhaps we should proceed without him?"

The meeting began informally. Photographs of Hilka Tolan's impersonator were distributed. Von Schleiben was told that the woman had already taken Hilka's place in Isolation Four, B Barracks. Phone communication with the operations area was established. The six rings of interior security were in place. The exterior rings outside Oranienburg were poised. On orders from the Council the final phase of the Webber Proposition was ready to be put into effect: all outgoing movement in the thirty square miles surrounding Oranienburg would be stopped. Anyone trying to leave the perimeter would be seized. Entry was open. Departure impossible.

"Very much like a lobster trap?" von Schleiben noted.

"Exactly, Herr Obergruppenfuehrer," Platt replied.

Von Schleiben was full of questions. Was everyone certain that the last stage of the plan should be put into effect? After all, since Gestapo had been elevated to co-sponsor of the operation and almost every police and intelligence agency—with the exception of Abwehr—was deeply involved in it, a failure would be most humiliating. Perhaps they should stop and reassess the situation.

"Herr Obergruppenfuehrer," Platt rejoined, "the plan, whatever its merits, has been executed to perfection. No one will be able to leave that area."

"Even so," von Schleiben said, "I feel a vote should be taken."

The show of hands in favor of proceeding was unanimous. Von Schleiben smiled and signaled his agreement. Platt called in the order by phone. Confirmation that Webber Proposition was in full initiation was received within ten minutes.

Von Schleiben led the members of the Council to the adjoining underground mess hall, where a lavish champagne supper had been prepared. The officers held up their glasses and waited for a toast from their leader.

Von Schleiben smiled without amusement and snapped his fingers. The provost hoisted the famous locker in front of the General. Von Schleiben lifted the lid, peeked inside and tilted the metal container forward. Webber's decapitated head bounced out and rolled along the table. For some inexplicable reason the monocle over his left eye was still set firmly in place.

PART TWO

The
Julian Proposition

13

Goebbels Seduces His Own Twelve-Year-Old Illegitimate Daughter! Hitler Sets Up Special Tribunal!

—Headline from the *German Popular Gazette*,
printed 17 January 1944, for release 6 April 1944

THE O.S.S. Lysander liaison aircraft skimmed over the moonlit Channel swell, cleared the English coastline, banked sharply and droned due south.

A melody was heard. Hilka Tolan began to stir. Her lips moistened. Her eyes flickered open and slowly focused on the back of the pilot's neck. She tried to shift position, then looked down. She was strapped into a bucket seat. There was a gentle tug at her left arm. Hilka glanced to the side. A lean man with beret and leather cycle jacket was sitting cross-legged on the cabin floor humming to himself as he filed the steel manacle encasing her wrist.

"Where are we?" she finally asked.

"Aha," Spangler cried out expansively, looking up, "awake at last! And how does your jaw feel?"

Hilka studied the violet-eyed, sharp-nosed windburned face. The cheekbones were high. The thin lips curled in a tight, curious smile. She found something crudely handsome in him. Something childlike. Something unrevealed and brooding. "Where are you taking me?"

"Excuse the sock in the face, lass. I'm not one to be hitting the ladies. But you *was* kicking up one helluva ruckus back there in Germany—and anyway, I was forced to reach some messy conclusions with that Webber, conclusions you might not have found overly appetizing. But that's all done with and now, as you see, you're safe and snug."

"Am I expected to thank you?"

Spangler laid aside the file and began bending the blood-caked handcuff. "If your right arm's a little sore, don't worry, it'll wear off. I had to inject you with a sleeping drug—easier to travel without you clawing at me. Do you feel up to some Coca-Cola and doughnuts? They're not bad at all."

He strained harder to snap the manacle. The metal wouldn't give. Filing resumed. So did the humming.

Hilka turned away and rested her head against the cold perspex of the canopy. "Take me back," she said softly.

"Take you back?"

"To the camp. To Oranienburg."

"Why, did you leave something behind?"

"You had no right to come for me. I told them I didn't want to leave. Take me back," she begged desperately, as a solitary tear trailed down her cheek.

"If I were you, dear child, I'd stop the play-acting and try one of these doughnuts."

Hilka glowered at Spangler. "Who are you?"

"A myth."

Spangler swung his legs up and draped them over the auxiliary gas tank in front of him. He handed the file across to Hilka. "Here, you saw for a while. It'll take your mind off things. And anyway, it's your wrist, not mine."

Hilka looked down at the file she was holding and then stared back at Spangler. He was checking his watch. His hand darted into his pocket, withdrew a small box and poured the last of the orange capsules into his other palm. Spangler examined them with obvious dissatisfaction and gave the container an extra shake. Nothing came out. He tossed the box away and put the pills into his mouth. He chewed with obvious relish as the plane dropped sharply.

"Coming in," the pilot called back over his shoulder.

The Lysander bumped down and bounced forward over the rough landing area. The engine cut and the craft braked to a stop.

"Boyo," Spangler said to the pilot with a yawn, "I've had me one helluva long night. Be a good fellow and deliver our pretty lump of weeping cargo here, will you, and pick up my things. A suitcase and envelope will be ready. I'll wait here and spin meself off an erotic dream or two until we leave."

"Sorry, sir, we're not leaving. This is the end of the line."

"Don't be ignorant, man. You're to turn this flying tin pile around and take me to Dundalk."

"Orders just came over the radio, sir. This is as far as we go."

"Far as we go, is it?" Spangler muttered as he pushed out of his seat. "You stay where you are and wait for me."

He unbolted the cabin door, lifted it and jumped down onto the thick, moist fairway grass of the abandoned golf course.

"Get me Julian," he shouted to the solitary mechanic hurrying toward him.

"Major Julian isn't here, sir. He's—"

"Then get Hanson or Green, and put some snap into it."

"They're not here either, sir. No one's here. The entire operation moved out two days ago."

"Moved out? Where?"

"Don't know, sir. But there's another plane waiting for you on the third fairway."

"The hell with the other plane. Get this one refueled and load on my things."

"Sir, there are no things. There is no more gas."

"There's a suitcase. There's an envelope. Now get them for me."

"Sir, nothing is here, nothing at all. I wouldn't lie to you, honest. Everything is gone."

Spangler stiffened, then dashed through the rough, up the overgrown path and into the unlit gabled clubhouse. The main floor was stripped bare. He took the stairs two at a time and raced down the corridor. The padlock and hinge were missing from his private room. He threw open the door and rushed in. Everything was gone. The room was empty.

There was a grunt of rage as Spangler's fist crashed through the plaster wall. He rolled back against the doorframe and fought for control. His breathing eased. He checked his watch, thought for a moment and then darted from the room.

The mechanic was pulling camouflage netting off an American twin-engine Beechcraft parked under the trees off the beginning of the third fairway. Spangler boosted himself through the fuselage door and hurried forward to the pilot's compartment.

"A small case?" he demanded. "Did you bring a small black case for me?"

"No, sir," the captain replied.

"Anything else? Was anything else left? Any other package?"

"Only food and beverage, sir. But I do have a bottle of rye here, if you'd care for a taste."

"Are you taking me to Julian?"

"I'm not acquainted with the name, sir."

"Well, find out, dammit, find out. Radio ahead and ask if Julian is waiting. Major Julian."

"Can't use the radio, sir. Security silence, you know. But even if I could, I wouldn't know what signal to send." He pointed to a small metal box attached to the instrument panel. "I'm being directed by ground control."

"You mean you don't know where the Christ we're going?"

"That's about it, sir."

Two lines of facing bucket seats were fastened to the cabin walls. Spangler sat across from Hilka. The propellers whined, the aircraft taxied forward and turned. The pilot opened the throttle and released the brakes. The lift-off seemed to relax Spangler.

He closed his eyes and breathed deeply. The drone of the Cyclone engines began to lull him. He felt a lightness, a certain drift. The smell of fresh bread grew more distinct. He saw himself in the distance descend the stone steps and start down the narrow cobblestoned street. His stride was long and determined. It stopped before the bakery. He turned and continued on past the line of lead-paned shop windows. He stopped again by the green copper Goethe statue in the small square. Organ music came from within the single-spired medieval church opposite. He gazed at the columned building to its right, bolstered his courage and started across.

"Are you all right?" Spangler heard the voice call urgently. "Do you hear me. Are you all right?" He felt the hand on his leg. He blinked down. Hilka was kneeling before him.

"What's the matter, luv?"

"You were shouting," she replied in relief. "You must have been having a nightmare."

"Don't have nightmares."

"But look at yourself. You're soaked through with perspiration."

"Always work up a good sweat sleeping."

"You were shouting."

"Shouting what?"

"Something about Forst. Is that the city Forst?"

Spangler inadvertently touched his face. The skin was cold and moist. "Go roll your bandages somewhere else," he snapped.

"Excuse me?"

"Get away. Scram. Stop bothering me."

Hilka rose and backed off in confusion. She started to turn, but hesitated. "Your accent?"

"Now what?"

"Your accent has changed. When we talked before you had an English accent."

"I guess that makes us a matched pair of Sunday liars, eh?"

"Liars? I don't understand."

"How long are you supposed to have been in a concentration camp?"

"Almost . . . three years."

"Three years at Oranienburg?"

"I was at Belsen and Mauthausen before."

103

"Come here."

Hilka came closer.

"Take off your clothes," Spangler ordered.

She didn't move.

"Take them off."

"Why should I?"

Spangler reached up and tore away the front of her dress. Her naked breasts jutted high and firm. She covered herself and spun away.

"Baby," Spangler said indifferently, "women who've been in camps only a *month* don't hesitate when they're ordered to take off their clothes. Women who've been in camps for almost three years don't have any breasts left. They're all dried up inside and out. And, lady, they don't cry, they never never cry—there just aren't any tears left."

"I can explain—"

"Explain to someone who gives a damn. I'm finished with all of you. I'm out of it. I'm stepping away for good. So just sit down and keep quiet—and stop your goddam staring."

14

JEAN-CLAUDE pulled his knees tight to his chest and wedged himself into a sitting position between the twin chimneys on the roof. The bricks radiated a slight amount of heat. He pulled tight the lapels of his stolen Luftwaffe overcoat in a vain attempt to keep out the early-morning snow.

Six, he reminded himself, breathing on his ungloved fingers. I mustn't forget. There should be six. Six.

He waited less than an hour. The rumbling came from the north. This was good. Spangler had said they would come from the north. If they came within a day it probably wasn't a decoy. If they came within a day and there were six men, not five or seven, then the transfer was in effect. Spangler had told him the quicker they moved, the more reliable the indications. If the Germans took their time, then watch out for a trick. A trick would take time to plan.

Jean-Claude inched up and along the roof crest until he could look directly across into the yard of the ancient prison. Two SS motorcycles preceded the windowless Gestapo van up the narrow, snow-choked street. Three more motorcycles followed. The iron gates opened, and the convoy turned in. The van swung around and started backing toward the prison building. Jean-Claude focused his binoculars as the canvas was unfastened and the rear of the truck unlocked. Two shadowy forms were pulled down and shoved into the prison. Jean-Claude counted under his breath as the third and fourth appeared. Then the fifth. He strained at the eyepieces. The sixth finally emerged and disappeared inside. Six shadowy forms. Six faceless men.

Jean-Claude started down the roof and suddenly stopped. Should he wait? If this was only a transfer point the trucks might stop just long enough to refuel. They might leave again shortly. The prisoners would be coming out of the building then; they would be coming out in his direction; he might be able to see their faces: he might be able to discover if the Orator was among them. But the message from Spangler had been specific: *Count the prisoners.* That was the most important thing. Identification was secondary to the count. If there were six, get word through to the north. There were only two routes the Germans could follow from here. Let the north find out who was in the shipment.

But what if it really *was* a decoy? Jean-Claude asked himself. Why not wait a little longer and see if this is a decoy or the real thing? The men up north were American agents. Does Spangler trust American agents? They were new, were they not? What if they bungled it?

Jean-Claude moved back between the twin chimneys. Yes, he had better wait a little longer. Not till daylight, but just a little longer. After all, what else did he have to do?

The SS emerged within the hour, formed a large ring in the courtyard and held their machine pistols at hip level. Jean-Claude raised his field glasses over the roofcrest and followed the first prisoner out the door and into the center of the circle. An order was shouted. The prisoner, hugging his arms to his body, began running in place in the ankle-high snow. On command he executed four awkward knee bends and a far from successful push-up. Another order was called out. The prisoner scrambled into the rear of the van.

Jean-Claude swung the glasses back to the doorway and watched the second prisoner go through the same procedure as the first.

The third prisoner was somewhat more defiant. He stepped from the building and hesitated. The order was repeated. The man raised his head and stared up into the snowfall without moving forward.

106

Jean-Claude strained at his binoculars, etching into memory every detail of the wide nose and the dense eyebrows. The hair seemed silver-blue and was cut close to the square skull. The man's complexion was sallow, his jaw tight and obdurate. It was the eyes that differed from one of the six photographs Jean-Claude had taped to his wrist. They were hardly eyes at all, mere dark depressions above the flat cheeks. Perhaps the insufficient light caused the effect, but Jean-Claude had no doubts—he had found the Orator.

A third command was shouted. Still the Orator did not move. He was truncheoned to his knees and dragged into the van.

Jean-Claude bicycled for more than an hour before reaching the convent grounds. The greenhouse was a shambles. Table after table of seedlings had been overturned. The floorboards had been torn up. Smashed radio equipment was scattered among the debris. Guenther was nowhere to be found.

Jean-Claude rushed up the ice-covered path, circled the main buildings, cut through the orchard and started for the chapel. He heard the chanting of morning Mass and ducked behind a row of snow-laden bushes. The final blessing was given. The doors opened and the long line of nuns trailed silently out. Jean-Claude crouched lower to give the column time to pass. He peeked up. Sister Brendon was standing above him.

"Get away from here," she said gently.

"But Guenther—"

"They have taken Guenther. They have taken the Mother Superior and ten of the sisters. Now go."

"You have to get word through to—"

"We don't know *anyone,* don't you understand? We don't know you or your friends or anybody. They have taken the Mother—and ten of the sisters. The soldiers will be coming back for more of us. We have done all we can. So go, go. I'm sorry, but go."

15

TEAMS OF SOLDIERS began extinguishing the blue-flamed fog torches lining the landing strip cut in the forest. Spangler settled uneasily into the back seat of the Lincoln. His teeth began to chatter as the car moved forward. He clamped them shut and glanced out the rear window. Hilka was descending from the Beechcraft. A second limousine and a contingent of guards waited for her.

Spangler's car swerved onto a forest road.

"Where the hell are we?"

"Hunting preserve, sir," answered the white-helmeted driver.

"Hunting preserve where?"

"Westerly, sir."

"What the Christ is Westerly?"

A glass shield rose out of the top of the front seat and sealed shut in the roof bracket. Spangler leaned forward and pounded against the thick pane. The driver ignored him. Spangler tried the rear doors. They were locked from the outside.

The first traces of a headache began throbbing at his temples. A slight spasm in his left shoulder was followed by a dull, lingering pain. Spangler clutched his arms tight to his chest and stared out the window. He would see nothing but forest and haze for the next half hour.

The limousine pulled to a stop. The single-lane dirt road had ended. A fifteen-foot-high barbed-wire fence lay directly ahead. The white-helmeted driver got out and presented his pass and an envelope of credentials to a yellow-helmeted guard. A yellow-helmeted driver moved behind the wheel. The fence gate was pulled open, and the car crept through. Another fifteen-foot fence loomed twenty yards ahead. The gate pushed back. The car passed through and stopped at the edge of a single-lane asphalt road. The yellow-helmeted driver climbed out and handed his papers to a blue-helmeted guard. The inspection was thorough. A blue-helmeted driver got into the front seat.

The Lincoln gained speed and shot along a broad causeway. The ground fog grew thicker. Spangler's teeth began to chatter. The headache worsened, so did the shoulder pain.

The road ended. A double line of fences could be seen ahead. Credentials were again inspected. A red-helmeted driver took the car through the gates and up to the lip of a two-lane road. The driver waited until a large circle of gold-helmeted sentries were posted around the Lincoln before getting out and disappearing into the drifting fog.

It was several minutes before another man emerged from the grayness. Spangler watched as the form neared. The mist obscured the helmetless face, but there could be little doubt that he carried a small square case. A guard opened the front door. Julian slipped into the driver's seat and picked up the intercom.

"Good to see you again, Erik," he said nervously from behind his fogged wire-rimmed spectacles.

"Give me the case," Spangler shouted at the glass partition.

Julian shook his head and pointed to the receiver on the back seat.

Spangler snatched it up. "Give me the goddam stuff."

"Only if you agree to behave yourself," Julian's voice replied over the rear speaker.

"Stop playing idiot games."

"It is no game, Erik. It is merely self-preservation. We both realize how unpredictable you can be when you're in this somewhat tense condition."

"I wouldn't be in this condition if you'd left my medicine."

"But then you wouldn't be here now, would you? Or at least I couldn't be certain you would respond to an ordinary request for a meeting. And, Erik, it is most important that we have such a meeting."

"Give me the stuff."

"Your word to behave?"

Spangler hesitated, then nodded. The visor lowered six inches, and the case was passed over. Spangler snapped it open, spun the tops off medicine bottles and began swallowing pills.

Julian put aside the intercom, took off his glasses and began drying them. "Sorry I couldn't have met you at the aircraft, but security is cumbersome. This establishment has only been functioning for two weeks, and certain kinks are still to be ironed out."

He replaced his glasses. "You see, the old unit, IRAP, the one which had you bring out Vetter and Miss Tolan, is now part of something much larger and quite spectacular," Julian explained as he watched Spangler roll up a sleeve, dab his arm with alcohol and adjust the syringe. "I know your distaste for organizational undertakings, but this operation is rather different. It might tickle your fancy."

Spangler injected himself with the insulin.

"Yes, Erik, I think we're onto something that will catch your imagination. Might even swerve you from your intention of retiring."

Spangler dropped back in relief.

"The new organization is called G. P. G., Erik—General Projects Group. That's only a cover title, of course. Its actual meaning is—"

"Where's the envelope?" Spangler demanded.

"Envelope? Oh, yes," Julian recalled. He handed the thick packet over the visor. "You'll find everything in order. Tickets, check, an absolutely official discharge from the Army—or is it the Navy?"

"The passports aren't here."

"There was a delay at the Peruvian Embassy. You know how those Latin Americans are. But it's all been worked out. Sent a spe-

110

cial messenger to London. The passports should be at my office when we return."

"They'd better be."

"Erik, are you implying I misuse the truth?"

"Truth? You wouldn't even know how to spell it."

Julian pulled his knees onto the seat and rested his back against the front door. "You see, Erik, it was G. P. G. who wanted both Tolan and Vetter. And now let me tell you *why*. They wanted them—"

"I know why." Spangler said, closing his eyes and massaging the back of his neck.

"That's ridiculous, Erik. How could you know? I thought most of it up myself."

"I know why. Von Schleiben knows why. Any Mongolian idiot who can find his way into an outhouse knows why."

"I don't believe you, Erik," Julian said tentatively. "I don't believe you at all. You're pulling a bluff. I'm calling that bluff. I don't think you have the vaguest."

"My boy," Spangler began, "it's nothing more than a matter of big political fish, little political fish. Vetter and the Tolan girl are little fish—nothing more than bait. You're hoping their escapes will frighten von Schleiben into tightening camp security—transferring some of his big political fish to more secure areas. And while the switch is on, you'll get an idea of who and how many important political prisoners are available for future netting." Spangler opened his eyes, leaned forward and pressed his nose against the visor glass. "How am I doing?"

Julian's lips twitched.

"Now shall I tell you *why* G. P. G. needs German political prisoners with such a black and furious passion? Or would you rather not hear?"

"Erik, must you use that superior tone?" Julian said, trying to regain his composure. "You sound like a constipated Cary Grant."

Spangler laughed and moved back on the seat. "The reason G.P.G. must have political prisoners—"

He lunged forward with tremendous speed. His finger shot up and gripped the edge of the glass dividing visor. The pane snapped. Julian was halfway out the door when Spangler dove into the front seat, grabbed him by the ankle and dragged him back. The gold-helmeted sentries started for the car.

Spangler seized Julian's ear and began to twist it. "Tell them to stay where they are or off it comes."

Julian shouted the order.

Spangler jerked him up in the seat and gave the ear an extra turn. "Now, you chicken thief: you've got thirty seconds to tell me what this is all about."

"Jean-Claude," Julian gasped in pain and panic.

"What about Jean-Claude?"

"He—he won't be waiting for you in Ireland."

"Why not?"

"We had to use him."

"Use him?"

"You were right about our forcing the transfer of German prisoners. We set up a network of observation points near each prison—prisons where we thought important prisoners might be held. We were short of observers. Terribly short."

"So you sent Jean-Claude?"

"He volunteered. I talked to him myself on the short wave."

"But you've never met him."

"No. I only talked to him once—when he was sending in your information."

Spangler jammed Julian against the steering wheel. "You moron! You treacherous moron! Couldn't you tell? From his voice, couldn't you tell?"

"Tell *what?*"

"How old do you think Jean-Claude *is?*"

"He sounded young. Seventeen, eighteen."

"He's *twelve!* He just turned twelve years old. Now order one of your flunkies out there to get on the radio and get him out of wherever he is."

"We don't *know* where he is. He's missing."

Spangler grimaced and tried to think. His grip on Julian's ear eased. "Where was he when you last heard?"

"Outside of Hamburg. He was covering the Kurtweig jail—a prison relay stop. He was supposed to contact his controller every twelve hours. But the radio is dead—all radio communication in that area is dead—"

Spangler pushed Julian behind the wheel. "Drive me back to the airstrip—and you had better have that plane ready."

Julian's ear was released. The major breathed in relief. "Stay here, Erik. Don't go to the plane. You have a better chance of finding him from here."

"Start the car."

"Erik, listen, please listen," Julian said breathlessly. "We have the facilities to find him. That's why I forced you to come here. I want to help. I'll keep a plane ready. I swear I will. Once we have any information, you will be flown wherever you want. At least come and look at our facilities. I feel badly about this, Erik. I'll do everything I can to help. It wasn't *my* idea to use Jean-Claude. I tried to avoid it. You must believe me—it wasn't my idea."

"Then whose *was* it?"

"Kittermaster. Colonel Kittermaster."

"Who the hell is he?"

"The chief of G. P. G. But he's not a bad sort, Erik. It's just that he's new to espionage. He's had no intelligence training."

Julian started the limousine up the road, past convoy after convoy of trucks, bulldozers and cement mixers. The fog lifted. The verdant rolling valley was thick with well-camouflaged construction. The overcast began to burn off. On a high hillcrest, shrouded in scaffolds, stood the Great North Hall, the South Hall and the connecting main house: the massive and venerable center of an estate known as Westerly.

16

SUITE VIII-WHITE on the fifth and uppermost floor of the Great North Hall consisted of a bedroom, a sitting room, a dressing room, a bathroom, a dining room, a kitchen and a library. The furniture and carpeting had come by air from Sloane's, the drapery and the wallpaper from Schumacher. Neiman-Marcus had designed and shipped the bathroom. All the windows were steel-grilled.

The closet in the dressing room contained five sizes of lingerie flown in from Bonwit Teller and Henri Bendel, and four sizes of hosiery from Marshall Field's.

Hilka slid on white panties and a white half slip.

"Not this?" the maid asked, holding out a brassiere.

Hilka studied the undergarment hesitantly. "No," she finally concluded. "I think not. I've lost too much weight. I have no need for it."

"Miss Tolan, your figure is excellent. Your breasts are high and full. Turn around and look for yourself."

"No."

"Then trust my word and take the bra."

"No. I am not used to it any more. It would itch."

"So will a blouse or sweater."

"No."

"Then what about stockings?"

"No. My legs are too skinny for stockings."

114

"Your legs are lovely. Any woman in America would be envious of legs like yours. Please, judge for yourself. Turn around and look in the mirror."

"No—I do not look into mirrors."

"Then how will you be able to put on your makeup?"

Hilka studied the large selection of unopened bottles and boxes on the dressing table. "I only need lipstick. I can put it on by touch."

"And your hair? Can you do your hair without looking in a mirror?"

"Could—could you do it for me? And cut it in the back, please?"

The closets were filled with dresses, suits, skirts, blouses, sweaters, coats and shoes from Bergdorf Goodman and Hattie Carnegie. They came in four sizes. Even so, the smallest beige turtleneck was slightly baggy and the plaid skirt had to be taken in by the maid.

The maid unlocked the entrance door, paused and gave a final touch to Hilka's hair.

"Am I—am I at all pretty?"

"Very pretty," the maid told her, pressing the buzzer. "Just like Jean Arthur."

A WAC with a gold-and-black armband guided her up two flights of marble stairs, through an electrically opened sliding door and out onto a steel catwalk. A vast modern printing complex was spread out below. At one end, workmen in yellow overalls scurried about unpacking new equipment, making final tests and adjustments. At the other, two dozen blue-coated linotypists were already busy at their machines.

The metal walkway led past room after room of glass-enclosed offices. All were fully equipped. All were fully staffed by men and women in blue jackets. No one looked up as Hilka and her guide walked by.

The two women entered the last door. A fragile elderly man with a goatee, wearing a smartly tailored long blue dust coat, was waiting.

"Vetter?" Hilka uttered in disbelief. "Martin Vetter?"

"Welcome, little Hilka—but I see you are not so little any more."

"Was ist—"

"No, no, Hilka," Vetter counseled gently, "English. You must acquaint yourself with the rules. If you wear blue—and you *will* be wearing blue—it means that you are German, but you must speak English. They listen in with devices to make sure."

"I thought you were dead."

"I am. You will find this establishment rich in ghosts—German ghosts. But enough of that. Sit down, sit down! Let me look at you."

Hilka settled on the deep-blue satin couch as Vetter pressed a button on the desk. A man appeared from the next room with a tray of coffee, rolls, cream, sugar, butter and jam.

"Now tell me, where were you? Where did they bring you from?"

"Oranienburg."

"I do not know of Oranienburg. Is it a camp?"

"Yes."

"And the Americans freed you?"

"A man freed me. I am not sure if he is American. He brought me here."

"Just one man?"

"That's all I saw. He stopped the car I was in. He knocked me unconscious. Then he gave me something to make me stay asleep. When I awoke he was in the airplane beside me."

"Did he put you to sleep with a needle? In the arm?"

"I think so. My arm was sore."

"And this man, was he thin and tall? About six feet? Did he have violet eyes?"

"His eyes were violet. He was thin and tall."

"You don't know his name, by any chance?"

"No, he avoided answering that."

"Excellent. Excellent." Vetter nodded, bit into a sweet roll and ate quietly. He sipped his coffee. "They sent Spangler for you, and that is excellent. You see, Hilka, the social strata here are most usually determined by the degree of difficulty the Americans went to in procuring you. Konrad Lottman had to be more or less abducted from Mexico. He certainly didn't come of his own volition. It took time and money. That makes him important. Thomas Hutch and Reinhard Teller were requisitioned, with considerable resistance, from South America."

116

"Hutch? Who would want anything to do with Hutch?"

"He is German, isn't he? In exile? A *well-known* German!"

" 'Infamous' would describe it better."

"Infamy is a relative concept, particularly here. Do you remember Nebel? Oswald Nebel?"

"The mayor who—"

"Who fled to Canada and was soon back to his old proclivities? My old antagonist? Yes, the same Nebel. Well, it is a well-known secret that the Americans went to extreme measures in convincing the Canadians to release him. Thus Herr Nebel enjoys more than his share of prestige in our present environment. But you and I, Hilka, are the most exclusive of the elite. We were brought back by Spangler. The only two, so far. We stand above Nebel. Spangler does not like the Americans, and I don't think they like dealing with him—so you can see how very important we must be. They have you on the fifth floor, no doubt—in the Great North Hall? You must have either Suite Seven or Eight on the fifth floor."

"I'm in Eight."

"Good, *good*. That means we have only one suite to wait for, Number Seven."

"I don't understand."

"Neither do any of us. Not that the Americans are intentionally deceptive, they simply limit the amount of knowledge allowed us. Certain things are obvious—the printing press and the radio studio. But something else is going on. Something dealing with whatever it is they are building on the first three floors of the main house." Vetter paused. "Tell me, Hilka, what news of your father?"

"He is dead, for all I know—or care."

"Now, now, we mustn't—"

"Mustn't what? Speak the truth? Why were any of us arrested if not because of him? You dealt with him. You fought him for years. Why must we be polite at this stage?"

"Certainly your father and I disagreed, but he was honorable in his—"

"He was despicable, and you know it. There was little difference between Himmler and him."

117

"I would have preferred your father to succeed rather than Herr Himmler."

"And I prefer to drop the subject." Hilka put down her cup and glanced about the modern office. "What do they have you doing here?"

"I am ostensibly the publisher."

"Publisher?"

"Of a newspaper. The *German Popular Gazette*."

"But what do you know about newspapers?"

"Nothing. There's no need to. They tell me what to do. They supply the important stories."

"And me? What do the Americans expect of *me*?"

"Why, you are to be one of my editors. You are to be responsible for all matters relating to German women within the Reich. In addition you will have your own little chitchat column. This is your office we're sitting in. You've been assigned a staff of three. In between your newspaper assignments, you'll be expected to make radio transcriptions upstairs at the German Popular Gazette of the Air."

"I know nothing of this type of work."

"Then, to quote our benefactor, Colonel Kittermaster, what an opportunity to learn!"

"What *kind* of newspaper? What kind of radio program? What is their purpose?"

"While Major Chumley was running things, that was rather easy to answer. We had thirty-five issues ready for distribution. In fact, if you look out that window you'll see the three warehouses where they are stored. But that was yesterday. Now Colonel Kittermaster has taken over personally. New equipment has been moved in and our purposes are somewhat obscure. You will find, my dear, that when Colonel Kittermaster is directly involved, purposes are *always* somewhat obscure. So there you have it."

Vetter reached into the desk, brought out a sheet of paper and handed it to Hilka. "This is about as much as I know about the good colonel's policy, for the moment."

Hilka glanced down.

118

Printer's Sample   For Translation
(Note: *German Popular Gazette* will always
appear in 75% type size.)
Composed and Approved by: L. B. Kittermaster

Type size

75%	ATTENTION ATTENTION ATTENTION ATTENTION ATTENTION
100%	TRUE PATRIOTS OF GERMANY: TAKE HEART!
100%	TRUE PATRIOTS OF GERMANY: YOU ARE NO LONGER ALONE!
100%	TRUE PATRIOTS OF GERMANY: FREEDOM IS AT HAND!

75%   TRUE PATRIOTS OF GERMANY:

50%   On this day is born the GERMAN POPULAR GAZETTE.

75%   TRUE PATRIOTS OF GERMANY:

50%   The GERMAN POPULAR GAZETTE is a weekly newspaper
written and published by loyal and patriotic Germans
in exile for their freedom-loving brothers trapped
under the boot heel of the insane tyrant Hitler and his
Nazi horde.

75%   TRUE PATRIOTS OF GERMANY:

50%   10,000,000 copies of the GERMAN POPULAR GAZETTE
will be printed and air-dropped throughout your enslaved
country each and every week.

75%   TRUE PATRIOTS OF GERMANY:

50%   For the first time in 10 years the lies of Goebbels
will be exposed and the truth told. Here are some
of the revelations to be covered:

100%   HITLER'S RECENT ATTEMPT AT SUICIDE
EVA BRAUN'S RECORD OF PROSTITUTION
GOERING'S DOPE ADDICTION
HIMMLER'S JEWISH ANCESTRY
BORMANN'S HOMOSEXUALITY

75%   TRUE PATRIOTS OF GERMANY:

50%   Watch for the first issue of the GERMAN POPULAR
GAZETTE. Stay tuned to your short-wave radio sets—bands
078 and 081—for the first broadcasts of the GERMAN
POPULAR GAZETTE OF THE AIR.

119

17

JULIAN BEGAN Spangler's tour at Communications, a vast complex of recently completed camouflaged Quonset huts and wooden structures at the base of the hills to the rear of the Great North Hall.

C-1, Monitoring, was the largest of the eight self-contained divisions comprising Communications. Bilingual radio operators were already tuned in on every conceivable area of Europe and North Africa from which reception was possible. The general monitoring of German domestic broadcasts took five buildings by itself. Wehrmacht communications required an additional six Quonset huts. Three wooden structures covered the French radio. Belgium and the Netherlands were assigned a building each, as were Norway, Denmark, Portugal, Spain, Morocco, Algeria, Tunisia and Libya. Eighteen buildings were devoted to British radio communications, and three more for this purpose were under construction. Switzerland and Italy had two Quonset huts each. Every monitored broadcast was wire-recorded. The personnel which manned the three daily eight-hour shifts were billeted in twenty-one barracks. A massive Quonset hut served as both mess hall and recreation area. C-1 was completely enclosed in barbed wire. No one could leave or enter without undergoing an arduous credentials inspection.

Internal Security was known as C-4. The compound contained

seven buildings and was linked to the primary alarm systems at Westerly. Any penetration of the area would be recorded on its machines. C-4A was the nerve center that kept in constant contact with guard teams patrolling the one hundred and twenty miles of perimeter fencing enclosing the estate.

C-4 and C-4A, Julian pointed out, for some reason had no contact with the six-building complex known as I. P. D., Independent Penetration Detection. I. P. D. was an elaborate secondary alarm system Colonel Kittermaster had ordered installed in the three main buildings on his arrival ten days before. No one really knew its purpose.

C-5 was still under construction. This was the complex which would be fed the propaganda broadcasts emanating from the studios now nearing completion in the main house.

"What propaganda broadcasts?" Spangler asked.

Julian replied offhandedly, "Oh, didn't I mention it before? 'General Projects Group' is just a cover title. G. P. G. is actually German Propaganda Group. This is all a propaganda operation. Our two main fronts are the *German Popular Gazette* and the German Popular Gazette of the Air."

"All this just for propaganda?"

"Colonel Kittermaster is very well connected in Washington."

"What's that over there?" Spangler asked, pointing to the most heavily guarded building he had yet seen.

"A new innovation they just sent in from the States—something called the Monster Machine. I don't know much about it myself, but we'll find out soon. They should have it working any time now."

They finally arrived at C-8, "Dark Channels," located on the third floor of the South Hall. The twenty-by-twenty-five-foot table-top terrain map of Germany was divided into sixteen different-colored sectors. Sixteen headphoned DC-radio operators were seated in a horseshoe around the north, west and south perimeters, listening for signals from clandestine short-wave transmitters from their assigned zones.

"Those sixteen white flags stuck in the map," Julian explained, "are agents who have been heard from in the last twelve hours.

121

Those nine blue flags designate where contact was made twenty-four hours ago."

"What are those?" Spangler asked, pointing to the five red and six black flags arching from Hamburg toward the east.

"The black, Erik, are radio operators out of action—and the red are missing agents." Julian reached out and pulled a red flag from a spot slightly west of Hamburg. "This was the last contact with Jean-Claude."

"What are you doing to find him?"

"This room represents only agents and radios watching for the German prisoner transfer. We are calling agents in from other operations to investigate. Those are the green flags you see moving up from the southwest."

An officer leaned over the table and placed a black flag on Frankfurt.

"Who's that?" Julian demanded.

"Pedro, sir."

"What about Pedro?"

"He stopped transmission in the middle of Harmon's message. The stoppage coincides with a British air strike on Frankfurt. It looks as if he's been tagged, sir."

"Why wasn't I given an Early Report?"

"But you *were,* sir. I made it out myself when Pedro went off the air forty minutes ago."

"I never received it."

"But Colonel Kittermaster said he would give it to you, sir."

"What are you doing sending our material to Colonel Kittermaster?"

"I didn't send anything, sir. Colonel Kittermaster was here and took it himself."

"He was here—in this *room?*"

"Yes, sir. He was conducting an inspection."

"He has no authority to be in this room."

"But, sir, he is the commanding officer."

"Did he take anything else?"

"Yes, sir. He took a copy of every report we filed today."

"What reports? Be specific! I want a complete list, do you under-stand? A complete list of—"

"Major Julian," an aide called, rushing into the room, "they need you upstairs. They've finally got the Monster Machine working."

18

THE BRIDGE was partially destroyed. Convoys were backed up for miles. The van, two motorcycles in front, three behind, had already been waiting five hours when the whistles and the shouting began again.

Volunteer traffic patrols frantically waved trucks and cars off the road. Drivers and soldiers dove desperately for cover as R. A. F. Mosquito bombers swept down, angled off and began the strafing. Tracers streaked along the concrete, shredding men, machines and foliage. The aircraft banked gracefully and prepared for a second run, their twin engines muted by distance, vapor streaming from their wingtips.

Jean-Claude leaped from the culvert, darted across the road and zigzagged along the line of abandoned vehicles. The planes opened fire as he slid under the front wheels of the van. Shells tore into the metal above him. Gasoline began to drip and flare. Flames burst out around the cab. Jean-Claude rolled sideways and scrambled for the tree line.

Guards jimmied open the side door of the van. The dazed prisoners jumped to earth and were led into the woods.

Jean-Claude heard the shouts. He dashed to the cab and pulled open the door. He tugged at the dying driver, whose face had vanished into a bloody pulp, and looked up through the smoke and the flames at a map pasted on the roof. Its edges were burning. A blue line traced the route into Poland.

19

JULIAN ENTERED the glass-enclosed studio and seated himself at the makeshift desk. Three telephones, one red, one white, one blue, rested before him. At the base of each instrument were a white and a yellow light. He glanced at his wristwatch. The "last-minute" adjustments had taken over three hours.

"How soon can we make contact?"

The monitor looked up from the operations manual resting on the control board at the opposite end of the room. "Oh. Sorry, sir," he said, throwing a switch and adjusting his earphones. "We already *have*. Relay is waiting on the Blue Line."

The white light on the blue telephone was flashing.

"Relay? What is Relay? I want to talk to VFW."

"You *will*, sir. But we have to go through something called Relay first. I don't know why, but that's how it's set up. Take the Blue Phone, sir."

The major raised the receiver. "Julian here."

There was no answer.

"Julian here!"

Still no response.

"Sir, maybe you should talk louder?" Monitor suggested.

"JULIAN HERE!"

Static rose in the earpiece and subsided. "Who?"

"JULIAN."

"Please repeat."

"JULIAN GODDAMMIT, JULIAN!"

"Julian? We don't know any Julian."

125

"Sir," the monitor called out, "I think they want your BLI."

"My *what?*"

"Your BLI—Blue-Line Identification, sir?"

"Make some sense."

"Your code name for the Blue Phone, sir."

"Well what the hell is it?"

"Don't you know, sir?"

"Do I sound as if I do?"

"Oh." The monitor hurriedly checked the identification sheet. "You're Oop, sir."

"Who?"

"It says Oop, sir. O-o-p."

"OOP HERE."

Static again rose. "We read you, Oop. Relay reads you and welcomes you aboard. Security Delay now operative. Repeat, Security Delay now operative. Stand by for transfer."

The white light went off. The phone was dead.

"What is Security Delay?" Julian asked.

"I'll look it up, sir," the monitor replied, riffling through the operations manual.

The white light went on. The earpiece crackled.

"Oop?" called the Voice from Washington, "Do you read me, Oop? This is Sweet Pea calling. Do you read Sweet Pea, Oop?"

"I HEAR—I READ YOU."

The phone went dead. The white light was off. Julian shook the receiver. "We've lost bloody contact."

"Have we, sir?" the monitor asked, looking up from the manual.

"Aren't you watching? What the hell are you doing here if you're not watching?"

"Trying to look up Security Delay, sir."

The white light flashed on.

"Oop," the Voice from Washington said, "what do you think of the spanking new communications system they've set up for us? Only one like it in the world, I'm told. Cost better than half a million. Quite a contraption, what? Quite a thing, wouldn't you say?"

"HILARIOUS."

126

The white light went off.

"Here it is, sir," the monitor shouted triumphantly. " 'After each and every exchange of normal conversation between the participants, a *Security Delay* of exactly twelve seconds will be effected during which time both instruments will be inoperative.' "

"Why?" Julian asked.

"I'll look it up, sir."

"Yes, hilarious," the Voice from Washington chuckled as the white light flashed on. " 'Hilarious' is precisely the word. Now tell me, Oop, how is England these days? Been up to London lately? Must get up to London, Oop. First-class city. I know a superlative tailor there. Owe it to yourself to drop in and see him. His name is . . . is . . . Now what the devil is that man's name? Well, better not dawdle on things like this, right, Oop? Time is money you know. Let's get down to it, Oop. Oop, did we pick up Olive Oyl?"

"Sir," the monitor called out before Julian could ask, "Olive Oyl is BLI for Hilka Tolan."

"SHE WAS DELIVERED THIS MORNING."

Julian checked his watch. The white light remained off exactly twelve seconds.

"Splendid, Oop, splendid. And what of Daddy Warbucks? Have we found ourselves a Daddy Warbucks?"

"Daddy Warbucks is the Throne, sir."

"EVERYONE'S IN PLACE. NOW IT'S A MATTER OF WAITING."

Again Julian clocked the delay. The white light came on in ten seconds.

"But how long, Oop? How long a wait?"

"THE NEXT THIRTY-SIX HOURS SHOULD TELL."

The delay took fourteen seconds.

"And if nothing appears in thirty-six hours, then where do we go, Oop? What alternatives do we have, Oop?"

"WHY NOT USE THE RETRIEVER—"

A shrill, high-pitched buzz pierced Julian's ear. The white light was off. The yellow was flashing frantically.

"Sir," the monitor said, with the first vestige of authority, "only Blue-Line Identification can be used."

"Then you'd better give me Spangler's code name—rapidly."

"Absolutely, sir," the monitor replied, quickly checking his chart. "Spangler is Dick Tracy, sir."

The yellow light went off; the white was on.

"Don't be evasive, Oop. Answer my question. If nothing breaks in the next day and a half, then where are we off to?"

"WHY NOT USE DICK TRACY? I'M HOLDING DICK TRACY—JUST AS WE DISCUSSED."

The delay was eleven seconds.

"You took him, Oop? You actually have Dick Tracy in hand?"

"YES. AND I'D LIKE TO MOVE HIM OUT OF HERE RIGHT AWAY."

"Masterful, Oop, masterful," VFW stated as the white light came on. "Never thought you could manage it. But why move him?"

Julian put his hand over the phone. "Who is Kittermaster?"

"Colonel Kittermaster is Mandrake, sir."

"I DON'T WANT MANDRAKE TO GET TO HIM."

The white light was off eight seconds.

"Oop, are you spatting with Mandrake again? You must stop, Oop. I know your feelings about Mandrake, but you must understand—we *need* him! His group still holds the upper hand. Not that our stock hasn't risen here on the Potomac. It has, Oop, it has risen sharply. Many of the right people are starting to overcome their fears about us. Bringing in Olive Oyl will add to our prestige and position. Finding a Daddy Warbucks quickly might push us over the top. But until then, bide your time. Keep Mandrake happy. Do you understand what I'm saying, Oop?"

"I STILL THINK WE SHOULD MOVE TRACY."

"Trust in me, Oop. You know your end of this and I know mine. Trust my judgment. While we're about it, just how is Mandrake doing with the little leftovers we've thrown him?"

"HE'S STILL A PAIN IN THE ASS—" The alarm blasted into Julian's ear. The yellow light went on. The phone was dead.

"Transfer Time, sir," Monitor announced.

"What in the name of Christ—"

"The Red Phone, sir. It's time to transfer to the Red Phone."

"Why?"

"I don't know, sir. It seems to be up to Relay. We're ready on the Red Phone, sir."

The white light is flashing on the Red Phone. Julian picked it up. "MANDRAKE IS—"

The blast in Julian's ear was even louder than before. The yellow light was on.

"Oh, sorry, sir," the monitor said. "Red-Line Identification is now in effect. Colonel Kittermaster is Clark Kent. You're Charlie McCarthy. Sweet Pea, I mean VFW, is Edgar Bergen. Spangler is—"

"Give me that damn code sheet!"

The monitor raced across the room and handed it over the desk. Julian looked down.

TOP SECRET   *TOP SECRET*

M. M. IDENTIFICATION

For: Conversation No. 1   5 February 1944
    Copies Restricted to: LBK   RELAY
                      VFW   MONITOR I
                      JJ   MONITOR II

NAME	G.P.G. CODE	RED LINE	WHITE LINE	BLUE LINE
KITTER-MASTER	GEORGE	CLARK KENT	CAPTAIN BLOOD	MANDRAKE
VFW	TEDDY	E. BERGEN	MICKEY ROONEY	SWEET PEA
JULIAN	ULYSSES	C. MCCARTHY	BEN TURPIN	OOP
CHUMLEY	WOODROW	CLAGHORN	ARBUCKLE	GOOFY
GAZETTE	G.P.G. 1	EDWARD GEE	TRUE SCREEN	KING COMICS
GAZETTE-OF-AIR	G.P.G. 1A	SINGING LADY	SPENCER	LOTHAR'S DRUM
ROOM NINE	G.P.G.	SANCTUM	MANDALAY	MOORE'S
WESTERLY	PHILLY	WISTFUL VISTA	TARA	GASOLINE ALLEY
1ST CHAIR.	DOC	DOC	DOC	DOC
2ND CHAIR.	SNEEZY	SNEEZY	SNEEZY	SNEEZY
3RD CHAIR.	SMILY	SMILY	SMILY	SMILY
4TH CHAIR.	GRUMPY	GRUMPY	GRUMPY	GRUMPY
5TH CHAIR.	HAPPY	HAPPY	HAPPY	HAPPY
6TH CHAIR.	DOPEY	DOPEY	DOPEY	DOPEY
7TH CHAIR.	BASHFUL	PORTLAND	THEDA	OLIVE OYL
THRONE	SNOW WHITE	COUGHLIN	LIVINGSTON	DADDY WARBUCKS
SPANGLER	RETRIEVER	MR. KEEN	STANLEY	DICK TRACY

"Sir, VFW is waiting on the line," Monitor said cautiously.

Julian raised the receiver.

"You didn't answer my question, McCarthy. Just how is Clark Kent doing?"

"MAGNIFICENTLY. HE'S BLOSSOMED INTO A FULL-FLEDGED CONSTRUCTION MANIAC. HE'S BUILDING FIVE TIMES THE FACILITIES WE NEED. HE'S ALSO DUPLICATED OUR ENTIRE SECURITY ALARM SYSTEM WITH ONE OF HIS OWN. I THINK HIS MOTHER WAS FRIGHTENED BY THE W.P.A."

"Go easy on the W. P. A., McCarthy. The W. P. A. is well thought of here. When the elders on the Hill allocate funds they expect them to be spent. The more you spend, the better—as long as they see tangible results. Nothing is more tangible than construction. Don't let Clark Kent get the edge on you in this area. Get out there and do a little spending of your own. Now what other news of Clark Kent."

"NOT TOO MUCH. HE GOT RID OF CLAGHORN YESTERDAY AND PERSONALLY TOOK OVER EDWARD GEE AND THE SINGING LADY."

"Edward Gee? The Singing Lady? He *can't* do that, McCarthy. That's not his jurisdiction!"

"HE'S IN COMMAND ISN'T HE? WHO CAN STOP HIM? AND HE'S ADDED A RATHER RUSTIC TOUCH TO THE PAPER. THE HEADLINE TO HIS FIRST ISSUE DEALS WITH THE SEX LIVES OF THE NAZIS. CLARK KENT'S PERSONAL GENIUS IS BEST REFLECTED IN THREE NEW COLUMNS: 'COOKING TIPS UNDER AIR ATTACK,' 'BARGAIN GUIDE FOR WARTIME SHOPPING' AND, LAST BUT NOT LEAST, 'HOUSEHOLD HINTS DURING A SIEGE.' WHO ELSE BUT CLARK KENT WOULD HAVE THOUGHT OF CROSS-BREEDING A PRIMER ON SODOMY WITH 'POPULAR MECHANICS'?"

"This can't be, McCarthy. It simply cannot be."

"BUT IT IS."

"McCarthy, don't you *understand?* Can't you *see?* The aim of that publication is to foment unrest and insurrection among the German population. Sympathetic citizens must be instructed in sabotage techniques. You can't do it with menu suggestions. You can't blow the roofs off their homes and advise them on decorating bomb shelters at the same time. You must *do* something, McCarthy! We must

130

get back to the original format. What about the back editions? Clark Kent hasn't tampered with them, has he?"

"NOT REALLY. HE'S ONLY BURNED HALF OF THEM."

"Why are you telling me all this, McCarthy?" VFW wailed. "Why are you ruining my day?"

"I THOUGHT YOU MIGHT LIKE TO KNOW THAT CLARK KENT IS RAPIDLY BUT SURELY TAKING OVER."

"Ridiculous, McCarthy. He's not taking over anything. He wouldn't know where to begin. Keep your personal feelings out of this. What makes you think he's taking over?"

"HE HAS DEMANDED TO MEET WITH MR. KEEN."

"What was that? How could he know we were using Mr. Keen? How could he even know who he *was*?"

"CLARK KENT HAS A WAY OF FINDING OUT EVERYTHING."

"Well the meeting mustn't take place. Do you understand, McCarthy? *No meeting!*"

"HOW CAN I STOP IT? CLARK KENT IS MY SUPERIOR OFFICER."

"You must stop it, McCarthy. I know you can. Stall him. But nothing impolite. Epps!" VFW shouted. "Carlton Epps."

"WHO?"

"You know," VFW said with relief, after the delay, "that tailor I was telling you about earlier? His name is Epps."

The line went dead.

"Transfer Time, sir," the monitor proclaimed. "White Phone now operative. White-Line Identification now in effect. Sir? Where are you going? VFW is still on the line, sir."

Julian stopped at the door and turned back to the monitor. "Where did that code sheet come from? I don't remember approving anything like that."

"Clark Kent sent it over, sir."

131

20

THE DRAWING ROOM was resplendent with antiques. A scale model of Westerly rested on the table under the tall leaded windows looking out over the restored formal gardens of the main house. Workbenches and drafting tables were lined against the adjacent wall. Blueprints were tacked to the beaverboard covering the oak paneling. Models of ships, airplanes, automobiles and buildings lay thick on every available surface. A crystal chandelier hung over the Victorian billiard table in the center of the room. A punching bag was suspended from the balcony. Barbells lay in the corner. At one end of the luxurious room stood an incongruously shiny drugstore soda fountain.

Spangler stepped across to the opposite wall. Steel-framed photographs spread from ceiling to floor. The smiling Presidents, senators, mayors, celebrities and well-known public dignitaries were easily identifiable. The other man in each of the photographs was not.

Spangler studied the freckled square face with wide nose, low bushy eyebrows and eternal grin. He estimated the man to be well over six feet. The thick short neck rising from the massive shoulders indicated some type of athletic conditioning.

"Is that our boy, Julie? That the Retriever you got there with you?"

Spangler looked up as the officer descended the staircase. His hair was crew-cut and was blonder than it had seemed in the photographs. The freckles were hardly visible under the ruddy complexion. His age was deceptive. At first glance Spangler put it between thirty-five and forty. As the colonel strode toward him he guessed it might be fifty.

"Kittermaster at your service, sir—and mighty proud to make your acquaintance."

"I don't like that name," Spangler said, ignoring the outstretched hand.

"Which one, son? Lamar, Buford or Kittermaster?" the colonel asked with a grin. "I hope it's the first or the second. You see, I've grown kinda fond of Kittermaster. Now, Lamar's a whole different tale. Not that Buford's much of a tickler, either. Nope, I gotta admit that the only advantage to being called Lamar Buford is that you start learning the godly art of self-defense at a very tender age."

"I don't like being called Retriever."

"The hell you say. And after all the trouble Julie here went through picking it. Friend, if you don't like it, we'll just have to change it. Won't we, Julie old buddy?"

Julian smiled.

"Why did you send Jean-Claude into Germany?" Spangler demanded.

"Hold on. I'm the one who's supposed to be asking questions."

"Why was he sent on field assignment?" Spangler persisted.

"You know something, friend, I'd like to clear that one up myself. Yes *sir,* that one and maybe a few more, but I feel crowded. Hey, Julie, you planning to haul ass and get some of that work of yours done, or do you hold it in mind to hang around and snoop?"

"Anything you have to say to me," Spangler said, "you can say in front of him."

"That a fact? That's deeply touching."

"Why did you order Jean-Claude into Germany?"

"Hear that, Julie?" Kittermaster asked. "Hear how the fellah's talkin'? *Tell* him, Julie friend! Tell him all about it."

"Certainly, Colonel. You sent Jean-Claude to Germany."

"Mr. Whoever-you-are," Kittermaster said, throwing an arm

133

around Spangler, "let me tell you something. I wasn't supposed to know who you were, let alone know anything about this Jean-Claude. Why, it's taken me two whole days of threats to get to *see* you. Every time I asked, good old Julie here claimed he never heard of you. Now, if he never heard of you, I assume he wanted me to believe you don't exist. And if you don't exist, how can your friend Jean-Claude exist? And if Jean-Claude doesn't exist—exist for *me,* that is—how could I have sent him anywhere?"

Spangler broke the grip and moved away.

"Colonel Kittermaster," Julian asked quietly, "then how do you know they *do* exist? How do you know about Spangler and Jean-Claude?"

"Spangler? So that's his name." Kittermaster grinned. "Mighty glad to meet you, Mr. Spangler."

"I repeat, Colonel Kittermaster, if you had no knowledge of either of them, how do you know about them now?"

"I got my ways, Julie. Like you got your ways, I got my ways."

"And you didn't send Jean-Claude in?"

"You know I didn't, Julie."

"Colonel, with the exception of Spangler here, who is a contracted agent, every other person in my department is listed and subject to your approval. Jean-Claude was listed—and approved."

"Jean-Claude was listed in code, Julie. All your people are listed in code."

"But you knew who he was, you just admitted that." Julian took a sheet of paper from his pocket. "Colonel Kittermaster, these are Jean-Claude's orders—with *your* name at the bottom."

Kittermaster took the sheet and examined it. "Julie boy, you are a marvel! There's no denying that's my signature. How did you manage it, Julie? No, let me guess. You slipped it in with a lot of routine papers."

"Colonel, remember our so-called jurisdictional agreement on orders. You sign administration orders for my department, but I handle operational orders."

"That's the agreement, Julie boy."

"Administration orders are yellow, Colonel; operational, green. You're holding a green sheet."

"Julie, I sign so many orders I couldn't tell one from the other. I got mountains of orders. You just put them there, and I sign them because I trust you—more or less."

"And who brings you the orders from my department?"

"You, Julie, only you."

"Colonel Kittermaster, not only is your signature on a green order, but I couldn't have brought it to you. I wasn't even *here* at the time. If you'll look at the date you yourself stamped on it, you'll see that it was while I was away on the boat."

Kittermaster faltered, then moved behind the soda fountain. "Anyone for a shake? How does a big, thick shake grab you? No? Then what do you say to a black cow?"

"Why did you send him in?" Spangler demanded.

"I *didn't,* friend, I swear I didn't. I had no knowledge of it until a few days ago. I can't deny that's my signature, but I don't know how it got there. I'll figure it out in time. Everything Julie does you can figure out in time. But one thing's goddam obvious to me—and it should be to you—Julie's gone to a lot of trouble to rig this. And my question is, *why?* What's behind it? That's why I wanted to talk to you alone."

"Shall we go, Erik?" Julian asked.

"Stay, Mr. Spangler. Hear me out. A tug of war is going on over you—and I think you should know about it."

"Ready, Erik?"

"Let's hear what he has to say," Spangler replied.

"Now, I got no proof to lots of this," Kittermaster began, "so you'll have to bear with me a minute. But, as I see it, Julie used Jean-Claude to hoodwink you into coming here to Westerly."

"For what conceivable reason?" Julian asked.

"Julie was out on a boat all right—he was over in France meeting with a Kraut named von Schleiben. He and von Schleiben cooked something up. Something dealing with *you,* because right after the meeting Julie tried to contact you and call off the Tolan escape. But

I intercepted the message. It wasn't relayed on to you."

"You did *what?*" Julian gasped.

"That's right, Julie, the message came to me. You were away, remember. Anyway, Mr. Spangler, Julie got awfully upset when you took out Hilka Tolan. The question is, why? You see, Julie's in kind of a bind—he's got to locate another man, another prisoner, awful fast. I got a hunch von Schleiben offered him just that in return for you. But now it's too late. The search is on, but if it falls through, then what? And it looks as if it has fallen through. So, as I see it, Julie's holding you here until he can arrange to turn you over to von Schleiben."

"Don't listen to him, Erik," Julian said nervously. "He's trying to distort everything. He's trying to get you to work directly for him."

"Mr. Spangler," Kittermaster said, scooping up a ball of ice cream and dropping it into a tumbler, "I don't want you to think that Julie and I ain't the closest of friends. When he's fifty per cent right, he's fifty per cent right. I *do* want you to come over and work for me. What about it?"

"I don't work for Americans," Spangler said.

"But you worked for Julie."

"I didn't know whom he represented until I arrived here."

"What have you got against Americans?"

"The same thing I have against the British and the French."

"You ain't a Commie, are you, boy?"

"Not even that."

"Wait a minute, wait just one minute. Are you a Nazi sympathizer?"

"They're no better or worse than anyone else."

"What kinda talk is that?"

"You all wanted this war, you all got this war. It could have been stopped if anyone cared, but no one did. So go fight it—but not with *my* help."

"Oh no. You don't pull that one on me! If you're so damned above it all, how come you keep returning to Germany? Why do you keep taking out prisoners?"

"Whatever the reason, it has nothing to do with governments and slogans. And, in any case, I'm breaking the habit."

"Look, boy, you want to get on a high horse, be my guest. I ain't peddling patriotism or medals. You need me and I can sure as hell use you. Now what do you say?"

"Not interested."

"Not interested in Jean-Claude? Not interested in the fact that Julie can finger you for the Nazis? Julie isn't stupid enough to think he can hold you prisoner forever. He brought you here to keep an eye on you. Von Schleiben has no idea where you are or what you look like. Julie can supply that information and a photograph too— and he *will*. Even if you escape the Germans here, you'll still have von Schleiben on your trail the rest of your life.

"There's no one who can stop Julie but me. Still not interested? Uh-uh. Don't sell yourself short. You're Man of the Hour here. Key man. The most important single commodity going at present. You bounce one way or another—to Julie or to me. You're too valuable to too many people for too many reasons not to get involved."

"What other reasons?"

"Come take a look for yourself," Kittermaster said, starting across the room."

"Don't go, Erick!" Julian shouted. "Just by knowing, you'll be part of it. He'll have you locked in for good!"

"He's already locked in," Kittermaster said, holding open the elevator door, "but at least I'm offering to show him why. I'm allowing him to see what's behind all this. After that he can make up his own mind. Coming, friend?"

With a sudden shrug of interest, Spangler stepped into the elevator. The door closed in Julian's face.

21

THE CARD was tacked to the front of St. Olaf's Church in Sonderborg, Sweden, among the other obituaries, and read:

> BLEGVARD, Havdaen—devoted husband to Gunella, beloved father of Arn, Gustav, Lars, Nora and Britt. Born January 1, 1881, Ustak, Poland. Died February 14, 1944. Body arriving on noon train. Services at home, 3 P.M. unless otherwise notified.

The short-wave message received from Norway five hours later and rushed to Crypto was:

> Gunella, Arn, Lars, Gustav, Nora, Britt—February fourteen, three P.M.—one add one—rail.

The report relayed to Dark Channels within fifteen minutes stated:

> Tolan and five unidentified prisoners arrived Ositz by train, 3 P.M. February 14.

138

22

THE DOOR in the construction wall on the first floor of the main house opened and four sentries stood back. Spangler followed Kittermaster through, up the staircase to the left, past more lines of sentries and into the most closely guarded chamber in Westerly.

Spangler stepped out from under the gallery and looked around. He was standing in a precise replica of the United States Senate. Desk, chair, ceiling, window, molding, whatever the detail, was an exact copy of the prototype on Capitol Hill. There were, however, two immediately noticeable additions to the original. A blue-satin-draped platform had been erected just below the speaker's rostrum. On it rested a large mahogany table flanked by three blue-upholstered chairs on one side and four on the other. At the head of the table stood a throne covered in gold and blue.

The second addition was more prominent. A fifteen-by-twenty-five-foot silk flag was stretched high on the wall behind the Vice-President's podium. The banner bore a coat of arms on a field of blue and gold stripes. The crest contained a lion's body surmounted by two silver eagles' heads, facing in opposite directions, their eyes blazing red. An inscription below the crest read "GERMAN PROVISIONAL GOVERNMENT."

Spangler broke into laughter. "Whose brainchild was this?"

"Julie's."

"And you think you can get away with it?"

"Get away with what?"

"Double-crossing your allies and making a power grab?"

"Power grab? Are you a history professor?"

"It doesn't require much history to know that setting up your own secret postwar German government breaks almost every agreement the United States has made with England and Russia."

"I don't see any promises being broken."

"Why not start off with America's agreement to the postwar military occupation of Germany on a three-zone, three-nation basis?"

"Sounds promising. I can't wait for it to happen. Hell, we're all for it. Fact is, that's why we're here. To hurry it along. That's exactly the purpose of the G. P. G.—the German Propaganda Group. We've put together the largest and finest and *most expensive* printing presses and radio studios you'll ever see. We brought in hundreds of Germans to run them for us. Why, the first newspaper and broadcast are already waiting to go. We've gone to no end of trouble and expense so we can convince the Germans to mend their ways and dump Hitler."

"And this proposed Provisional Government," Spangler said good-humoredly. "It couldn't, by any chance, be made up of some of the better-known radio and newspaper personalities? Some of the more stalwart anti-Nazi exiles, like Vetter and the Tolan girl, who might be able to build themselves a following in Germany—with the aid of your newspaper and radio?"

"You do amaze me," Kittermaster called down in delight. "You are a *singularly* bright boy."

"How many people know about this room?"

"No one—officially. Officially it doesn't exist. Unofficially, I'd say fewer than a dozen."

"And if someone were to find out—say a Russian or an Englishman or even the wrong American general or politician—you could claim the Provisional Government is just a promotional device in reserve? Something you're saving up in case the initial propaganda needs beefing up?"

"Goddamned if you haven't hit it again," Kittermaster boomed.

140

"That's exactly what I was planning to say if someone comes stumbling along. The Provisional Government is just a slick PR stunt to trick the German people into thinking they've got their own politicians they can trust—and that they can trust us to back them."

"When in fact it's your allies whose trust you're betraying."

"Now, that's not a very neighborly thing to say, friend."

"But it's true."

"Truth depends on how you look at it."

"And how do *you* look at it?"

"Well, kind of opposite from you. I don't think it's a question of whether the Russians and English trust us; I figure it boils down to whether we can really trust *them*. Now, you take that Communist crowd. Do you really believe they'll let free elections take place in Poland if they think they have a chance of losing?"

"You're at war with Germany, not Poland."

"Well, then, let's take the British: if they're so intent on honoring the postwar zones, how come they're holding some top German political exiles in isolation without wanting us to know about it? And," Kittermaster continued, "there's another and much more important point. If our allies are so true to us, how come there are absolutely no German political exiles to be found anywhere in the world? How come they simply vanished?"

"Maybe there weren't any to begin with," Spangler suggested. "Maybe the Nazis got rid of their political opposition a long time ago."

"You don't want me to believe that out of fifty thousand anti-Nazi politicians, no one escaped?"

"It's more like a hundred and fifty thousand political prisoners— and very few got out."

"But that's the point—what happened to those few?"

"Perhaps," said Spangler, "if you had been concerned with what happened to the many at the right time, it wouldn't have happened in the first place."

"You one of those atrocity nuts, my friend?"

"No. I gave that up a long time back. I decided to turn it over to people who could do something about it, like yourself."

"Good. Glad to hear it. Glad you're not part of the rumor-monger clique."

"You mean rumors claiming that German political exiles have been secretly picked up by the Russians and the English?"

"Well, then, bright boy, you tell *me* where they are. It's taken us four months to get our hands on seven of them, and we still can't find one with real influence or stature. What happened to the fat cats?"

"Maybe de Gaulle's hiding them."

"You bet your ass he is, and so is every other damned Allied country. Well, friend, they're not going to catch us short this time. We've got our own insurance policy right here, to make *sure* our European buddies play it straight."

"And where do I fit into all of this?" said Spangler.

"Good question, friend, damned good question," Kittermaster said, sitting at a senatorial desk. "If you count the chairs around that table you'll see we got eight. Only seven are filled. It's that last chair that tells the tale. The question is—who'll come up with the man to fill it, Julie or me?"

"Why is that so important?"

"Because Julie and I both miscalculated," Kittermaster said. "You see, we started off having a little contest on who could bring in the most people. Of the seven we've got in hand, the score reads: Julie, five; me, two. Now, that doesn't look too good for me, because the boys in Washington are very big on figures and statistics. And they might just say, 'Look what Julie and his espionage fellows did, they whopped old Lamar B. five to two—so let's give Julie the reins and boot old Kittermaster out along with his politicians, and let the spy-boys take over.' Well, Mr. Spangler, needless to say, I don't find that a very gratifying prospect."

"If Julian has that much of a lead on you, there's not much you can do now, is there?"

"But he isn't *using* it, friend, that's the point. And I'm wondering why not. Believe me, Julie *wants* to take over. I don't think the answer's so hard to come by. What it really boils down to is the eighth chair. Whoever produces the man for it takes the ball game."

"And you want me to produce him—for you?"

"Let's put it this way: I don't want you to produce him for Julie. If you switch over to me, you throw a wrench in Julie's plans: he can't trade you off to von Schleiben or send you in for the eighth man. That's going to give you and me a little time to work out a scheme or two."

"Like sending me into Germany to bring back the eighth man for you?"

"You can go along if you like, but it really isn't necessary. What I've got simmering in the back of my brain will knock those boys in Washington right up into the bleachers. Oh yes! They're really going to see something! So there it is," Kittermaster concluded, "and I'll open the bidding for you here and now. Whatever deal Julie made for your services I'll triple. Triple, hell! You can name your own price."

"How about a share of the gravy?"

"What gravy?"

"Postwar Germany. That's what this whole thing is about, isn't it? Whoever ends up with G. P. G. may very well end up with most of postwar Germany. That means a lot of power and a lot of money for someone. What's my percentage if it goes your way?"

"I *like* you, boy! I certainly do like you."

"What's my percentage?"

"We'll work it out—if you say yes."

"And if I'm not around to use it, can it be transferred to whomever I say?"

"As long as there's a Switzerland."

"And von Schleiben? How will you stop Julian from letting von Schleiben know where I am?"

"No problem at all. You say yes and I've got my ways."

"Just a simple yes and the world is mine?"

"You're damn right."

"No questions asked?"

"I'm bargaining for your services, not your autobiography—though I wouldn't mind knowing what gives between you and Julie. Has Julie got something on you?"

"Maybe. He also thinks I'm insane."

"Are you?"

"I'm not sure."

"Then why worry?"

23

THE WHITE LIGHT flashed on.

"Oop? Do you read me, Oop? This is Sweet Pea calling. Do you read me, Oop?"

"YEP."

"I am beside myself, Oop, utterly beside myself. Beside myself and vexed, Oop—and all because of you. I return to the office this morning after a weekend of fishing, and I am besieged by phone calls from the other members of the Committee. Phone calls about *you*, Oop. You have brought us to the brink of disaster, Oop, do you realize that?"

"YEP."

"On whose authority did you decide to have a confrontation with Mandrake, Oop? Mandrake has circulated a rumor among the Committee that he had to intercede to keep you from selling one of our agents to the Germans. Do you understand the implications, Oop? He made it sound as if you and I are a pair of white slavers! White slavery doesn't sit well here on the Potomac, Oop. The Committee is up in arms. Do you realize the implications when the Committee is up in arms, Oop?"

"YEP."

"Just thank the Lord for my quick-wittedness, Oop. I gave the Committee my personal guarantee that the story was confused. Now, listen, Oop, and listen carefully. There is little doubt that Mandrake was referring to Dick Tracy, so I want sworn affidavits from both Dick Tracy and you that it *isn't so!* We must make Mandrake out to be a bold-faced liar! Get me those affidavits, Oop. Get them fast. Then move Dick Tracy out of there and away from Mandrake. Dick Tracy should never have been allowed near Mandrake! Do you understand what you have to do, Oop?"

"IT'S TOO LATE. MANDRAKE HAS ALREADY LIFTED DICK TRACY. I'VE BEEN TRYING TO REACH YOU FOR THREE DAYS TO TELL YOU. I WASN'T ABLE TO FIND YOU. HOW WAS THE FISHING? CATCH ANY BIG ONES?"

Julian waited for the delay to end.

"What was that? What was that you just said?"

"I ASKED HOW THE FISHING WENT. DID YOU CATCH ANY BIG ONES?"

"Not that," VFW squealed as the white light went on. "What did you say about Mandrake and Dick Tracy?"

"MANDRAKE MADE A DEAL WITH DICK TRACY. DICK TRACY HAS MOVED OVER TO MANDRAKE AS HIS PERSONAL ESPIONAGE ADVISER."

"God in heaven, Oop, do you realize what you have done? You have made me out a liar, that's what you have done. I promised the others sworn affidavits denying this whole ridiculous matter. I'm a trapped liar, Oop—all because of you. Do you realize that, Oop? You got me into this. Now you get me out of it. What about Daddy Warbucks? Have we located a Daddy Warbucks? If we could bring him in fast, that might regain control of the situation."

"WE MAY HAVE SPOTTED ONE. THERE'S SOME CONFUSION OVER THE EXACT LOCATION. WE THINK HE'S BEING TAKEN TO EITHER A BALTIC ISLAND OR NORTHWESTERN POLAND. WE HOPE TO PINPOINT IT SOON. BUT IF IT IS HIM, I DON'T THINK IT WILL HELP OUR SITUATION MUCH, SINCE IT'S DICK TRACY'S MAN WHO IS ON THE TRAIL."

"Oh, my God. That can't happen, Oop. That simply cannot happen. Oop, *suggest* something."

"WHY NOT LET ME HANDLE MANDRAKE MY OWN WAY?"

"Don't be insane. Another incident could wipe us out completely

146

back here. You keep away from Mandrake. I want you to come up with a positive solution."

"WHAT ABOUT GIVING UP OUR JURISDICTION TO MANDRAKE? WHY NOT LET HIM BE BOSS OF THE ENTIRE OPERATION? THAT WILL STOP THE MANEUVERING FOR CONTROL AND GIVE US TIME TO THINK."

"Absolutely not. Once you give something up, you never get it back. Mandrake is much too clever for that. We have to come up with the unexpected, the flamboyant. Something— Hold it, Oop, hold it. Give me time. I'm having flashes. I've got it, Oop. I've saved the situation once again. Call a meeting of the Seven."

"THAT'S MADNESS. ABSOLUTE MADNESS. YOU KNOW WHO WE HAVE AND WHAT THEY ARE. A MEETING IS THE EXACT THING I'VE BEEN TRYING TO AVOID. YOU'LL BE PLAYING DIRECTLY INTO MANDRAKE'S HAND. THIS IS WHAT HE'S BEEN WAITING FOR. HE KNOWS BETTER THAN ANYONE THAT WITHOUT A DADDY WARBUCKS A MEETING WOULD BE A COMPLETE DISASTER FOR US. ONCE THE COMMITTEE READS THE TRANSCRIPT WE'LL LOOK LIKE THE INCOMPETENTS OF THE CEN-TURY."

"Don't exaggerate, Oop. The trouble with you and your fellows is congenital exaggeration and a complete lack of political sophistication. I know of what I speak. A bold stroke is half the battle. Rely on the unexpected. Charge the Valley of Death. Trust to my instinct and guile, Oop. Wield the big stick. If Mandrake objects, it makes him out the wilting violet. Trust my years in the Potomac jungle, Oop. I am ordering you to convene the meeting. Do so, posthaste. I won't abide any dillydallying. This is war."

24

KITTERMASTER and Spangler seated themselves in the first row, Julian and his aide in the last. The Cipher Chief snapped on a slide projector. "TOLAN AND FIVE UNIDENTIFIED PRISONERS ARRIVED OSITZ BY TRAIN 3 P.M. FEBRUARY 14" flashed on the screen.

"The problem with this message," the code expert told his listeners, "is that we simply cannot find a place called Ositz. None of our maps, charts or directories show it. None of our people has ever heard of it. Our first assumption in a situation of this sort is that the transmitting agent, in this case a Jean-Claude, has made an error. Jean-Claude was employing the Triangle Cipher, a rather simple system. The most common cipher mistakes are usually connected with the spelling of foreign names. We believe Ositz is a phonetic attempt to spell a name, but we can't be certain since we know nothing of Jean-Claude or his message-sending ability."

"If it's any help," said Spangler, "he's only a boy. He's just turned twelve."

"How would you evaluate his spelling skills?"

"Not too highly. He's had three years of formal schooling and that's it."

"Thank you very much, sir." The Cipher Chief stepped to the wall map of Europe as the lights went on. "Since Jean-Claude sent his message to St. Olaf's in Sonderborg, we know he was employing the

Death Priority, so our most immediate assumption is that he is out-of-zone, somewhere in this area." The finger arched from the Baltic coast down through northern Poland. "As I said before, we have come across no location called Ositz, but if I might call Captain Wolsky, another possibility can be examined."

Permission was granted, and the stout, balding former University of Chicago Polish historian entered. He walked directly to the rack of maps and pushed two aside. The geography of eastern Germany and western Poland lay exposed.

"When I was a very young child," he said, removing his glasses, "I remember being taken to an Austrian Army cavalry training post to visit a great-uncle. He was a bear of a man who insisted on throwing me up in the air and covering me with kisses. It was a very uncomfortable day. I remember passing that way some years later and being delighted to find that the post had been torn down. I imagined that some great avenging hand had reached down from heaven and swept Great-Uncle and all his comrades from the face of the earth. The avenger had done an excellent job. All that was left at the site was a railroad station. Actually it wasn't even a station, it was just a siding on the Sola River. Yes, here—here is where it was," he said, pushing a red pin into the map. "You see, it is so insignificant that it isn't even shown, but it may still exist. In Poland, railroad facilities, no matter how small, are usually preserved. What I remember most specifically about this place was the name it bore after the cavalry post was gone and only the railroad siding remained. It was one of those silly, inconsequential names that sometimes linger in the memories of children. The siding was called Auschwitz."

Spangler rose slowly, crossed the room and studied the tiny red pin.

"I realize it is only a hypothesis," the ex-professor continued, "but in this entire area it is the only name even vaguely similar to Ositz. It is also a name that is difficult for strangers to pronounce, let alone spell, but a child might just remember it as I did."

"Ever heard of it?" Kittermaster called to Spangler.

"Yes. It's one of their newer camps."

149

"Ever been there?"

"No. I've never operated in Poland."

"What else do you know about it?"

"Rumors say it's big."

"How big?"

"Big."

"Political?"

"No," said Spangler quietly. "Not exactly political. . . ."

25

UNITED STATES and G.P.G. flags hung alternately from the gallery rail of the Senate Chamber. Pairs of blue-and-gold-striped helmeted guards with white gloves stood to strict attention at every door. Julian was leaning over the speaker's rostrum, Kittermaster was seated on the dais above him.

The wire-recorder operator spoke into a microphone and gave the clearance. Kittermaster looked up toward the hidden observation booth, nodded and pointed in the opposite direction.

Martin Vetter was the first person ushered into the chamber and given a place at the rectangular table. He sat rigidly and tried not to look around him. Two minutes later Konrad Lottman was seated beside him. Lottman's attempt at composure was betrayed by his amazement at the room and his recognition of Vetter.

Thomas Hutch was next to enter the Senate. Two minutes later Reinhard Teller appeared, and two minutes after that Hilka Tolan. Ernst Zahn was followed by Joseph Winder.

Oswald Nebel was last. He took his place between Hutch and Lottman, smoothed his moustache and leered across at Vetter. Mutual distaste was more than evident.

"You take it, Julie boy," Kittermaster said jovially. "It's your show, Julie. Give these nice folks the pitch." Kittermaster motioned. The silent guards moved out of the chamber.

Julian's speech was short and precise. The seven persons in the room were to be the seven Ministers of the German Provisional Government. The Cabinet of the government in exile. Each would receive an annual salary of twenty-five thousand dollars, plus expenses and maintenance. Payment was retroactive to 1 January 1944. G.P.G. had originally been slated to have an eighth member, a Chancellor to whom the seven Ministers would be responsible, but due to the time factor it had been decided to proceed with the seven people at the table.

Germany was to be geographically divided into seven regions. Each region would be the specific domain of one Minister who would represent that region in all matters. In addition to his geographic function each Minister would hold an executive office, such as Interior, Labor, State, Finance, and so on. These would be assigned later.

At present the German Provisional Government had only one mission: to expedite the fall of the Third Reich. This would be accomplished in a series of phases.

Phase One would be the mounting of a massive newspaper, radio and leaflet propaganda offensive aimed directly at Germany itself. The campaign had four primary and simultaneous intents: to pit the top Nazi leaders against one another, to create violent anti-Nazi opinion among the German people, to stimulate pro-American sentiment among Germans, and to condition the masses for a representative government in the form of G.P.G.

Phase Two would be more overt and would depend in part on the success of the propaganda efforts. As the first signs of disquiet were detected within the Reich's population, G.P.G. agents, many already waiting in Germany, would move in to organize and equip resistance movements. These would be handled on a regional basis, with each Minister advising on subversive activities within his zone of influence. Restlessness among Nazi politicians or Wehrmacht officers would be handled directly by a joint council comprised of the G.P.G. Ministers and United States G.P.G. liaison personnel. When the Third Reich finally collapsed, the German Provisional Government must be ready to move into any part of Germany—including Berlin.

When Julian finished speaking, the meeting was thrown open for ten minutes of questions.

"Major Julian," Vetter said without rising, "is either Russia or England involved in this operation?"

"You know they are not."

"Do you expect them to be?"

"Not at present."

"Are you aware that I am a Communist?"

"Aha, so he finally admits it for one and all to hear," Oswald Nebel jeered. "He finally comes out in the open and says what he is."

"I am not as lucky as you, Herr Nebel," Vetter replied. "The world already knows what *you* are."

"Of course they do—the rightful winner of a mayoral election."

"If honest votes were counted you wouldn't have been elected to an outhouse."

"If by honest votes you mean the twenty thousand duplicate ballots you and your Red traitors had printed, I quite agree."

"Herr Nebel, go find yourself another little boy to molest."

"I *object*," Nebel blustered. "I demand a formal apology. I *demand*—"

"Not on your whore mother's life."

"What did you say?"

"I called your mother a whore, but you must excuse me. I was hasty. We all know she wasn't a whore. She was a professional Lesbian."

Nebel dove across the table, seized the startled Vetter by the goatee and began pulling. Vetter struggled to free himself. His chair tipped over backward and both men crashed to the floor. Still Nebel held his grip. By the time the others reached them Nebel was banging Vetter's head against the table leg.

Nebel was dragged back to his place and held down. Vetter was lifted into his chair and revived with water.

"Gentlemen, gentlemen, gentlemen," Thomas Hutch admonished as he rose, "this is neither the time nor the place to reenact our ancient German political rituals. We have much more pressing matters to confront. Individually we can solve nothing, since our fate lies in the hands of our new masters. United we may be able to sue for more propitious treatment.

"Sir," Hutch said, grasping his lapels and turning to Julian, "let us all face reality, the reality of the people you have assembled in this room. Only sheer desperation could have brought together such a pathetic group.

"If you were looking for politicians, what a sorry course you have run! Only three of the persons at this table ever ran for elected office; the other four held only minor political appointments. Two of the three who *did* run for office were involved in one of the most scandalous electoral contests ever held in Germany. The loser was jailed for fraud, and the winner was subsequently impeached on so many counts that no one can remember them all. The one remaining elected officeholder, myself, won a minor post when his heavily favored opponent dropped dead the day before balloting. Our combined electoral strength—legal and illegal—could hardly elect a respectable zoo keeper.

"If you are thinking of us as *exiles,* then the picture is slightly more optimistic. Five of us had to flee Germany, but not necessarily for political reasons. If you hope that we are anti-Nazi exiles, then the picture is bleaker still. Three of us here have served happily under the Nazis. Two were fired for simple incompetence, and the third, Hilka Tolan, was jailed because of her father's personal enemies, not political enemies.

"But you knew most of this before you went to such trouble to bring us here. So then I must ask: Why bother in the first place? The answer is self-evident: There was no one else left.

"Good Major, why waste time with questions and answers? Most of us are so politically inept we really don't know what to ask you. Tell us, and we will do what we must. We will sign what you want, say what you want, endorse what you want, legislate what you want, do everything and anything you want—with one exception: we will not submit to hypocrisy.

"We admit to our ineptitude—and it is our strength. Kind Major, if you had to come to us, how utterly desperate your situation must

154

be. And since it is so desperate, we must be more valuable to you than you care to admit.

"I therefore submit the following recommendations on behalf of myself and my colleagues. First, that our yearly salaries be doubled, and extended to the natural lifetime of each one of us. Secondly, I submit that should the Provisional Government in fact become the governing body of postwar Germany, our positions as Ministers should not be subject to election. The Ministry can simply be an appointed body—something like your own Supreme Court, for example? And, as with your Supreme Court, our appointments should also be for a lifetime. Next, I believe it only equitable that when a Chancellor is subsequently appointed, he should be selected from the six men here. After that I feel—"

Julian left the room.

Hutch looked up at Kittermaster. "Did I say something wrong?"

"You're doing just fine, my friend, *fine!*"

"Then may I continue the negotiations with you, Colonel?"

"The negotiations just ended."

"Sir, in the best interest of our future—"

"Tom, in the best interest of your good health, I've got a little suggestion: Do what you're told."

"Or what, Colonel?"

"Or you get your head blown off, that's what."

Kittermaster stepped to the ornate door and waved his hand. The lights dimmed and the guards reappeared. Within a minute the chamber was empty and still, the only light a bright projection lamp shining on the unused Throne.

26

It was a curious raid.

Thick February storm clouds had crept down the Continent, enveloping northern Europe. From the upper end of the Latium plains to the Aller the blizzards raged. The Luftwaffe knew the American bombers were on their way as soon as they passed over Umbria, seventy-five planes in all—and this is where the confusion began.

The Americans generally preferred to attack during daylight. Now they were coming three hours before dawn. The Americans had always preferred clear weather for their strikes. Now they were buffeting through a storm. Only northern Germany was clear. The Luftwaffe would have expected the attack there to come from the long-range bombers, the B-24s. But the Americans were sending over their B-26s. Only one B-24 had been spotted.

The fighter escorts turned back near the Adriatic coast. The Messerschmitts attacked minutes later. Twelve B-26s spiraled down in smoke. Still the medium-bomber wing droned northward.

At 0400 hours the storm was easing in the west. Friedrichshafen, Ulm and Freiburg were visible. This, the Germans concluded, was where the strike would come now. Preparations were made. It was 0430 hours and sleeting in Munich when the first bombs exploded. Two passes were made. The aircraft circled and headed back to Italy with one exception: a solitary B-26 in the armada dropped altitude and continued north into the storm.

It was dawn when the pilot alerted the crew. The aircraft descended under the thinning clouds and leveled off. The bomb-bay doors opened and the aerial cameras were readied. A moment later they began photographing the terrain along the Sola River in which a railroad siding known as Auschwitz should appear.

27

HILKA STOOD beside the portable bar. She took a cigarette and lit it. "Would you care for a drink?" she asked.

"I don't drink."

"Neither do I," Hilka said, pouring half a glass of vodka. "Or, more correctly, neither *should* I." She took a deep swallow. "Well, what do you think of my apartment? You haven't told me."

Spangler glanced around. He saw Hilka's reflection in the wall of floor-to-ceiling mirrors. She was loosening the bodice of her brocade dressing gown. "Is that why you asked me here, to get my opinion of your apartment?"

"No, I'm sorry. That wasn't what I meant to say at all. There are other things. Important things."

"I told you before, I'm not interested, lady."

"Hilka! My name is Hilka!" she shouted. "And you *have* to be interested. You *must* be interested. You are *responsible* for me!"

"My responsibility ended when I brought you out."

"No it didn't. It began then. I didn't ask to be freed. I didn't *want* to be freed. When the camp underground offered me an escape I refused. I was better off inside and I knew it. But you changed all that without thinking twice, without even asking me. Well, here I am, and *you* are responsible, so where shall we begin?"

Hilka began to drink, then thought the better of it. "Do you like my hair braided like this?"

"It looks all right."

"Is that all? Do you think I'm pretty?"

"Yes."

"How pretty?"

"Very pretty."

"As pretty as a motion-picture star? In fact, I've played in a picture or two myself, but I don't imagine you have seen them. I used to remind people of Jean Arthur. Do you think I'm as pretty as she is?"

"I have no way of knowing. I don't go to movies."

Hilka laid aside her drink and leaned back against the bar. "What do you intend to do about my situation?"

"What situation?"

"My rehabilitation. You brought me back to the conventional world. Now you must teach me to adjust to it. You understand what I'm saying, don't you?"

"More or less."

"How nice," Hilka replied, smoothing her gown. "How flattering to be understood. But that's one of your virtues, isn't it—understanding? You knew immediately when I lied to you about Belsen and Mauthausen. And you were quite correct—I've never been at either. I was somewhere else. Have you ever heard of Salon Kitty?"

"The place in Berlin?"

"The bordello in Berlin. The unofficial Gestapo listening point. Every room had hidden microphones so that they could learn more about the distinguished clientele, especially the foreign diplomats.

"Yes, Salon Kitty," she said in a musing tone. "It was the creation of Reinhard Heydrich, and Uncle Reini had no more enthusiastic admirer than my father. So when it became the patriotic and fashionable thing for young and beautiful Berlin girls to volunteer to take the places of the common prostitutes who originally staffed the establishment, my father felt it expedient for me to be included. That I was barely seventeen and still a virgin mattered little. I was taken from private school and sent to the establishment as a 'personal ward' of Uncle Reini. I ran away twice, but not because I disliked it. I was beginning to like it too much. You know how impressionable school-children can be.

"Then one evening when several other girls and I were performing the 'spectacular,' I was discovered by a certain Obergruppenfuehrer von Schleiben. Even Heydrich feared this man, so I was given to him. He became a most ingenious mentor. Like all great artists he eventually tired of me, but at least my life was spared. I was sent to Oranienburg, where I could cause no future embarrassment. When the SS guards reviewed my exceptional qualifications I was immedi-ately assigned to *their* private bordello—where my figure was not jeopardized by the ordinary camp fare.

"I was content in the bordello, because that's all I really knew. But you have taken me from it." Hilka moved around the couch and leaned against the chair next to Spangler. "Now what am I expected to do? I am accustomed to having six to ten men or women a day. Will that be supplied among the expensive clothes and furnishings here? My own pleasure is derived from more extreme activity. Will that be provided, too?"

"I'm sorry," Spangler mumbled.

"Don't be sorry, be *useful,*" Hilka said, letting her gown fall open. "Did you bring me back to be the whore or to portray a presentable woman? I have always lived under masters—so *be* my master! By your thoughtless action you have said, 'Forget the past, live in the polite world.' Well, then, show me how. Take me into the bedroom and show me how one man can effect the transition."

"When it's time for the bedroom, I'll make the decision, not you."

"No, no," she cried desperately. "We mustn't wait. There isn't time. Don't you see, nothing will be left if we wait."

She moved forward and stood before him. Her gown fell to the floor. "Well, is it in the bedroom or here? I really don't know where proper people perform the ritual. Forgive my abruptness, but it's all I am accustomed to. How do we begin? How do nice people begin? Would you like to whip me? Or do you prefer it the other way around?

160

"Don't look away, damn you. Show me! I am twisted. I am a freak. Cleanse me of all of that. Change me," she pleaded, dropping to her knees and clasping Spangler's hand.

Spangler reached down and touched her head. He raised her chin, wiped away a tear and gently pulled her to him. He stroked her forehead. Suddenly he pushed her away and jumped up. He shuddered involuntarily, raising his hand as if in a blessing, his lips moving as if in prayer. Tears came to his eyes.

"What is it?" she asked in bewilderment. "What have I done?"

Spangler turned and walked quickly to the door.

Kittermaster sat alone among the movie cameras and the recording equipment in the red-lighted secret observation corridor between Suites Seven and Eight. He watched Hilka stare after Spangler as he left the room. She went to the bar, nervously lit a cigarette and put it out after one puff. She picked up another and struck a match. She moved the flame close to her face and studied it hypnotically. She blew it out and entered the bathroom.

Kittermaster moved down to sit in front of a floor-to-ceiling, one-way bathroom mirror. Hilka stood facing him as she examined the reflection of her angular body. He could see the small round scars on the firm breasts and around her lower stomach.

She turned both taps on full blast, climbed into the tub and swung her legs up around the faucet. Water jetted down into her open thighs as her body arched and began to tremble. Her teeth clenched and her neck strained back in tension. Her body continued to struggle. Nothing was resolved.

Hilka rose from the tub and stood dripping in front of the mirror. Water and tears streamed down her face.

Her fingers clawed tentatively at the mount at the base of the abdomen. She reached for a cigarette and lit it. The first two puffs seemed to bring relaxation. She began to tremble again. Her arms dropped limply to her sides. Her head shook slowly and helplessly. She stared down at the cigarette. In one rapid motion she spread her legs and plunged the burning tip up between her thighs. Her scream was low and guttural; her body shook uncontrollably. The explosion

161

came. Hilka fell forward against the mirror. Her arms moved slowly down the surface as she slipped to the floor. She curled up into a tight ball on the bath mat. Relaxation had arrived. So had hysteria.

Kittermaster silently made his way to the end of the observation room, opened the floor hatch and descended the circular metal staircase. He unlocked the door leading out into the fourth-floor corridor. He pulled back the knob. Two helmeted security guards sprawled motionless on the floor. He was starting to bend down over them when a hand clamped on his throat and lifted him from his feet. He gasped for breath and tried to break the grip. The single hand was too powerful. His head jerked forward and he stared down into Spangler's face.

"Never, never let me catch you watching me again," Spangler told Kittermaster, and released his hold.

28

THE PHOTOGRAPHIC MONTAGE of the Auschwitz area covered three walls of the Strategy Room. The military and Air Force analysts on exclusive assignment to G.P.G. studied it most of the morning. Agreement was reached before lunch.

Kittermaster was the first to arrive. A bright-blue ascot concealed the bandages on his neck. Julian arrived a few minutes later.

"Been on those fancy phones of yours, Julie boy?"

"Yes."

"Your big-shot buddy in Washington have anything new to say, or just the routine back-alley plotting?"

"You've won."

"Won what?"

"Everything. The Committee has ordered my operation transferred to your direct command. I'll stay on to brief your new intelligence chief, then leave."

"How long do you think that briefing will take?"

"It depends on whom you select as my replacement."

"Spangler."

"He's new to organizational work. I can probably show him everything within three weeks."

"Do it in two, will you, Julie? Spangler's a bright boy, and having you around makes me nervous."

The Air Force analyst moved in front of the enlarged montage of aerial photographs. "This picture covers a seventy-five-mile area in the Sola River vicinity along the old Polish border. As you can see, we've found two major independent complexes and five or six minor ones. The reconnaissance plane reported seeing at least two dozen smaller installations, but we don't think we need any further overflights. What we have here tells us enough.

"The first of the two major installations covers the area Professor Wolsky had designated as the Auschwitz railroad siding. As you can clearly see, it is a thirty-building complex enclosed by cement or brick walls and ringed with guard towers.

"Here, a few miles away, we see the second and by far the largest installation. Our maps indicate that this complex has enveloped a small village known as Birkenau. These paths show that the Birkenau and Auschwitz complexes are linked, as are the minor satellite compounds to the north, east and west."

Spangler entered the room and sat beside Julian.

"Whatever your expectations may have been, gentlemen," the analyst continued, "our experts seriously doubt that these installations represent either prisons or detention areas."

"Why not?" Spangler broke in.

"Sheer mathematics, sir. If you examine the Birkenau complex you'll find that the exterior perimeter encloses some twenty-eight to thirty-six square miles. Contained within this area are some three hundred and twenty-five buildings which appear to be prisoners' barracks. If we estimate fifty prisoners per building this gives us a total of over sixteen thousand inmates. If we went to a maximum of seventy-five per building the total would rise to more than twenty-four thousand."

"And what if you had one hundred and fifty to two hundred prisoners in a barracks?"

"Sir, you simply cannot fit that many into those barracks. You can see the size for yourself."

"But what if there *were?*"

"Then it would further prove my point. Even at the lower totals the basic ratio of detention doesn't work out."

"What ratio?"

"Guard ratio, sir. If you count these exterior buildings, which the Germans want us to believe are the guard billets, you'll see that there is simply not enough accommodation for a guard force large enough to control sixteen thousand to twenty-four thousand prisoners. You see, sir, in all detention systems there are basic ratios between the number of prisoners and the number of guards required to control them. Employing the most extravagent of these ratios, we can see that this could not be a detention area."

"If it isn't, what are those guard towers doing around it?"

"They're decoys, sir. They are actually defense posts to protect against outside attack, but the Germans have made them look like prison guard towers."

"How much do you know about concentration camps?"

"We've made discreet inquiries in Washington, sir, but they seem very reluctant to release any material on the subject. We can't press the issue, because of our own security problems here. But even if we *did* have more data, it wouldn't make any difference. We are quite certain what we are looking at."

"You're looking at a concentration camp."

"We are looking at a secret divisional staging area camouflaged to *look* like a camp, sir. Air Intelligence has known for some time that the German military has been constructing a ring of concealed staging camps in preparation for their counteroffensive on the eastern front. We have come across some of the smaller ones recently, and all of them are quite similar to this. Not in size, but in layout. All you have to do, sir, is to count the buildings here, then compare with the structure of Wehrmacht military units. The Auschwitz compound accommodates a German mechanized division. The existing Birkenau facilities can handle some twenty thousand recruits. Even more telling is the construction under way in the upper part of Birkenau. As anyone can see, the sites are being cleared for another hundred and thirty barracks. I would say this indicates the Germans are expecting another ten thousand recruits, rather than thirteen to fifteen thousand prisoners. Sir, have you considered what shipping thirteen to fifteen thousand new prisoners to this area would do to their already overloaded transport facilities? This area is in the heart of their advance supply lines to the front. No German general is going to let this transport be interrupted. It's basic military logistics, sir."

"The Army has nothing to say about it," Spangler snapped. "It's in the hands of the SS."

"Sir, if you let me continue I can pinpoint many more facts that definitely establish this as a staging area."

"Adviser," Kittermaster interrupted, as he leaned forward and looked over at Spangler, "you're certain this is a camp?"

"Yes."

"Adviser, I'm starting to get a vision—a vision of the biggest and most stunning scheme those boys in Washington ever did see. It'll be just the extravaganza they've been looking for. So I want you to take your time. I want you to *think*. Are you really sure that is a camp?"

"Yes!"

"How sure?"

"I'll bank my percentage on it."

"Deal!" Kittermaster started for the door. "We're going to have us some fun," he shouted. "Get me Black Buck!"

29

HILKA HEARD the rumbling. She slipped on her dressing gown and went to the window. The moonlit road was jammed with traffic. As far as the eye could see, vehicles of every description were thundering toward the hunting preserve. She pressed closer to the pane. Suddenly she realized she was not alone.

She spun around. Kittermaster was standing beside the bed.

"How did you get in here? The door was locked!"

"There's no door in this entire place that's locked to me, dear child," he said, lighting a cigar.

"Get *out!*"

"Do you know something? You look a little drawn. What you need is some good night air. What do you say?"

"I want you to leave."

"Sure thing—in a minute. You aren't going to toss a man out till he's finished his smoke, are you? After all, I'm only interested in your well-being. Say—has anyone ever told you you look just like Jean Arthur?"

"Please leave me. Please go."

Kittermaster surveyed the room. "You know something, I owe you an apology. Why, this place of yours is nothing more than a glorified jail. Now, you just trust me and do as I say. Grab your things and we'll get you away from Westerly for a spell. What about a nice, long drive out of this trap? When was the last time you saw the ocean? We'll just drive and talk—or not talk if you'd rather not. Come on, it'll do you good."

Hilka rubbed her hands. "Maybe I should. Yes, maybe it would be a good idea. Thank you, yes. I have been a little nervous lately."

"Nervous or tense?"

"Both, I guess. Let me get my things and I'll be with you in a minute."

"Well, we can't have you being nervous and tense, can we? I'll tell you what," he said, blowing on the glowing cigar tip. "I'm personally going to make sure you get yourself untensed. I've got just the home remedy."

"What are you talking about?"

"Just trust me. Put your faith in Big Daddy. Yes, *sir,* he's going to fix you up as you're begging to be fixed!" Kittermaster gripped the glowing cigar in his fist, pointed it at Hilka, lowered his arm and began walking slowly toward her. "Yes, sir, Big Daddy is going to fix you up just *fine!*"

30

THE BULLDOZERS lumbered down the forest hillside in waves of ten. Dredges and scoops moved along the muddy creek bed and cut out a wide, deep river basin. Engineers worked on two dams at either end. Mobile workshops rolled into a newly hewn clearing. Portable generators were connected to lathes, saws and drills. The convoy of lumber trucks arrived on schedule. Three hundred carpenters did the cutting, two hundred the fitting and nailing and five hundred the erecting and assembling. Squads of soldiers began to enclose the buildings with a twelve-foot fence and built nine guard towers. Barbed wire was strung within the compound as electricians laid cable, spliced feed lines and started connecting the banks of floodlights. Powerful searchlights were hoisted into the guard towers, mounted and connected. The inner compound was completed three hours ahead of schedule. The eleven buildings on the outside of the wall and the electrified exterior barbed-wire fencing came in three hours and forty minutes before the deadline. Railroad crews began laying track along the freshly built roadbed on the western exterior of the compound. Only the paint crews were delayed. Their color charts had been misplaced, and others had to be sent for. They arrived an hour and ten minutes late. Yellow would be for stone, gray for concrete and brown for wood. The twelve-foot-high fence was sprayed gray, its nine guard towers brown, the buildings within yellow.

One of the dredges was stuck in the completed river bed. Salvage cranes were called for. When they had not arrived by the next day the engineers could wait no longer. The floodgate to the upper dam was thrown open. Water rushed into the basin, swirled about the abandoned machine and began backing up against the second barrier wall. Within an hour all but the top of the dredge lay submerged. The Sola River had been completed. The senior electrician threw the first master switch, and the buildings and the street lights were illuminated. The second switch came down. The full-scale reproduction of Auschwitz glowed in the misty twilight of Westerly.

The railroad gang continued laying a single line of track, which fanned out after three and a half miles into a triple-pronged siding. Here work continued on the second and more massive installation. More than two hundred buildings already stood complete within the fourteen fence-divided compounds. Another two hundred and fifty structures were at various stages of construction. When, shortly thereafter, work was completed, it was named Birkenau Concentration Camp. The name proved to be officially correct, although Extermination Camp would have been the more accurate title.

3 1

Major D. W. "Black Buck" Cogan jammed his foot onto the brake pedal. The jeep skidded to a stop in a puddle before the guardhouse. He flashed his identification and emergency orders. He pressed the accelerator to the floor. The back wheels spun deep into the mud, hit tight earth and lurched forward onto the three-lane Westerly Freeway.

Cogan's staff of officers, all wearing the screaming-eagle armpatch, were already studying the table-top scale models of Auschwitz and Birkenau in the Strategy Room when the major arrived. Cogan was briefed, and Kittermaster was called. He arrived shortly afterward with Julian and Spangler.

"Hitting the target will be no problem," Cogan told Kittermaster. "Overrunning the installations will be no problem, if we're given enough time and bodies. Finding your man and the boy, if they're in there anywhere, will be no problem. Getting them out by light plane will be no problem. But how are we going to bring back the fifteen hundred men it will take to do the job?"

"I don't have the foggiest, friend," Kittermaster answered. "I thought that was *your* department."

"It is. And my suggestion is to go north to the Russian lines. But I'm told you say no to that?"

"Correct. No contact with the Russians. They can't know we were there."

"Colonel, *everyone's* going to know you were there. You don't make a raid this size without everyone knowing it. The Russians will probably know as fast as, if not faster than, the Germans. What they won't know is *why* we were there, especially if we bring out a couple of decoy prisoners and say we were after them. Not that there aren't problems going east. First we have to get through German lines, and if we *do* reach the Russians there's a chance they won't let us out for quite some time. Even so, we have to go east."

"We can't."

"Then you tell me, Colonel Kittermaster, how we do it. Shall we go south through Czechoslovakia, Austria and Jugoslavia to the Adriatic? What about west through Germany and occupied Europe? North? It is three hundred and twenty miles through occupied territory to the Baltic. If you match this against an eastern escape, you'll see it's only a hundred and eighty miles to the Russian lines, and at the rate the new offensive is going, they may be as close as ninety or a hundred miles by the time we go in. It's our only way."

"What about coming out by air?" Kittermaster suggested, "I thought you found an airstrip in the vicinity."

"The photographs show a workable field sixteen miles to the south, but this would require several additional elements. First we'd need an extra thousand men to take and hold the airfield until our return. With the European invasion shaping up so quickly, I'm surprised you got *us,* but asking for another thousand men would probably be laughed right out of Supreme Headquarters. Even if you *did* have the additional men, we'd have to get the Air Force to land there. They don't mind letting you jump out of their planes, but it's a different story when they have to land them deep in enemy-held territory."

Spangler smiled thinly and spoke for the first time. "Put your men in trucks and head for the Baltic."

"And what are the Germans going to do when they suddenly see fifteen hundred American soldiers driving down their roads?"

"They're going to think their Army has just won a great victory

172

and is transporting the prisoners somewhere—especially if the drivers and the soldiers guarding these prisoners are wearing German uniforms. And if the prisoners themselves ripped off their collars and insignias and rolled around in the dirt a little, you'd be amazed how difficult it would be to tell them from Russians. Also, you wouldn't have a language problem, would you? No one expects Russian prisoners to speak German. But I would suggest that the men you pick for the drivers and guards speak German perfectly."

The silence was immediate and prolonged. It was finally broken by Kittermaster.

"You know what this accommodating fellah's just done for you?" he shouted ecstatically to Cogan. "Why, in one sentence he's opened up not one or two, but *three* escape routes for you. He's shown you how to go north and south—and, if I ever get a change of heart, even east—without the Germans ever giving it a second thought. I think the least you can do is say thanks."

"It will never work," Cogan said grimly. "You'll never be able to disguise our uniforms to make them look Russian."

"Tell you what you do, Major," Kittermaster replied jovially. "You send the measurements of every last one of your men, because I'm not only going to have the best goddam Russian uniforms ever made, I'm also going to give each man a German uniform to boot— just in case you decide to go south. On a long trip they might do better as Germans."

Cogan's staff avoided his glance. The major turned back to Kittermaster. "I want one thing clearly understood. From this point forward I'm in sole command of this rescue operation."

"Haven't you always been, pal? Haven't you always? Now we have to discuss our little rehearsal. Yes, your boys get a crack at jumping down on the real thing right here at home. We've *built* it for you, life size."

For the first time, Cogan felt fear.

Spangler stood watching the alarm clock. At one minute past midnight, February 8, he lit the nine candles on the mantelpiece and began pacing the room. He felt the pains begin in his head. New

173

symptoms he had never imagined began to develop. His hands opened and contracted out of his control. The throbbing rose at his temples, an invisible band tightened slowly around the top of his head. The spasms started and mounted in intensity. The agony grew sharper. His scream was low, guttural and long. It was barely audible above the roar of the endless convoys coming from the road below his window.

When he opened his eyes daylight was streaming through the windows. The candles on the mantel had completely burned out. He rose unsteadily and tried to take a step. His knees buckled, and he fell to all fours. He crawled cautiously to the desk and reached for the phone.

"What day is this?" he asked weakly.

"Tuesday, sir."

"Not the day, the *date!* What's the date?"

"The tenth, sir."

It's getting worse, Spangler told himself, much worse. "Get me a doctor," he cried into the instrument.

32

SPANGLER HOBBLED down the hospital steps and climbed into the waiting limousine. The evening drive to the hunting preserve was uninterrupted by gate checks.

Cogan was busy on the field phones as Spangler climbed to the observation post along the ridge. Kittermaster stood with raised binoculars farther up the path, directing combat photographers in their documentation.

"Sorry I couldn't drop in on you," he said as Spangler reached him, "but the medics say there's nothing wrong with you. Meantime, as you can see, we've been kind of busy. Here, have a look for yourself."

Spangler took the field glasses and focused. The lights of Auschwitz and Birkenau glowed in the forest below. Red-helmeted sentries paced the complexes, others leaned over their machine guns in the guard towers, still others patrolled the outside fences. A locomotive chugged and whistled and slowly backed its twelve cars onto the first siding at Birkenau.

"What do you think?" Kittermaster asked proudly.

"That I'd like to go back and get some sleep," Spangler said, lowering the glasses.

"And miss all the fun and fireworks? We got a great big dress rehearsal just beginning. Not that we're using planes tonight. The jump comes tomorrow. Even so, you'll see quite a sight."

"I'm not well, I need rest. I have to get back."

"Not a chance. I need your opinions, adviser."

"Get Julian's opinions."

"Oh, you mean good old Julie. Haven't you heard, Julie isn't with us any more? He sort of misplayed his hand. Nope, Julie's probably landing in D. C. this very minute. So you see, it's important you stick by—I've elected you his replacement. How does it feel to have all those spies under your command?"

"Find someone else."

"It's un-American to turn down a promotion."

"Find somebody else. Now will someone drive me back? I'm tired."

"The medics said you need plenty of exercise. I wouldn't think of going against the doctors' orders. Why not just watch a little? It should be a hell of a show."

Spangler heard shouting. He glanced along the ridge. Cogan was barking orders into a walkie-talkie.

"Beautiful," Kittermaster chuckled from behind his binoculars, "absolutely beautiful. Those Rangers sure have class—not a patrol to be seen."

Spangler raised his glasses. All the exterior red-helmeted guard patrols had vanished. Powder flashes caught his eye. The white lights of Birkenau went off. A moment later the camp was illuminated by red bulbs.

"They're in darkness," Kittermaster said proudly. "The red lights mean darkness—thought of it myself."

Spangler shifted his glasses to the tree line beyond Birkenau. Waves of blue-helmeted paratroopers rushed from the forest toward the exterior fence.

"Okay, I've watched," Spangler said, putting down the binoculars. "Now can I get some sleep?"

"But the fun is just beginning."

"Tell me about it tomorrow."

"Don't you want to see how they identify Tolan and Jean-Claude?"

176

"I know."

"The hell you do."

"Once you take the camp, the prisoners will be brought out, lined up and moved past inspection posts until Tolan and Jean-Claude are found."

"Who told you?"

"Nobody. It fits, that's all. And it won't work." Spangler walked off, suddenly looking healthier, as if pessimism were a restorative.

33

THE "SILENCE" SIGN went dark.

"Can we take that last part again, Miss Tolan?" the control-room loudspeaker asked. "Pick it up from the beetroots. Take your time, you're doing fine."

The sign went on. Hilka cleared her throat and stepped closer to the microphone. ". . . then add the beetroots and let the mixture come to a boil," she said in German. "If you prefer a darker shade, a teaspoonful of soot can be added. After half an hour the dye will be ready and you can put in any garment you like. Once the garment is immersed, allow it to boil another fifteen minutes and then remove it. And so, brave women of Germany, another meeting of—of Household Hints comes to a close. We patriotic Germans abroad salute you and pray that God will soon ease your plight. Until next time, *auf Wiederhören.*"

Hilka pushed through the studio door to the Green Room.

"Well, Hilka," Vetter said, handing her a container of tea, "how does it feel to be a radio star?"

"If advising women to put soot in their dye is being a radio star, I must say it's not very good. Can you imagine putting soot in dye?"

"It will all come out in the wash." Vetter smiled, waiting for a reaction. None came.

"What do I do next?" she asked, looking out the window. Parachutists could be seen dropping in the distance.

"Fifteen minutes rest, and then your bedtime story."

"Bedtime story?"

"For the children, Hilka. They will be the Germans of tomorrow —if any of them survive. They must learn to love and trust us."

"Do you have the script?"

"It's being translated now."

"Are they actually going to broadcast all of this?"

"How can we tell? Seven warehouses are now filled with newspapers that have never been dropped on Germany. The storage room next door is crammed to the ceiling with radio transcriptions that have never been aired. Someone somewhere must be optimistic. Perhaps the colonel can give you the answer. Why not ask him next time?"

Hilka turned hesitantly.

"There's no need to be upset, Hilka. I doubt if any of the others know."

"Know what?"

"Why, that the colonel often takes you driving at night."

"What's wrong with that?"

"Nothing, Hilka. In fact, I'm rather jealous. I am most curious to know what the world has come to look like beyond the fences."

"Still the world. No better, no worse." She turned back to the window.

"Where does he take you?"

"Up the coast."

"Oh, that must be most scenic. Now I am even more envious than before. Do you ever see *people*? Ordinary people? Do you ever stop in towns?"

"Yes. He's rather good about that. He lets me walk about the villages if I choose. Nothing is open that late, but it is nice to walk through them."

"Tell me, Hilka, are there mailboxes in these villages?" Vetter asked, moving up beside her.

"What do you want mailed?" she said without looking at him.

"Just a postcard."

"You know the regulations."

"Achh, Hilka. You truly are becoming the colonel's lady. Is there anything so wrong with a father writing to his son?"

"Rudi? You told me he was dead."

"It is best for us here to say our loved ones are dead. After all, who knows how this whole thing will turn out? Who knows what the Nazis might do when they find out about this?"

"Is he in Germany?"

"No, in Africa with the British Army, but that insures nothing. Will you mail it, Hilka? You can read it." Vetter brought out the postcard. "There's nothing secret between the lines, believe me. Major Julian used to let me send them, but he's gone now. Look, it isn't even signed, so you can't get into any trouble. I just want Rudi to know I'm still alive."

Major Black Buck Cogan sat in the number-two bucket seat beside the open door and adjusted the chin strap of his helmet. He stretched around and looked out. Thirty more transport planes droned forward through the evening sky in wing-tip formation. Behind him a contingent of Blue Attack paratroops sat on both rows of facing seats. Each had his chute cord attached to the static line overhead.

Cogan flipped open the attack plan and began reviewing it. The daylight jumps had gone well. Now he was faced with the moment of truth: night assault. Casualties were his main concern. Field judges would be waiting on the ground to estimate "projected losses." The losses must not exceed five per cent. If fewer than seventy-five men were declared wounded or killed in the mock battle, the operation would be a success—provided Auschwitz and Birkenau could be overrun and the two prisoners found within the estimated margin-of-safety time period. Cogan checked his watch. The Rangers should already be on the ground. They should be setting up the drop zone, "taking out" the exterior guards and preparing to cut off the camp's power and communications.

"Sir," the co-pilot called, hurrying back to Cogan, "there seems to be some trouble with the ground flares. They're not in the same positions we have here on our charts. The skipper suggests delaying until we have clarification."

"We jump. Correct with aerial flares."

"But, sir, wouldn't it be better to—"

"Correct it with aerial flares. We jump on schedule!"

"Whatever you say, sir."

The formation of transports descended and spread into the approach pattern. The red lights above the open doors glowed on as the jump masters moved down the aisle checking the hooks on the static line. The men were ordered to stand. Flares dropped, ignited and drifted slowly down through the night. The transports jogged slightly. The green lights switched on. The paratroopers crowded forward. Cogan lunged through the open doorway of the lead plane with a yell.

The target area had been miscalculated. The treetops were littered with chutes and dangling soldiers. There was no need for the field judges to tabulate the "projected losses"; the actual casualties came to three hundred and two injured and eighteen dead.

34

THE SECLUDED gabled resort hotel lay twenty-three miles down the coast road. Five cars and a lorry on blocks stood in the parking area. The ancient desk clerk slept behind the desk. Spangler glanced around the fake Tudor lobby. Two sets of curtained glass doors opened off it. A string quartet was playing Ivor Novello from behind the first. Spangler pushed through the second. The dining room was oaken, low-beamed and gas-lit. A young couple leaned face to face against the bar in the near corner. Julian was seated across the room at a table overlooking the ocean.

"I thought you were in Washington," Spangler said, pulling up a chair.

"Good! That's what I wanted everybody to think. Actually, Erik, I'm not in Washington. Actually, Erik, I got no farther than here. Felt I needed a few days of rest and meditation—and, come to think of it, drink. I am intoxicated, Erik. Smashed. Polluted. Zonked. But *lucid,* Erik; always lucid. Just can't walk too well, that's all. Care for a bite? The fish is almost edible."

"I don't have the time."

"No English accent, Erik? How disappointing. That means you're in low spirits. Pity."

"This meeting was your idea, not mine. If you want to talk, talk. If not, I'm going."

"Erik, Erik, Erik, I'm ashamed of you. You know how I am. Never have been able to get directly to the point. Love to thrash around a bit first. It's my ritual, Erik. It's like your symptoms. Erik, it's extremely nice of you to drop by." Julian flashed a sad smile and pushed his glasses higher on his nose. "Now tell me, how is it all going at Westerly? Everyone still jumping out of airplanes?"

"More or less."

"And the little calamity, Erik—how has it affected events?"

"What calamity?"

"You know, Erik, all those silly men coming down into the poplars and the oaks. Something about misplaced flares?"

"How do you know about that?"

"Stop looking at me with that expression, Erik. You know that my patterns of intrigue and deception are always mundane and predictable. Why, when was the last time I came up with such a complicated idea as misdirecting an air drop? I expect last night's little bloodletting will hold things up for a bit, won't it?"

"Replacements are on the way. Cogan has a broken ankle."

Julian frowned, lifted his glass and sipped. "In that case, Erik, he must be stopped."

"Who?"

"Kittermaster. Yes, Erik, he must be stopped. He's quite mad, you know. Thinks he's Busby Berkeley. Obsessed with staging an extravaganza—a great big extravaganza for a grandstand of five or six Washington potbellies, and the price be damned. What do you think the price will be, Erik—one thousand, two thousand, five thousand men?"

"He might not lose that many."

"That coming from you? Erik, which one of us has been doing the drinking? Can you really sit there in full sobriety and tell me that those released concentration-camp prisoners and those pathetic would-be marauders draped in American uniforms won't be slaughtered like swine?"

"What are you talking about?"

"You know precisely what I'm talking about: Kittermaster's latest scheme. He plans to dress the camp prisoners in the discarded Amer-

183

ican uniforms, arm them and send them around the countryside to sabotage and create diversion—to give the paratroopers a better chance of getting out unnoticed."

"If you're so damned concerned about the prisoners, why didn't you do something about the camps before?"

"I tried, Erik, I tried—as you know better than anyone. But Washington's a little vague on the subject. After all, if our government has still not officially recognized their *existence,* what can one insignificant major do? But perhaps this is our opportunity, eh? Perhaps now we can do something to save them."

"No one has to save them in this situation, because nothing's going to happen to them."

"Does God plan to intervene?"

"C.-c. prisoners are conditioned to passivity. The outside world doesn't exist for them. It's beyond their comprehension. It has to be if they hope to survive. No more than a handful would ever leave even if the gates were thrown wide open. And those few who *would* go out could hardly stand, let alone carry a gun and fight."

"I see your point, Erik, and I will take your word on their physiological and psychological condition. But, Erik, isn't the safe retreat of the American soldiers based on the prisoners' acting as a decoy? What will happen if there *is* no decoy?"

"They have a chance to make it through."

"How much of a chance?"

"That depends on their luck."

"What a curious word for you to be using, Erik. You and I aren't the type to put much stock in luck. We wouldn't be alive today if we were. Let's not dwell on luck, Erik; it makes me feel as if someone has trodden on my grave. Let's deal with something else—with premeditation and skill. Erik, do you believe that if the air drop is launched in Poland the paratroopers can overrun the camps, locate Jean-Claude and Tolan and get them into the escape plane?"

"Maybe."

Julian pondered. "Erik, are you counting on thirty-two hundred Americans to bring out Jean-Claude regardless of how few of them survive? Are you subscribing to the Kittermaster credo: Get me

184

what I want and damn the corpses left behind?"

"We don't know if Jean-Claude is in there."

"He's been missing for three weeks now, Erik. Where else would you expect him to be?"

"Maybe he's lost. He's a child, children can get lost. Or maybe he was captured and taken somewhere else."

"Erik, isn't the reason you've remained at Westerly quite simply based on one belief—that Jean-Claude is at Auschwitz or Birkenau?"

"I don't know where he is."

"I think you *think* he's at Auschwitz or Birkenau, Erik. Why waste time? Why don't you go in and find out for yourself?"

"You know I can't. I'm set up for Germany and the West. I have no contacts in Poland—you know I work through contacts."

"Only recently, Erik. In the old days you had a way of not relying on anyone. Those were the good days, Erik. Those were your golden days. Perhaps you can do it again?"

"Look, if you want to steal Kittermaster's thunder, do it anyway you like, but just keep me out of it. I'm finished with the camps. Through. I shouldn't have gone in the last time. I'll never go in again."

"And your apparatus, Erik? All your little devices and techniques, are you just going to let them sit and rot?"

"Yes."

"Erik, I've always meant to ask you this. Just what is your relationship with Jean-Claude? Is it that he's the last human being on this earth you feel an obligation for?"

Spangler rose. "I've had enough of you—enough to last a lifetime."

He walked quickly from the dining room, stopped at the desk, woke the clerk and bought a roll of throat lozenges. He bit off the top of the wrapper and sucked two into his mouth.

"What the hell are you doing now, boy, following me?" Kittermaster's voice blasted out. "Never figured you for the poor sport. After all, you had your shot at her and muffed."

Kittermaster was grinning down at him from the staircase, holding

185

a small valise. Hilka had stopped two steps above. She gazed at Spangler, turned sharply and continued climbing.

"You were her first choice, boy," Kittermaster said evenly. "No doubt about it. You were number one, but you just weren't up to it—just couldn't cut the mustard. So why ruin another fellah's good time, eh? Why should we have any hard feelings over a dizzy Kraut cunt? Just you stay off my turf and I'll keep clear of yours, okay?"

Julian swayed half hidden just inside the dining-room doors. He watched Spangler stare blankly up after the ascending colonel, turn away slowly, check the time and half run from the hotel.

Julian made his way down the hall, pulled open the door on his third try and squeezed into the telephone box. He hiccupped, placed a long-distance call and finally managed to deposit the required coins.

"Yes," a voice answered in a clipped British accent.

"This is Peppermint," Julian said thickly. "You remember Peppermint, don't you?"

"Yes."

"You wouldn't happen to know if Freddy was still in town, would you?"

"Yes."

"Yes what?"

"Yes, Freddy is in town."

"Then put the silly bastard on."

"Freddy isn't here. Could you leave a message?"

Julian paused, sighed and closed his eyes. "You tell Freddy I've changed my mind. You tell him I'm willing to sell the merchandise he wants. Tell him the object he wants is definitely for sale. But tell him he has to bring his own tobacco—I haven't any. He knows where to contact me. And you tell him he'd better make contact bloody damned fast—or I might change my mind again."

Julian hung up, leaned forward and rested his forehead against the coin box.

35

THE BACK OF the hand caught Hilka flush in the mouth and tumbled her backwards over the bed. Kittermaster raised her up by the hair with one hand and waved the postcard before her eyes with the other.

"Who is he," he shouted as he slapped the card across her face. "Who? Another boy friend, is that it? Trying to meet Spangler here on the sly isn't enough for you? Got to have another one, too? Got to have a whole stable, is that the story?"

The hair was gripped tighter and twisted. Hilka shrieked.

"Who is Rudi?"

"No—no one . . ."

Hilka jerked away, dashed to the door and began screaming and pounding. His fist smashed into her ear. She spun around against the wall. The second blow drove into her cheek. Hilka slumped to her knees and dropped sideways onto the floor.

Kittermaster raised her by the wrists and hurled her onto the bed. "Admit it," he said, slapping her cheeks to revive her. "Admit it. I want to hear—"

The pounding on the door was heavy and authoritative. "All right in there, open it up. Constabulary here. Open it up."

Kittermaster scooped Hilka in his arms, hurried her into the bathroom, laid her on the floor and turned the water on full. He could hear the pounding grow more insistent.

He unlocked the door and pulled it open. The constable entered.

The trembling desk clerk remained in the hall.

"All right, what's going on in here?"

"Just an argument, officer," Kittermaster said, sweeping a hand through his hair. "A lovers' quarrel."

"And where's the lady?"

"Taking a bath. She always takes a bath after we—after we've had one of our little go-rounds."

"Let us have your identification."

Kittermaster produced his ID card.

"A colonel?"

"Yes."

The constable took out his book and jotted down the information on the card. "And where are you quartered?"

"Westerly."

"Oh, one of them, are you?"

"I'm the commander."

"Are you. Well, a fine example you're setting for your men, wouldn't you say?" The constable put away his pad and glanced about the room. "Is the lady all right?"

"Yes, she's fine. She'll take her bath and have her cry and then be fine. That's how it always is."

"And we'll have no more trouble from you?"

"No more trouble. On my word."

"And I'll take your word, Colonel. But if there's any more trouble, I must warn you, in you go. They run a quiet place here."

"We're known for our quiet," the clerk added from the hall.

"I'll be quiet, you can bet. And thank you, officer, for your kind consideration."

"Constable. I'm no officer by a long measure. I'm a constable and proud to be."

"Thank you, *Constable*."

Kittermaster closed the door, locked it and hurried back to the bathroom. Hilka lay motionless. He leaned over and put an ear to her mouth. She was breathing. He turned off the water and carried her to the bed. He knelt beside her and began massaging her wrists. "Everything's going to be okay now, I mean it. Just don't you worry.

188

Everything's going to be dandy. Do you hear me? Hear that? Why, you can go and write to whoever you want, even him. Sure. I tell you what. If you want to see Spangler at Westerly, then you go right ahead. It won't ruffle me the slightest. Do you hear me? Hey, do you hear? Ah, come on, I didn't hit you that hard. You know I didn't. What are you trying to do, scare me? Don't do that to me, honey. Come on, will you, cut it out. Do you hear—"

The knocking on the door was sharper than before.

Kittermaster made no move.

The pounding continued.

He stood up as a key turned in the lock.

Two men in double-breasted dark-gray pinstripes entered. One carried a black leather satchel.

"Police inspectors, Scotland Yard," said the tall one in a clipped accent. "Don't mind if we see your identification again, do you? Been some trouble with forged papers lately. May I?"

Kittermaster reached for his wallet and brought out the card as the short man closed the door in the room clerk's face.

The tall inspector studied the identification and then handed it to his companion. "What do you think, Harold?"

The short man glanced from photograph to Kittermaster and back to photograph. "Seems proper to me, Freddy."

"Better check the list," the tall detective replied. Then he snapped his fingers and pointed to the bed. "Well, well, well, what have we here?" he said, stepping toward the motionless Hilka.

"She's—she's just sleeping," Kittermaster said nervously. "She fell down—and now she's sleeping."

Kittermaster stepped back as Harold joined Freddy at the bed. "She's damn near dead," Harold said without overmuch concern.

"She is, isn't she?" Freddy commented casually. "Better see what you can do for her, Harold. See if you can bring her round."

Harold opened his satchel, poked about inside and came out with a can of pipe tobacco. He reached further in and withdrew a hypodermic syringe.

"Getting back to your identification card," said Freddy. "Is Lamar your Christian name?"

189

"Yes," the colonel answered, watching Harold pull the syringe out of Hilka's arm and change the needle.

"Lamar Buford Kittermaster?"

"That's right," he said, turning back to the tall man.

"Are you sure it isn't Spangler?"

"Spangler?"

"Erik Spangler."

"Say, who the hell are you?"

"Friends of friends—*Herr Erik Spangler.*"

"What—why— Now, just a minute, you've got—"

Kittermaster's arms were jerked behind his back.

"Why, that treacherous little bastard," the colonel half laughed, "that little bastard Julian. Julie put you up to this, didn't—"

Freddy ripped open Kittermaster's shirt.

"Hey, you fellows just had a good one pulled on—"

The hypodermic needle drove into Kittermaster's heart. Death was instantaneous.

The corpse was laid on the floor and photographed repeatedly. Fingerprints and a blood sample were taken.

Harold slid the tobacco can between Kittermaster and the bed. The men locked the door after them as they left the room. They had driven almost half a mile before they heard the explosion.

190

36

THE DOCUMENTS were signed and sealed and copies given to Julian. The secret inquest conducted by the coroner and three local officials was terminated. The casket was loaded onto a guarded truck and driven off toward the R.A.F. airfield, where a special bomber would be waiting to fly it to the United States.

Julian followed the coffin as far as the first village before turning off onto a side road and pulling in behind the remains of a fire-gutted barn. He got out of the car, lifted the trunk door and reached in for his priest's clothing. He was changed and driving on within five minutes.

The fishing smack was moored to the jetty with its engines idling. Von Schleiben sat in the stern, dressed as a bishop. Freddy and Harold moved in behind him as Julian descended the steep path leading down to the isolated cove.

"Sorry to have missed Spangler's final benediction," von Schleiben called out cordially, with a wave of his ribboned miter, "but I find death slightly obnoxious. That is why I have never set foot in a camp. Did you know that, Peppermint? It is true. If the Fuehrer himself refuses to view a bombed German city, why should I sicken myself with carnage? Come aboard, Peppermint."

Julian stopped at the stone wall and tossed a manila envelope down into the boat. "These are the inquest papers, as well as Spangler's service record," he called, as Freddy opened the packet and spread the pages on the deck. Harold took out his camera and began photographing.

"The service record is sparse," Julian continued, "but that's the procedure with agents of Spangler's category. Activities and assignments are never reported. But it does include a photograph, fingerprints, blood type and other physical identification."

"Come aboard, Peppermint, come aboard," von Schleiben urged.

"I prefer it up here." Julian slipped one hand under his cassock.

"Don't you trust me, Peppermint?"

"Not with the engines running, I don't."

"But I've found some new prospects for you. How can you make the selections if you don't come aboard?" von Schleiben asked, displaying a typewritten list.

"Read them to me."

"Our understanding doesn't cover my reading off names."

"It doesn't cover my coming aboard, either."

Von Schleiben scowled, paused, then snapped his fingers and removed a list from his pocket. "There are two categories of prisoners to choose from—those being held in prisons and those in concentration camps. Those in prison can be delivered quickly and easily. The camps present a different problem."

"Start with the prisons," Julian said.

Von Schleiben held the paper out under his glasses and began reading. "Goetz, Speigle, Drosset, Stroud, Werner, Mandelbaum."

"No good. Who is on the other list?"

"Those I once offered you in France: Hauller, Brome and Tolan. You can also have Kapska or Boeck."

"What happened to von Rausch and Bengl? They were in the original offering."

Von Schleiben recalled, "So they were, Peppermint, so they were. That seems so far back now. Von Rausch and Bengl are no longer with us. Acute pneumonia."

"I'll take Kapska and Brome."

Von Schleiben turned to Harold. "Where are we holding them?"

192

"Kapska's at Sobibor, Obergruppenfuehrer, and Brome is in Grossrosen."

Von Schleiben shook his head. "Ach, Peppermint, I hope you are in no particular hurry? It will take time to get them out."

"How much time?"

"Six to seven weeks for Brome. Kapska? Perhaps two to three months."

"I need them faster."

"Impossible. And you have no one to blame but yourself. Had you given me Spangler when I first requested, the prisoners would not have been moved around. All the names on the camp list had to be moved—because of you. Now they are more closely watched by Totenkopf security. It is very complicated to arrange for their disappearance without creating suspicion."

"I must have Kapska and Brome within three weeks." Julian insisted.

"Harold," von Schleiben snapped, "where are the others?"

"Hauller's at Treblinka, Obergruppenfuehrer," Freddy replied, leaning over von Schleiben's shoulder and examining the list. "Tolan's at Birkenau and Boeck at Plazow."

Von Schleiben considered. "You could have Hauller in three weeks and Tolan in four."

"I don't want Hauller or Tolan. They're no use to me. I must have Kapska and Brome—and quickly."

"No one else will do?"

"No."

Von Schleiben shrugged. "Harold, get down to the radio room and contact Zieff. Tell him that Kapska and Brome are to be immediately executed." He turned back to Julian with satisfaction. "No reaction, Peppermint? You disappoint me. When I was outwitted in exactly this fashion, I was livid with rage. I lost several good men because I was naïve enough to let another enemy know my requirements.

"But that's how it is with us, isn't it, Peppermint? We learn from one another. The gambit you play on me today I employ against someone else tomorrow. Eventually our bag of tricks becomes the same, and then the game resolves simply into catching the other side off guard. Goals and causes become secondary; only the competition matters. How futile it is, Peppermint. We are jousting windmills, boxing with shadows. Our late friend Spangler was a real shadow-boxer, wasn't he? And what did he accomplish for all his trouble? But I suppose he enjoyed it. We all do, eh, Peppermint? Intrigue exhilarates us. Win or lose, there's never any rancor between adversaries. Is that why no one outside really understands us—or cares to?"

"You agreed to give me whoever I wanted in return for Spangler," Julian said coldly. "I want Kapska and Brome."

"Kapska and Brome were *suggestions,* not agreements. Our agreement was formulated that night in France when I demanded that Spangler should not go after the Tolan girl. You saw fit not to honor it. You imperiled my position, even my life. But now you have been outmaneuvered. Spangler is gone. Kapska and Brome will soon follow. Whatever the scheme you had in mind, it has been crippled. But, most important, I am safe. No one is left who can implicate me in anything treasonable to Germany. No one except you, Peppermint. But there's nothing I can do about that, not with a gun pointing at me from under your cassock. Do you intend to shoot? Wouldn't that be foolish, Peppermint? You would hit me, and my companions here would kill you. So we are at a deadlock."

"And Jean-Claude? You also agreed to release him."

"Suggested, Peppermint, not agreed. I was careful with my phrasing. I had to be careful not to lie. After all, we may be doing business again in the future."

"He knows nothing. He's only a child."

"Then we shall make good use of him, as I once promised," von Schleiben said with a snap of the fingers as Harold cast off. *"Auf Wiedersehen,* my friend."

37

"LET YOUR FANCY paratroops do the job," Spangler muttered, asprawl in the great armchair before the blazing fireplace in Kittermaster's office.

"The Army has called off the raid, Erik. The invasion has been moved up and they need the planes. With Kittermaster gone, we have no power to override the Army," Julian said from behind the colonel's desk.

"Just what did happen to Kittermaster?"

"We're still investigating. Erik, you have to go in."

"I won't."

"Then what will become of Jean-Claude?"

"We don't even know where he is."

"But we do, Erik. I went through Kittermaster's private files. I found this message he never showed us. Jean-Claude had gotten it out of Birkenau. He's in Birkenau, Erik."

"I won't go back."

"And forsake the boy?"

"I can't go back. I'm in no condition. I'm sick—I can't even walk."

"You're a hypochondriac, Erik, short and simple. You know that as well as I do. You're that locker-room cripple, that magnificent athlete who always complains of ailments—until the competition

195

begins. There's not a thing in the world wrong with you, Erik. Not physically."

Julian took a cigar from Kittermaster's humidor. "Erik, remember when we first met in France? You had been staying with Henri Tramont in the mountains, at his cabin. You and Henri had already freed those priests—the ones who had been friends of his at a monastery nearby."

"What has that to do with anything?"

"What order of priests were they, Erik?"

"I don't remember."

"Of course you do." Julian lit his cigar and inhaled appreciatively. "That's one reason you went to visit Henri so often. Those particular priests fascinated you, didn't they?"

"I went there to hunt and ski."

"Those priests were flagellants, weren't they, Erik? And that's why they lived in such isolation in the mountains—they had been banished by the Church, I believe."

"I don't know what they were, outside of being friends of Henri."

"Was Henri a flagellant?"

"How would I know?"

"Are you a flagellant?"

"You must be out of your mind," said Spangler.

"It's odd that you should say that, Erik. You see, I've talked to some medical people. Erik, did you realize that under certain circumstances hypochondria is a form of self-flagellation? Instead of punishing yourself physically, you do it mentally."

"When I want a psychoanalyst I'll pick my own," Spangler said, rising and limping to the desk. He glanced down and read the message Jean-Claude had sent from Birkenau.

"I found out a good deal about those priests, and a great many things start fitting in place. The numbers, for instance. The dates that Henri also liked for his raids—the eighth, the seventeenth and the twenty-sixth—remember them, Erik? Remember how we decided to set patterns to confuse the Germans and make them think it was one man engineering all those escapes? Eventually only one man did, Erik—you. But at the beginning there were to be many. Henri picked those numbers, and I never gave it another thought. But you knew what they stood for. Those were the dates on which the priests would flagellate themselves—inflict pain on each other and expiate their sins. It was a private joke between you and Henri, wasn't it? "But your own symptoms—your pains are the worst on those three days, aren't they?"

"None of your goddam business."

"Go back to the camp, Erik—bring out the boy."

"I can't."

"You still have your contacts, you can get across Germany without trouble. You can get into Poland. You'll conceive a method to get him out."

"You don't understand."

"They're not searching for you any more, Erik. It will be much easier. Look, Vetter is a Russian agent. I've known it all along, and I've let him send out messages—but I've changed them. They have a description of you that belongs to a man who is now dead. The Russians have passed the information on to von Schleiben. Von Schleiben has confirmed it through another source. Von Schleiben thinks you're dead, Erik. So you see there's nothing to worry about. They won't be expecting you."

"I won't do it."

"Henri was Jean-Claude's father."

Spangler remained silent.

"And now you're repaying Henri for deserting him—letting him go on a raid alone and get captured. You have officially adopted his son. You *are* the protector of Henri's orphaned child?"

Spangler turned away.

"You have to go, Erik. You have to go for Henri's sake—for letting him die. But you owe it even more to Jean-Claude himself—von Schleiben has threatened to use him as a Bubel."

Spangler's head dropped and his eyes closed. Teeth and fists clenched. He remained motionless for many seconds. Then he began to sob.

197

"And while you're there, Erik, you'll have to bring out Tolan as well. I'll help you, if you help me. Tolan must come out. And if you don't do it, Erik, I'll turn you over to von Schleiben myself."

Kuprov sat cross-legged on the low wide hassock, reading the coroner's report while harem-clad serving girls draped a Grande Armée cape over his business suit. Von Schleiben, resplendent in Roman toga and myrtle wreath, with open sandals and painted toenails, reclined on a divan beside a lily pool.

The Russian picked through the other documents Julian had provided on Spangler's death. He studied the pages carefully and suddenly stopped with a harsh laugh.

"Idiot!" he shouted at von Schleiben. "They have made an idiot out of you. You have slaughtered my agent."

Von Schleiben waved the girls from the salon.

"Spangler your agent?" von Schleiben replied languidly. "How ingenious—and how unfortunate."

"No, you fool," Kuprov said savagely. "You've murdered my primary agent at Westerly—Hilka Tolan. Vetter was the decoy. We knew the Americans would be watching him. We wanted them to watch him and intercept or tamper with his messages. With their attention on Vetter, the Tolan girl could operate more freely. But you put an end to that. You killed her for me, didn't you? And before she got out anything useful *except* for some random details—like who her lover was."

"As I remarked before, how unfortunate."

"The man you murdered was her lover, the colonel in command —a man named Kittermaster—*not* your precious Spangler."

Von Schleiben paled and grew rigid. *"Where is Spangler?* You provided his description—it checks with the coroner's report."

"A description concocted by the Americans. I told you they were tampering with Vetter's messages. His description of Spangler had been changed to fit Kittermaster."

"I should have been told."

"We didn't know for certain until two days ago."

"I want accurate information on Spangler."

198

"Then this is what you do, my little shrunken Caesar," Kuprov said, rising and ripping off his cape. "Go do your own handiwork and find out. Go whisper in the corpses' ears—Tolan now, Vetter shortly. Maybe their dead lips will reveal a secret."

Kuprov stopped at the door and turned back to von Schleiben. "You are a vain, stupid little peacock, Goliath. You don't even have good jokes any more. I am beginning to tire of you. Don't let me tire of you, Schleebund. Now that you've slaughtered my agents, *you* find out what the Americans are up to at Westerly—or you'll be strutting from the end of a rope when we overrun Germany."

Von Schleiben watched at the window as Kuprov descended into the blacked-out side street. The German General nodded. Four men emerged from doorways and started after the Russian.

PART THREE

The
Spangler Proposition

38

THE THREE-CAR "express" from Copenhagen ground to a stop outside Flensburg. Teams of green-uniformed Frontier Police hoisted themselves into the carriages and started along the low blue-lit passageways.

The compartment door squeaked open. A gloved hand shook Spangler awake.

"Passport. Papers," a youth with peaked felt cap and leather elbow patches demanded in German. "Passport! Papers!" he repeated in Danish.

Spangler reached into his rewoven, threadbare wool jacket and handed up the packet. The boy thumbed through it with practiced efficiency.

"Hans Kieland," he droned as his confederate standing in the doorway began printing on the form attached to the clipboard. "Danish. Passport number 2735." He started on the other documents without dropping the chant: "Volunteer worker permit S-1521. Point of departure: Copenhagen. Point of arrival: Hamburg. Destination: Zermastoff Labor Battalion." A thin paper was unfolded. "Travel permit issued Copenhagen, 19 February 1944, Gestapo, Amt Four E Four. Ration card and currency receipt in order." The documents were stamped with various seals.

"Luggage?" inquired the youth.

Spangler pointed to the rack over his head.

"Get it down."

Spangler did as he was told. The battered cardboard contained a worn, colorless shirt, two pairs of mended woolen socks, suspenders, a straight razor, three apples, a half-eaten loaf of dry brown bread and a pouch of ersatz coffee.

The youth nodded and pasted a customs sticker to the side of the box. "Are you all right?" he asked, gazing at Spangler.

"Yes."

"You look warm. Don't sit so close to the window or you'll get a chill. We can't afford to have our volunteers sick. Heil Hitler!"

The inspection team descended on the next passenger.

An hour and a half later the flag was waved and the switch thrown. The train began to rattle slowly forward.

Flares stopped the locomotive just before Neumuenster. Spangler could see German police officers on the tracks below his window talking with the conductor and pointing to the north. The compartment doors were open.

"Outside," the engineer urged him. "Everyone outside. Kiel is being bombed. The British might pass this way on their return. Everyone out."

Spangler lowered himself to the roadbed and limped into the field with the other passengers.

"If you hear engines," a one-legged Wehrmacht captain in a muffler told them, "lie face down on the earth. Do not light matches."

"What about the flares?" said Spangler. "If you're worried about British planes spotting matches, what about the flares burning out in front of the locomotive?"

The officer turned and shouted an order. The flares were extinguished. The man studied Spangler momentarily, nodded and left.

Faint thuds were heard in the distance. Suddenly the ground beneath them shuddered. It was almost a full minute before a red glow flickered in the north.

"Petroleum," whispered one of the passengers.

"Perhaps it was ammunition," offered another.

204

"No, it is petroleum. Little ammunition is kept in Kiel these days."

"Petroleum," a third confirmed softly. "Only petroleum burns that high or hot. If it was ammunition the glow would not linger in the distance. There would be a white flash and that would be that."

More explosions were felt, then heard. The red glow in the north grew brighter and higher. Distinct bands of blue shimmered across the sky. Gentle pillars of black began curling upward and drifting into the red, like ink into blood.

"It's petroleum," the dissenter conceded.

The concussions lasted another twenty minutes. Half an hour later the officer returned. "They have left. You can go back to the cars," he told them.

"I heard no aircraft," the first passenger said, almost in disappointment. "They usually pass back this way."

"They've gone on to Hamburg."

"Hamburg?" the passenger muttered to Spangler as they started back to the tracks. "What is there left in Hamburg to bomb?"

The train moved steadily through the night. The rails had been destroyed beyond Ulzburg, so the "express" was shunted west to Elmshorn and then southeast through Pinneburg.

Spangler's headache spasmed from time to time. The pain in his left shoulder was easing but noticeable.

The Elbe was sighted by dawn. The outskirts of Hamburg appeared a few minutes later.

Spangler stared out at the ruins of the Hanseatic city. Two seared cranes were all that remained standing of Europe's largest shipyards. The train reduced speed and wound among gutted oil tanks, razed refineries and twisted machinery. They moved along an elevated track and entered Hamburg proper. Hardly a building remained standing. Block after block of dust-covered debris and neatly piled brick passed the window.

The elderly woman sitting opposite Spangler gasped in disbelief at the vast destruction.

"Don't be so concerned," her husband said, patting her on the knee. "Just think what we are doing to London."

205

Whistles blew. The train slowed and pulled into the roofless terminal.

The bus was late. Spangler arrived at Lueneburg in early afternoon. He paused outside the post office while he had a mild attack of asthma, then he entered and presented his receipt.

"The parcel arrived five months ago?" the clerk asked curtly.

"I have been on a work battalion. We were kept longer than anyone expected."

"Even so, we are not a storehouse."

"I would have been longer," Spangler tried again, "but I lost my brother. He was with the Reich Division. They let me attend the funeral. He had won four Iron Crosses."

"Four?"

"Four."

"You will still have to wait. The parcel is in 'no claims,' if it hasn't been returned. I don't have time to look for it now."

It was midafternoon before the suitcase was located in the cellar storage room. It was addressed "Hans Kieland, care of General Delivery." The sender was listed as Hafdan Kieland, SS Division Das Reich.

"The one with the four Iron Crosses?" the clerk asked, reaching for Spangler's passport and identity papers.

"Only two. This is my other brother. We think he's still alive."

The postal form was quickly signed, stamped and recorded. The suitcase was released.

Spangler caught the evening bus to Dannenberg. He arrived slightly after eleven and limped to the woods beyond the town limits. He stripped off his clothes, opened the suitcase, took out an SS major's uniform, boots, cap and overcoat and put them on. He oiled the Luger, checked the clip, and pushed it into his holster. The wallet contained five thousand Reichsmarks. The passport and papers were in the name of Richard Wendorff, *Obersturmbannfuehrer* SS, R. S. H. A. Spangler opened a packet of cigarettes he had brought with him, peeled off the inner layer of paper, slid out a photograph of himself and pasted it in the passport. He transferred his Danish clothing to the suitcase, folded the carton inside and started back to Dannenberg.

The inn was full. The proprietor could find no other room in the city. Spangler demanded to see the local Kripo representative. The officer was called to the inn. When he arrived Spangler presented his credentials and ordered him to find immediate sleeping quarters or else arrange transportation to Wittenberge. The Kripo man ran back home and returned with his car. Little was said during the drive. Even after he had deposited Spangler at the Wittenberge hotel, the officer never thought of asking how he had managed to get stranded in Dannenberg in the first place.

Spangler slept late, breakfasted in the hotel dining room, sat for a haircut and shave, and stole a car. That night he slept in Berlin.

He was at the post office by eleven the next morning. The cardboard carton with his Danish clothes and papers was mailed to Major R. Wendorff, General Delivery, Luebeck. The rest of the day he spent leisurely touring Berlin.

After a mediocre dinner he took a walk. What he had hoped for happened: air-raid sirens began to wail. By the time the first bombs hit, Spangler had broken into the offices of Amt IV-B-4, Department of Jewish Affairs, R. S. H. A., and was studying the transportation files. He moved on to the storeroom of the Documents Division, located the blue forms, filled one out and returned to the outer office for the stamp.

After the all clear, Spangler stole another car and started driving east. Despite his chills, he stopped only for gas until he reached Budapest. There was no time for sleeping. He ate breakfast at 7 A.M. The shop opened at eight.

"I would like something for my nephew," he told the clerk. "He's just about my size."

"Work clothes or dress?"

"Something in between," Spangler answered, placing the ration book on the counter.

39

THE BLUE SIGNS had been posted in Szogor for a week. They were
printed in both Hungarian and Yiddish.

ATTENTION!
SPECIAL REICH DECREE

to

ALL PERSONS HOLDING
BLUE PAPERS

Prepare for emigration to relocation settlements on
or before

FEBRUARY 23

Each emigrant will be allowed one suitcase and
should bring warm clothing and extra shoes. Money,
jewelry and other valuable possessions will be allowed. Artisans and professional men will be allowed
to bring the tools of their craft. A two-day supply of
food will also be needed for the trip.

The auxiliary police moved in at dawn. The local Jews were already queued up to show their blue papers and receive embarkation numbers. Columns of Jews from nearby towns began marching in for processing. The checkoff system was flexible. Certain persons were missing. They were searched for. Others carried blue cards, but their names did not appear on the lists; their names were added.

The Hungarian auxiliaries crowded the Jews into the seven side streets north of the main thoroughfare. All were ordered to sit or squat. Those who responded slowly were kicked or beaten. Speaking was forbidden.

Ragged columns of exhausted Russian war prisoners trudged into Szogor from the east and filled the side streets south of the main road. They were forced to lie flat on their faces. Infractions were dealt with harshly. One young boy was pummeled to death. Two prisoners were shot.

German SS officers arrived. The Hungarian auxiliaries guarding the Jews were curtly ordered to put their machine pistols back into their leg holsters. The SS moved among the terrified civilians apologizing for the Hungarians' stupidity. The Hungarians, they told them, treated everyone like war prisoners, like Communists. But the Jews were emigrants, not prisoners, the SS said, and Jews were free to stand or sit or do whatever they liked as long as they remained on the side streets. The SS officers began mingling openly with the yellow-starred civilians. They held friendly chats, offered sweets to the children, cigarettes to the adults. An old woman was escorted back to her house to retrieve the pet canary the Hungarians had so rudely forced her to abandon.

The tension eased. The SS officers continued their fraternization. They reiterated that the Reich had nothing against Hungarian Jews, or even the few Italian and Greek Jews among them. It was the Polish Jews who had forced them to apply restrictive laws; they had all suffered because of the Poles. But at last something could be done to ease the situation. The Reich was short of labor; the Hungarian and Italian and Greek Jews could prove their loyalty by working for Germany. It was a rare opportunity. They must do their utmost for the Reich wherever they were sent.

Picture postcards were distributed, depicting pastoral bliss, neat resort cottages beside tranquil lakes or verdant hillsides. The messages on the back were even more serene.

At the first sound of the locomotive a band began to play. No one knew it had been there. Now they could see the military musicians strut down the main street. The first selection was from Mendelssohn. The Jews filed out and fell in behind the music. The SS encouraged both spectators and marchers to wave to one another.

A festive mood began to germinate. The venerable village doctor ambled from the sidewalk to embrace his young neighbor, to give him his scarf and what little money he had in his pocket as a memento. An SS officer looked on smiling and even slowed the march so that the aged doctor could keep pace. The Germans commented audibly, and in impeccable Hungarian, on the beauty of friendship. Others from the village now dared call to their departing friends. The marchers responded with growing good humor. Laughter was heard, the paraders began marching in step. The Russian prisoners remained behind, lying face down on the side streets.

The Jews were marshaled into the stock pens at the railroad yard. The band continued to play. Neighbors and friends hung on the surrounding fences, calling out good wishes. The Hungarian guards looked on in confusion, the SS officers in satisfaction. Assigned numbers were called off. The emigrants were divided into groups of a hundred and ten, and moved into smaller pens. An officer passed among them with a large white sack. Blue transit slips were dropped in.

A gate opened and the first group of emigrants, clutching their belongings, hurried out over the tracks and clambered into the windowless boxcar. The door slipped shut and was sealed.

Spangler found himself a corner, squatted down and waited for the trip to begin. His headache had subsided somewhat. The pain in his shoulder remained.

40

THE TRAIN SLOWED, then stopped. The spotters at the peepholes reported that dawn was a half hour off, that the countryside was covered with deep snow, the thick hilly forests could be distinguished in the distance.

The cold was bitter; the emigrants huddled against one another for warmth. The two-day supply of food had long disappeared. So had conversation. Now they waited in darkness, chill and silence.

The train crept forward. The spotters announced that they were passing under a large wooden arch, passing through metal gates, that lights could be seen ahead, that the tracks had spread into three spurs, that the ground was frozen and littered with debris, that double lines of barbed-wire fences could be seen on either side, that barracks stretched endlessly beyond. The car bumped to a stop. Shouting was heard outside. The door slid open. The light was blinding.

"All out, good friends, all out," ordered the smiling man in striped cap and overcoat. "Welcome, and bring your possessions with you. Deposit them at the other side of the ramp. Claim them later. All out quickly, and form nice lines, five abreast. Do what you're told. Nothing to worry about if you obey quickly. Treat you better than you think here. Plenty to eat," he assured, patting his double chin.

The passengers poured out under the glaring shielded white and red bulbs strung over the long platform. Baggage and possessions were quickly deposited in front of a detachment of prisoners in striped uniforms.

"Achtung! Achtung!" a voice called through a megaphone as the new arrivals hurried to form in lines. "We must have silence. You will obey immediately on command. You have arrived at Concentration Camp Birkenau. The motto of Concentration Camp Birkenau is 'Work frees you.' "

Columns of prisoners in striped overcoats marched, arms swinging rigidly in unison, between the scurrying new arrivals and the empty carriages. SS men sauntered nonchalantly along, hands behind their backs, observing the proceedings, barking an order every now and then.

"If you work hard, there is little to fear," the voice from the megaphone continued. "Hard work and obedience are rewarded. Food and lodgings are abundant."

The prisoners in striped overcoats stopped, did a sharp right turn and walked briskly forward to begin searching the empty cars. The line of new arrivals already stretched well beyond the length of the train.

"A hot meal is waiting. You will fall into two columns to speed things. If your name is called, move to the left of the ramp. No talking in ranks. Eyes straight ahead."

The line to the right was still lengthening when the first seventeen names were read. Only sixteen men moved across the ramp. The missing name was repeated. Someone announced that the man had died in transit.

"All doctors, dentists and veterinarians move to the left."

Screaming was heard. The prisoners in striped overcoats were pulling a woman from a forward car by her feet. She clutched an infant close to her. Other striped prisoners moved around in a wall. The screaming stopped.

"All electricians, carpenters, mechanics, plumbers, masons, move to the left."

Spangler moved across the ramp and took his place in the new line.

Nine more categories were shouted through the megaphone. SS officers strolled up and down, picking people almost casually to go to the left.

Two more categories were called. The megaphone was laid aside. The line to the left was counted.

Spangler focused his attention at the head of the ramp. Two officers were conferring over a clipboard. The one with the riding crop stepped back and motioned over his shoulder. Then Spangler realized that the second officer was a brawny prisoner, whose striped uniform had been cut in a replica of the SS tunic and breeches. The face was too distant to be distinguished. The bright-yellow scarf at his neck and the SS boots were distinct.

The yellow-scarfed prisoner waved as he stepped forward. Other prisoners with SS cut uniforms followed him onto the ramp. Spangler counted eight in all. Jackboots clicking, the men strutted down the corridor between the two lines. As they neared, Spangler could see that all were massive and powerful. Their wrists were wrapped in white tape. Their huge faces bore scars and bruises. Most of them had broken noses.

The man directly behind the leader drew Spangler's attention. His hair was silver-blue and cut close to the square skull. The nose was wide. The deep-set eyes were crowded by thick bushy brows. The jaw was tight and slightly protruding. He stood a hulking six-foot-five, not as large as the leader, but bigger then the rest. He strode with fists clenched. Rings glistened on the fingers of both his hands. Spangler knew it was Friedrich Tolan.

The yellow-scarfed group split in half. One contingent began inspecting the line to the left; the other, including Tolan, examined the line to the right.

"Eyes straight ahead," a voice barked in Spangler's ear.

Spangler shot his glance forward, but not before glimpsing the yellow scarf.

"Occupation?"

"Mechanic." Spangler answered.

"Mechanic, *sir*. You say 'sir' to us," the voice snapped.

"Mechanic, sir."

Spangler's arm was felt, then his stomach and upper legs. "Step out."

Spangler moved to the side.

"Strip to the waist."

Spangler did as he was told.

"Drop your trousers and underwear."

Spangler obeyed the order. He stood naked as the man moved around him and studied his body. It was the leader of the yellow-scarves.

"No operations? Hernias? Things like that?"

"No, sir."

A chalk mark was made on his forehead and chest.

"Dress," the man ordered as he walked on.

Farther up the line, other prisoners were dressing or undressing for the yellow-scarves. Spangler could see that the inspection over on the right was somewhat different. Tolan had ordered a young woman to the side. When she hesitated he slapped her across the face. The woman slowly took off her clothes. Tolan studied the body, felt it and then made a chalk mark on the breast and the forehead. He pointed, and the terrified girl hurried across to the left line. Other girls were standing naked farther on while yellow-scarves inspected them.

An order was shouted. Spangler's line began to move forward.

41

THE COLUMN of new arrivals marched up the ramp, turned and continued along a frozen mud path through the opened barbed-wire gate and into the compound. They entered a large wooden building where six SS guards and two SS Totenkopf officers waited. The prisoners were arranged into five lines.

"Wer kann Deutsch?" shouted one of the officers.

Spangler could not admit that he spoke German. He must pretend to learn it slowly.

"Wer kann Deutsch?" demanded the second officer.

Three prisoners hesitantly raised their hands. The trio was moved forward and told to act as interpreters.

"They will keep at two-arms'-length distance from one another," the senior Totenkopf officer snapped at the interpreters.

The order was translated and followed. Spangler did not have to be told, he could anticipate the procedure, he had been through it before—in the early days.

The prisoners undressed and rolled their clothing into neat bundles and laid them at their feet. They tied their shoes together and deposited them in a designated corner.

Spangler could see that the Dachau system was being utilized. The dehumanization began on the train trip, now it would be continued and improved upon. The room was bitter cold. Frost covered the floor planks. The SS would let them wait, Spangler told himself, let the freezing sink in, let the humiliation and fear grow.

The naked men were ordered to stand at attention. The SS officers left. They returned two hours later. The naked new arrivals were orderd out into the subzero morning. Five times they were forced to run around the assembly field. Again they were ordered to attention. Finally they were led into a building adjacent to the one they had just left.

The prisoners moved along the supply counter. Spangler was issued a threadbare striped suit jacket, a striped pair of cotton trousers, a striped collarless shirt and a pair of torn shoes. His "underwear" had been made from a Jewish prayer shawl and was loosely sewn. His stockings were little more than strips of dark woolen cloth.

Spangler's squad of twenty was the second group into the shower room. No soap was provided. The water was tepid and remained on only two minutes. Spangler returned to the cold room and began drying himself with his striped uniform. He looked up. Tolan was staring at him from the door. Spangler went on drying himself. When he glanced over again Tolan was gone.

When all the new arrivals had finished their bath, teams of prisoners moved through the ranks spraying them with a delousing powder. The order was given to dress.

The jacket was tight, the trousers too loose. Spangler was given a piece of cord for a belt. He slid on the ragged stockings. One somehow held to his foot, the other would not. Luckily the shoes were almost his size.

He followed the slow-moving line around the room to the first table. The top was covered by stacks of neatly piled colored cloth diamonds. He knew from the past that red diamonds designated political prisoners; pink, homosexuals; green, criminals; yellow, Jews.

"Name!" demanded the prisoner behind the diamonds.

"Knebel, Emil, sir," Spangler answered.

"Knebel, E.," the prisoner shouted down to the next table.

"Juden. One fifteen dash three two seven," a second prisoner looking at the sheet called back.

The first prisoner marked the number on a piece of paper and handed it to Spangler. Next he picked up four yellow cloth diamonds. "You will sew them on your uniform like this," he said, laying one diamond over the other to form a Star of David. "One on the leg, one over the heart."

Spangler moved slowly forward to the next section. A finger was pointed. He sat on the stool and rolled up his sleeve.

"Name," called the prisoner seated behind the low counter.

"Knebel, Emil, sir," said Spangler, as a truncheon came down on the back of his skull. He fell to the floor. It took a moment for his head to clear. He sensed that an SS or a Kapo was standing behind him. He knew that if he looked he would be hit again. He was also aware that a new arrival would do just that—look to see who had hit him. Spangler glanced up to catch a view of his attacker. The truncheon came down on the side of his face.

"Onto the stool," the prisoner behind the counter ordered. Spangler slowly did what he was told. "Your name is One fifteen dash three two seven, do you understand? You have no name except that. Now we will try again. Name?"

"One fifteen dash three two seven, sir," Spangler said quickly.

"Left arm."

Spangler lowered his forearm across the counter. The prisoner on the other side gripped his wrist, pressed it tight onto the surface, pushed up the sleeve and raised the hot tattooing needle.

"Not this one, he has chalk, can't you see it," an SS officer said, stepping up beside Spangler and pulling him off the stool. "Over there with the others," the officer snapped.

Spangler joined four more new arrivals standing in the corner. They too had not been numbered. Spangler studied them. All were obviously in good physical condition.

It took the barbers an hour and a half to process the majority of the new prisoners. Only Spangler and the nine other men in the corner remained. Now they were ordered forward to the stools. Their beards were shaved. On orders from the SS officer their hair was not cut.

The new arrivals were then divided into three groups. Spangler and the nine other untattooed, unshorn prisoners joined twenty-five processed bald prisoners, merged into a double column and marched from the building.

The sun was bright and the sky a clear, cold blue. Ice-crusted ground, building and fences twinkled in the morning light. Spangler was impressed. Almost everything here at Birkenau was precisely the same as at Birkenau in Westerly: the ramp they had just re-crossed, the triple spread of rails that lay behind, the two crematoria they had passed to their left, the compounds beyond the interior fencing to the right with their endless rows of gray wooden barracks, the guard towers looming everywhere in the distance.

Spangler noticed only three variations from the Westerly reproduction. First, the barbed-wire fences here were one to two feet lower than those in England. Second, the lighting was different: there were more bulbs strung along the interior compound fences than had been allowed for at G. P. G. Third was the terrain: in England the earth was hard-packed; here in Poland everything rested on frozen mud.

The column marched deeper into the maze of Birkenau's compounds. Spangler became more relaxed. Gone was the pain in his shoulder, the tension, the intermittent fever that plagued him on the "outside." Gone, too, was the lingering headache that had followed him from England. He walked strongly and without a limp. His hands were steady, his countless other ailments had vanished. He knew it was February 26, but it didn't matter. Spangler took a deep breath. He had never felt better. He was where he belonged. He had come home.

42

SPANGLER and the other new arrivals stood in a single line along the north end of the roll-call field, in Compound II-D. Behind them were the stone kitchen buildings. Ahead lay a double row of brown wooden buildings, sixteen on each side. No SS guards were to be seen, only Kapos wearing the green triangles of convicted criminals. Kapos ordered them to stand to attention, and so they stood rigid in the cold and watching as the sun rose to its zenith and descended into dusk. No food was offered them. No relief given from the rigid posture. Strings of light bulbs along the interior perimeter fences glowed on. Darkness brought the smell of food. Darkness brought even sharper winds.

Chanting and the tramping of feet became audible. Spangler glanced out of the corner of his eye. He could see the adjoining compounds filling with the dark forms of prisoners.

The chanting and tramping continued interminably. He heard shouts directly to his rear.

Column after column of prisoners began trudging into the roll-call area, facing the line of new arrivals. Kapos' shouts and truncheon blows accompanied every movement. Soon more than five thousand weary, haggard prisoners stood marking time in place and chanting.

Orders were shouted. Marching stopped. Prisoners froze to attention. An SS officer and two SS guards walked briskly down the corridor separating the new arrivals from the mass of returning laborers. The officer raised a clipboard. Rolls were called. Work Kommando Kapos stepped smartly forward and shouted out the number of the newly dead. Corpses were dragged out and laid before the first line of prisoners. The officer strolled casually past the row of bodies. The order was given to remove them.

A second ritual began. The work Kommando Kapos reported the sick and injured. Prisoners struggled out of the ranks and formed a sagging line. The officer studied them from a distance. His finger began pointing. Some moved out and formed a column that quickly marched off. The majority dejectedly returned to their former positions and stood to attention again.

Spangler heard a movement to his right. All that could be seen there was the vague outline of large men huddled in the shadows.

The officer turned abruptly and faced the line of new arrivals.

"I am SS Hauptsturmfuehrer Klempf," barked the captain. "It is my *duty* to welcome you here—and so I do. It is your *honor* to be allowed here—and so you are. It is your *honor* to serve us—and so you shall. *Here* you will serve. Here you will work. Work cures all ills. *Past* and *future* no longer exist. The *present* is work. You *exist* only to work."

Captain Klempf spoke in German. No interpreters had been provided for the new arrivals. Very few could understand. It had not been expected that they would.

Klempf took to pacing back and forth. "Yes," he finally said, "here you will quickly learn that work and strength are the only virtues. *Work* and *strength* are progress. The Reich respects achievement. The Reich respects work and strength. It is *rewarded. Yes, here and now, before you,* we will demonstrate how well it is rewarded."

Klempf spun on his heel. "Read the list!"

An SS corporal raised his clipboard. Ten numbers were shouted. Spangler and the other nine untattooed, unshorn new arrivals were moved out between the two contingents of facing prisoners.

"At Birkenau there is no better position than that of cook. Yes, a cook leads a good life. A cook is of great importance." Klempf grinned at Spangler and his companions. "You few have been given a rare opportunity. These are the present cooks," he said, moving aside. "If you want their jobs, *take them!*"

Six massive prisoners led by a red-faced giant of a man charged out of the ranks to the left and started for Spangler and the other nine. Tolan and five more cooks approached them from the right.

Spangler was the first to be hit. He rolled with the blow, feinted and drove his fist into the neck of the leader. The giant let out a screech, clutched his throat and dropped to his knees, gasping for breath. The attackers stopped in disbelief and watched their comrade pitch face forward and writhe on the frozen earth.

At a shout from Tolan the cooks resumed their attack. One by one the new arrivals were bludgeoned into submission. Soon only Spangler and two others remained fighting.

Spangler knew that he must not win, that he must not be the last to fall, that he should submit now. Something kept him from it.

The cooks split into two groups and began to stalk. Suddenly they stopped. The wounded cook had risen unsteadily to his feet, clutching his neck. He pointed at Spangler. All the cooks started after him. He sidestepped, and two flew past. He caught the third full in the face with his knee.

Spangler decided to take his beating. When Tolan and three more cooks swarmed on him from behind he let them take him.

All eyes were on Spangler as he was dragged forward by Tolan and another cook to the felled giant, who lifted his club and brought it unsteadily down. Spangler knew he shouldn't move, but he couldn't resist. He tugged to his right, pulling Tolan under the plummeting wood. It caught him on the bridge of the nose. Spangler ducked, shot up an arm, knocked away the giant's hand and drove another fist into the swollen neck.

Four cooks held Spangler in position. Three more tried to raise the giant. When they couldn't, Tolan was lifted to his feet. Spangler was pulled forward. Tolan gripped the club and raised his arm. When it came down Spangler made sure he was underneath it.

Twelve motionless men lay sprawled on the blood-splattered ground. Klempf strolled casually through them and faced the ranks of stunned new arrivals.

"A Czech Jew once wrote a story," he said, with a faint smile. "In this story a man awakes one morning to find that he has been changed into a large bug. The story goes on to prove that if you put the mind of a man into the body of a bug, it will soon become the mind of a bug. The Czech Jew only had a *theory;* we have the *means!* Birkenau will soon turn you into bugs. But not *individual* bugs—you will be communal bugs! There is no more individuality; your ten fallen comrades are the last attempt at that. Now, you are part of a community. If one of you commits a crime, all will suffer. If one is good, all will be rewarded. And that is how it shall be— from this moment forward."

Spangler felt the tugging. He tried to open his eyes and couldn't. He knew vaguely that he was being dragged over the frozen mud. He was certain time was lapsing. He had the sensation of being lifted and carried. He felt a distant jolt as he was dropped on a hard surface and rolled over and over. Again he drifted. Sensations returned intermittently. He felt a chill. A stench was evident. So was a noise. He fought to open his eyes. Finally he did. Dimly he realized that he was on an upper shelf of a tiered bunk. Two other men were asleep beside him. Both were snoring. Both stank. The barracks was not heated. One thin blanket covered him and his bedfellows. Spangler tried to raise up. His effort stirred the man next to him. A somnambulistic arm engulfed him. He sank back with a far-off vision of tier after tier of bunks jammed with sleeping refuse. Cold and noise grew faint. Spangler fell back into unconsciousness.

43

WATER DRIPPED on Spangler's forehead. He opened his eyes and looked up into the grinning toothless face. The wide square head was covered with scars and bruises. One eye was permanently closed. The ears were cauliflowered tight to the skull. There was no neck, only massive shoulders set directly under the large battered jaw.

"Come," the Kapo uttered in low guttural German.

"I don't understand your language," Spangler answered in Hungarian. "We want you, come," the Kapo repeated, this time in pidgin Hungarian.

Spangler raised up on one elbow and looked around. The four-tiered rows of bunks were empty. He eased himself down to the floor and followed his guide out of the barracks.

The afternoon sun blazed bright in the steel-blue sky. Even so, the paradeground mud remained frozen. The compound gate was pulled open by the Ukrainian SS guard, and they started down the icy road. Barbed-wire fences stretched on both sides. Row after row of windowless barracks lay beyond. Directly ahead, thick black smoke curled from two tall chimneys.

After a quarter of a mile they turned through a gate. Here too a Ukrainian SS guard stood sentry. The compound they entered looked exactly like the one they had left. Spangler followed the Kapo around the long stone-block kitchen and into a whitewashed barracks.

Spangler counted twenty-four beds: four cots and ten double bunks. All were empty, with one exception: the giant red-haired cook he had fought the night before lay unconscious and breathing heavily on a far cot. Rewashed bandages bulged around the massive neck.

"His name is Vassili," a voice called out in accented Hungarian. "He was once chief cook here. Now I am—at least for the present. So I thank you."

Spangler wheeled about. Tolan stepped from the doorway. He too bore the bruises of the previous night's battle. Behind him waited a pair of scrawny prisoners laden with bedclothes.

"I am Friedrich, better known as Brilly," he told Spangler. 'Brilly' is short for *Brillenschlange*. Here we are no longer numbers. We can afford the luxury of names, but the SS prefers them to be nicknames.

"Your guide," Tolan said, indicating the Kapo who had accompanied Spangler, "is Anvil. He killed his wife and two infant children by dropping anvils on them, so we felt the title appropriate. If you last long enough we will find something appropriate for you. Yes, around here we all have nicknames—except that one," he said, nodding at Vassili.

Tolan moved across the room and slapped the mattress of a top bunk. "This shall be yours," he said. The two prisoners hurried forward with their load. "And look what I have brought you. Blankets. Three *woolen* blankets! That's something in this place, eh? And there's more. Look, a whole sheet. You'll soon learn there aren't many who can boast an untorn sheet or a pillow—with a pillow slip. Have you eaten?"

Spangler shook his head.

"Come," Tolan said as the two prisoners quickly began making up the bunk.

Spangler followed Tolan and Anvil through a well-equipped kitchen and out into the large front room. One wall was lined with lockers. Table and chairs stretched across the other. Spangler was seated opposite Tolan and Anvil.

"Do you speak German?" Tolan asked.

"Some," Spangler replied.

"Some is not good enough. You will have to learn quickly. Speak German always, no matter how badly. Soon it will come to you."

Anvil let out a short giggle and nodded.

The second prisoner came from the kitchen and set a tray of sliced meats, fresh bread, butter, cheese, coffee and sugar before Spangler.

"Slowly," Tolan counseled. "Eat it slowly. Your stomach is empty and the meat is tinned. Chew well and slowly or it will go off like a bomb in your gut."

Spangler took his advice.

"You fight well," Tolan said, rubbing the lump over his eye. "You move quickly. You know how to use the darkness. I thought I had you for a moment, but you slid into the shadows and the light blinded me. Ha, that was a good trick. Tell me, where did you learn to fight so well?"

"I grew up in an orphanage. Then I was in prison."

"Prison is a good place. That is where Anvil developed his techniques. Yes, prison is good, but not as good as the streets. I learned in the streets of Vienna, Berlin, Munich, a dozen other cities," Tolan said. "No one fought better than we did. You're Hungarian?"

"No, Russian," said Spangler.

"Why do you speak Hungarian? What were you doing on a Hungarian shipment?"

"I worked in Hungary before the war. I returned to Russia in 1938. They forced me into the Army. I ran away. They found me and put me in prison. Two weeks ago I escaped and made my way back to Hungary. The police stopped me. I had no papers. Worse, I was circumcised. They put me on a train and here I am. And you? How did you get here?"

"I was a Brownshirt," said Tolan.

"What's that?"

"S. A., Sturmabteilung—the storm troopers. We brought Hitler to power. There were two and a half million of us. I was a high official, one of the highest. It was we who conceived of the concentration camp. We built forty of them by the mid-thirties, for political prisoners. Ironic, eh? Then Hitler turned on us. Roehm, our leader was murdered. We fought back—and lost. I suppose I could have avoided all this if I had thrown in with Goering or Himmler, but I couldn't betray my men. They're still out there waiting. So I've bounced from camp to camp. I've seen them all, but this is the maddest."

"Why?"

"The Process—the functioning of Birkenau. The logic behind it. Especially this compound. We're different from all the rest. You'll find out, now that you're one of the elite."

"Elite?"

"A cook. The SS decreed that if any of you defeated a cook last night, you could take his place. You defeated Vassili. Therefore you take his place until he's well enough to fight you again. It's the Process. Come, let me show you around."

The compound was a long narrow rectangle stretching from the railroad track to the main interior road; the kitchens and the cooks' quarters stood at the road end, next came the roll-call area, then two rows of sixteen windowless barracks spreading to the railroad fence. It was bordered by identical compounds, each enclosed by a twelve-foot-high electrified barbed-wire fence.

The main kitchen building was painted a dull yellow. The stoves were ancient wood-burning relics. The solitary water tap worked irregularly. Utensils were damaged and patched. Only two large boiling caldrons seemed in any state of repair. It was obvious to Spangler that the most functional equipment had been requisitioned by the cooks for their own private kitchen.

The kitchen Kommando, Tolan explained, was a well-defined hierarchy. Four senior cooks constituted the top echelon. Spangler now shared that station with Tolan, Anvil and one other: Der Gronck. The senior cooks' responsibilities were limited to seeing that the others did their jobs, keeping the accounts and allocating food. Even these minor tasks were not really performed by them.

226

The senior cooks owned "Habes," or, more simply, slaves. The Habes did the work, except for allocating the food.

Spangler had seen that the senior cooks, the subcooks and the apprentice cooks were all large, powerful men. Most kept their hands taped and bore the scars and bruises of recent battles. All wore green triangles on their SS-fashioned prison uniforms, with one exception—Tolan. Tolan was a political prisoner, not a civil criminal. His triangle was red.

The sun was setting. Spangler watched the preparations for the evening meal. The potato shed to the rear of the kitchen was unlocked. Sacks of soft, spotted potatoes were carried in and dumped into the boiling caldrons, along with carefully measured bits of meat and a large can of starchy powder. Every ingredient was entered into two ledgers kept by Tolan's slaves. Even the empty potato sacks were accounted for under "assets" before being washed, flattened and returned to the barracks.

Kitchen security increased when the bread bunker was unlocked. The subcooks had the area cleared as the loaves were laid out and carefully cut. Every slice was recorded.

"Eighteen per cent of the authorized quota is never issued," Tolan told Spangler. "If the prisoners know we can't feed them all, the lines will move quicker. They're a cunning lot. They know the soup is thickest at the bottom of the pot, so they try to get to the end of the line. But if they're afraid the end of the line won't get fed, the problem is solved, isn't it?"

In the distance a band could be heard playing Liszt. The tramping of far-off feet followed soon after. Spangler watched the parade-ground fill with the hunched forms of returning labor prisoners. The roll-call procedure was the same as the night before, only this time there were no new arrivals to process.

Ranks were broken, and the inmates formed into endless lines. One by one the procession of gaunt, skeletal faces passed in front of the kitchen counters. Subcooks ladled out the thin soup. Each cup was carefully poured. Spangler watched as one portion was spilled. Prisoners dove to the ground and began licking the dirt. They were clubbed away by the Ukrainian SS.

Spangler noticed a second line forming behind the kitchen. He looked on as the subcooks and the assistant cooks worked directly from a ledger. Certain prisoners had already paid for extra rations. Their names were checked off as the accounts were settled. Spoons and cups, undoubtedly stolen from fellow prisoners, brought an extra ladle of soup or a piece of bread. If the utensils were in better-than-average condition the price might be doubled. Bits of soap were worth two thick slices of bread. A cigarette brought five. When the food ran out future orders were negotiated.

Spangler wandered out into the floodlit field. Five thousand exhausted prisoners were seated, devouring their evening meal. They all looked alike; the ragged striped jackets, the threadbare trousers, the torn shoes all appeared identical. So did the faces.

Spangler's eyes searched them. Perhaps somewhere among the countless thousands now squatting at Birkenau, Jean-Claude was at this very moment licking clean his cup and hiding it in his clothes so that it wouldn't be stolen.

Tolan called. Spangler followed him back to the barracks to the senior cooks' private dinner table. The plates were warm and the knives, spoons and forks shiny. The waiters wore white aprons over their prisoner uniforms. The meal began with a thick vegetable-and-beef stew. It was followed by sliced meat, baked turnips, Hungarian wine, butter, jam, honey, ersatz coffee with milk and sugar, and canned peaches.

44

THE HABES cleared away the dinner dishes and pushed the tables into line several feet in front of the wooden cabinets.

Der Gronck, the fourth senior cook, a former weight lifter, brought a set of ledgers from the back room and set them on the center table.

Anvil unlocked the first cabinet. Truncheons, five well-honed bayonets and two pistols were removed and distributed among the subcooks and the apprentice cooks. Anvil stationed the subcooks around the room and deployed the apprentice cooks outside the barracks.

Tolan opened the second and third cabinets, revealing shelves crammed with canned fruits, salt, pepper, spices, medicines, bandages, knives, spoons, cups, clothing, cloth and almost any other luxury item coveted within Birkenau.

Spangler was seated between Tolan and Der Gronck behind the center table. Anvil, truncheon in hand, stood leaning beside the door. The Bourse was declared open.

The first "suppliers" arrived at their scheduled time, seated themselves opposite the senior cooks, hoisted their sacks onto the table and quickly began unpacking their merchandise. These were the liaison prisoners from the Sonderkommando. Tolan explained to Spangler. The Sonderkommando was the prisoner contingent that operated Birkenau's four crematoria—the Kommando which could never leave its compound, the prisoners who were themselves disposed of every four months.

Spangler did not have to be informed that the goods being unpacked had been culled from the possessions of that day's quota at the gas chambers. Thick wool socks, sweaters, shoes, underwear, a pair of suede gloves, half a packet of cigarettes and a fleece-lined jacket were among the items examined and appraised.

Bargaining began between Tolan, Der Gronck, and the suppliers. Values were finally established and agreed upon. Shaving soap, flour and sugar seemed most in demand by the Sonderkommando prisoners this particular night. The items were brought down from the cabinet shelves and pushed across to the liaison prisoners. Goods that were not paid for at the time were left on consignment with the cooks.

Individual negotiations between cook and supplier representative got under way. The prisoner opposite Tolan passed across a leather wallet. It was swollen with Reichsmarks. Der Gronck was examining a small cyanide capsule, the type that could fit under the tongue. Both items were considered windfall merchandise. That the SS had overlooked them in their initial search of the victims was the sheerest luck. Agreement was reached and the inventory recorded in the ledger.

The next group of traders represented the ramp Kommando, those inmates who greeted Birkenau's incoming trains, carried the new arrivals' baggage to the warehouse and sorted through the possessions under careful scrutiny by the SS. Two trains had arrived in the last five hours. The suppliers' merchandise included fresh fruit and vegetables, bags of fresh coffee, cakes and loaves of rich Rumanian bread. The fresh milk, eggs and butter were immediately locked away. The two pairs of fur-lined boots drew smiles from all. The most startling item was a side of fresh lamb; how the ramp Kommando had sneaked it past the SS no one could guess. Negotiations opened as with the Sonderkommando. A new commercial wrinkle was added—future contracts. Vassili had received an order from

Bubel, one of his private clients, and had placed it with the ramp Kommando for filling. Now delivery was being made. Five fine lace-and-silk slips, five silk brassieres and five pairs of silk panties were pushed across to Spangler with three pairs of high-heeled leather shoes and six dolls. Payment was made in the official currency of the Bourse—bordello passes. Four passes to the officers' bordello and eight to the enlisted men's were handed to the ramp-Kommando suppliers.

The "special" supplier was last. A small prisoner with bifocals took a chair at the table, reached into a pocket and brought out two gold cigarette cases, a gold cigarette lighter and five pairs of gold-rimmed glasses. Tolan shook his head and pushed them back. The prisoner returned the items to his pocket, dug deeper and came out with a handful of ragged bits of gold filling. Again Tolan rejected the merchandise. The supplier emptied an inside pocket and handed across a small velvet pouch. Tolan untied the knot, and gems spilled over the table top. Bidding began. Ten SS-officers'-bordello passes and six loaves of bread were the final price. The "special" supplier was pleased. He reached into his trousers and spun his final item onto the table. Spangler watched as the round gold slug came to rest. It was almost two inches in diameter. Tolan burst into a broad smile. There was no haggling. The supplier demanded six passes to the Finishing School. It was paid immediately.

Then came the buyers. The first group came from the SS enlisted men's kitchen. They traded a pair of SS boots, a razor, half a bar of shaving soap, a quarter bottle of iodine and six passes to the enlisted men's bordello for Rumanian bread, four cakes and two sacks of coffee.

Security tightened. Truncheon-carrying subcooks lined the far wall. They were joined by six assistant cooks. Tolan and Der Gronck brought out their own pistols and laid them on their laps.

Anvil opened the door, and the room began to fill with Kapos representing black markets operating in other Birkenau compounds as well as in many of the subcamps. The auction began. Item after item was held up and bids were shouted in. There were arguments. Fights were stopped. A fleece-lined coat brought four officers'-

bordello passes and two dry-cell batteries. A cake went for a stolen rifle with three clips of ammunition.

Bidding on the bottle brandy was interrupted by a piercing scream. Anvil had caught a Kapo stealing and had just pressed out one of the thief's eyes. Trading resumed and was soon at high pitch. The brandy brought two cans of petrol for a barracks stove, and a stick of scented shaving soap. Wool socks, sweaters and suede gloves were exchanged for a repaired Luger, three pages of a month-old Berlin newspaper, three more dry-cell batteries and a pillow slip. A tin of milk went for two sheets, a completed crossword puzzle, a pair of scissors and half a dozen detonating caps. Within fifteen minutes the table top was bare and the buyers began filing out.

The furniture was pushed back. Subcooks, apprentice cooks and slaves withdrew for bed. Coffee, brandy and cheese were brought out, and a single place was set at the far table.

Klempf entered the barracks and stood at the door. "You sent word?"

"Yes, Hauptsturmfuehrer," Tolan said, standing to attention. "We think we have come across something of interest."

"Show me."

Tolan walked stiffly across and held out a leather wallet and the bag of gems.

Klempf studied the items, moved to the place which had been set at the table, seated himself, counted the marks in the wallet and carefully examined the jewels. "Quite extraordinary," he finally admitted. "What are you asking?"

"Our own bordello, Hauptsturmfuehrer," Tolan replied.

"You can place your whores in the camp bordello now. You're paid for them."

"If you'll excuse me for saying so, Hauptsturmfuehrer, it is not quite the same thing."

"Are you not provided with enough passes?"

"We would prefer our own establishment, Hauptsturmfuehrer."

Klempf pondered as he fingered the stones. "Out of the question," he finally concluded. "It would bring on complications. Other exchanges would want the same."

"Other exchanges are not as wealthy as we, Hauptsturmfuehrer."

"You are wealthy only because I *choose* for you to be wealthy!"

"Not to disagree, Hauptsturmfuehrer. We have grown wealthy since my arrival. I control the pick of the women, Hauptsturmfuehrer."

"Then if you want to make extra money, open up that Finishing School of yours."

"I doubt if that would please the *Obergruppenfuehrer*, Hauptsturmfuehrer."

"You will have no private bordello," Klempf stated emphatically. "Establish another price."

"Exterior passes. Sixteen exterior passes."

"No."

"Then we can do no further business, Hauptsturmfuehrer," Tolan said firmly. "The merchandise will have to be offered to the *Standartenfuehrer*."

"Seventy-five bordello passes."

"It is far too little, Hauptsturmfuehrer," Tolan replied. "There is better than five thousand marks in the wallet alone."

Klempf cut a slice of cheese and held it at knifepoint. "What about a radio?" he asked slowly. "Would a short-wave radio satisfy you?"

Tolan and Der Gronck tried to conceal their surprise.

Klempf barked out an order. An SS sergeant entered carrying a cumbersome apparatus.

"Do any of you know how to operate it?" Klempf asked.

Tolan and the other cooks looked at one another blankly and shook their heads. They turned to Spangler. He shrugged.

"Don't worry," said Klempf "you'll find someone who does. I guarantee it's in working order. That bag contains extra parts and tubes. If I were you, I'd set it up in the secret room under the potato shed."

Again Tolan and Der Gronck registered surprise. "Why are you doing this?" Tolan finally asked.

"Things are changing rapidly—as you'll find out from the radio. Who knows? In the near future it may be I who will be relying on you—and your secret organization. But be cautious," Klempf said, picking up the wallet and the gems. "Special detachments of SS are moving into the area just beyond the camp. They'll be watching for trouble."

He moved to the door. "I'll send over extra batteries tomorrow."

A movement near his face woke Spangler. He rolled back against the wall. A massive hand was slowly groping over the top of the bunk. Spangler inched to the end of the bed and looked down into the contorted face of Vassili. The giant was on his knees, clutching one hand to his bandaged neck, flailing the other aimlessly in search of his adversary. Spangler grabbed the index finger of the massive hand and bent it sharply back. Vassili fell to the floor with a groan. Spangler went back to sleep.

45

THE PRISONERS filed past the kitchen in the morning darkness, received their work rations, immediately re-formed in their respective labor Kommandos, picked up the chant as they stood marching in place and then, on command, tramped forward out of the compound to join the thousands of other prisoners high-stepping along the road.

Spangler followed Der Gronck back to the barracks. A tailor was waiting with a wooden box and a pile of cloths.

"First we get you a decent uniform," Der Gronck told him, "and then I'll show you the routes." He opened the center locker and started filling a sack. "Senior cooks own the routes, the trading areas. Or, I should say you, me and Anvil own them. Tolan isn't interested. He has the Finishing School—where they take the pretty young girls who are selected on the ramp. It's across in the Canada Compound."

"Is it a bordello?" Spangler asked, standing naked as the tailor measured him.

"It *supplies* the bordellos. The girls go in there for six to eight days and then are either sent to various houses here or put on the train." Der Gronck watched the tailor spread a woolen jacket on the table and begin cutting it apart at the seams. "A special railroad car comes once a week just to pick up the girls. You'll see for yourself, it's due in tonight or tomorrow."

"What happens at the Finishing School?"

"No one is supposed to know or even ask. Only Tolan is allowed inside, not even Klempf. But Tolan has made certain exceptions— for money."

"Have you been inside?"

Der Gronck broke into a jagged smile and watched the tailor baste the jacket back together.

"You're not answering," Spangler said.

"It's better to find out about the Finishing School on your own."

"Has it been here long?"

"That's a peculiar question."

"How else am I going to find out about things?"

Der Gronck chuckled. "It's rumored the school didn't open until Tolan arrived."

"I thought you were a veteran," Spangler said as the tailor slipped the jacket on him and began marking it.

"I am. I've lasted longer than most. But sooner or later someone beats you and you're shipped away."

"Did everyone become a cook by fighting?"

"Everyone but Tolan and Vassili. They *say* that Tolan and Vassili were the first cooks when the whole Process was conceived, but no one is sure. No one else has lasted longer than three weeks—and that's a ripe old age for most of us. If you want to stay around that long, you'd better kill Vassili."

"Why?"

"Because he has the right to fight you again when he recovers—so why risk it? If he were in your shoes, he wouldn't give it a second thought."

"How would the SS take my killing him?" Spangler slipped on a pair of trousers for the tailor.

"They *expect* it. Everyone expects it. That's how it is around here."

"If I wait to fight him again, when would it be?"

"In about a week. They usually give you a week after your first fight. But since Vassili is in pretty bad shape, they may wait till he's strong enough to make an interesting contest." Der Gronck watched Spangler step out of the trousers. "Klempf likes interesting contests."

"What's Klempf's position?" Spangler asked.

"He's in charge of our line of compounds. He's also with Camp Security, the Birkenau secret intelligence agency. But he spends his time running the black markets. I think he owns most of them. He's a bad one. Stay clear of him. If he does manage to corner you, act afraid. He likes people to be frightened of him."

"Tolan didn't act frightened."

"Tolan's different. I don't think he can be replaced."

"Why?"

"No one is certain. Some think because he's a red-triangle, a political prisoner. Others say it's the Finishing School—that he's needed here."

"What do you think?"

"That he must be important to someone high up. I doubt if even Klempf can touch him. Tolan's the only prisoner that Klempf is cautious with. Klempf is powerful. If he's cautious, there has to be a good reason for it."

"If Tolan is protected by someone, why does he have to fight?"

"He doesn't. He just likes to. And, after all, if he can't be replaced, what does he have to lose?" Der Gronck walked through the kitchen and into the dormitory. "Be back in a few minutes."

The tailor's needle flew through the cloth. Jacket and trousers were chalked and fitted twice more. Then they were spread on the table and carefully striped with white paint. By the time Der Gronck returned, carrying a pair of jackboots, Spangler was dressed in his new attire. The suit had been converted into an SS tunic and breeches.

"What kind of triangle?" the tailor asked, reaching into his work kit and bringing out a thick, worn envelope.

"Green," said Der Gronck.

"With authentic papers?"

"Yes."

"That will be expensive."

"How much?"

"A pass to the Finishing School."

"You can have half a loaf of bread," Der Gronck replied.

The tailor reconsidered. "Six officers'-bordello passes and a jar of preserves."

"Half a loaf of bread."

"Just the six passes and we can forget the preserves?"

"A full loaf of bread, and that's my final offer," Der Gronck said menacingly.

Erik Spangler was no longer a Jew.

46

THEY PASSED the last compound. A stretch of sixty snow-covered yards lay between it and the beginning of the "death-zone" trench before the exterior barbed wire. Spangler studied the concrete fence-posts topped by shielded lights as he moved along. The electrified wire was strung on both sides of the columns. He glanced up at the endless row of guardhouses. A sentinel stood on the deck of every third one. Spangler concluded that some guards must be pulled out during the daylight hours to form an outer perimeter around the labor battalions. At night when they returned, all the guardhouses would be manned.

Twenty feet beyond the towers ran a line of telephone poles. Spangler stared up at the sagging wires as two Ukrainian SS guards at the exterior fence checked the passes Der Gronck presented. Two lines were for the telephone, the other was electric. His eye followed the electric wire down to the switchboxes on each of the guard towers. No other feeder was visible. His search was interrupted when they were let through the gate.

Der Gronck led him around the officers' billets and into the mess hall. The sack was opened and the officers' cook was given fresh milk, eggs and butter. Payment was made in officers'-bordello passes.

The next stop was the enlisted men's dispensary. Der Gronck

brought out syringes, sleeping pills and a medical kit. Passes to the enlisted men's bordello were given in return.

Spangler and Der Gronck skirted the SS headquarters building, passed behind the bus shelter, moved along a walk and went up to a billet with portico and blue awning.

The door opened on the second knock. The face was round, the cheeks exceedingly puffy and heavily rouged. Lipstick was smeared thickly around the mouth. The false eyelashes were tinted green, the eyelids painted with eye shadow. The eyebrows had been plucked completely and replaced by thick green grease arcs. The wig was composed of various hair textures. The boy couldn't have been much taller than four feet ten, not much older than eleven. The dress he wore was open at the bodice so the stuffed brassiere could be seen. The skirt dragged along the floor as he led Spangler and Der Gronck into the room.

Two other Bubels were seated on the floor. Both looked similar to the boy who had led them in. One carried a Teddy bear. The second ran a crayon aimlessly over a sheet of wrapping paper.

"Little beauties, aren't they?" the sergeant said, entering the room and taking the sack from Der Gronck.

"I see you staring," the SS man said to Spangler. "Does this type of thing appeal to you? If so, take your pick."

Spangler said nothing.

"What a pity! You'll never know what you're missing. You owe it to yourself to try. I can guarantee that these little puppies are cleaner than anything the houses have to offer. Are you sure you wouldn't like to taste one?"

"I'm sure."

The sergeant reached for a bottle of schnapps, swallowed heavily and began unpacking the merchandise.

"Excellent, most excellent," he uttered as he sorted through the garments. "Those Rumanians have a way with silk."

The sergeant reached into his pocket, brought out a stack of bordello passes and began peeling them off to Der Gronck. "Fifteen more trains are due in from Hungary in the next three days," he said, toying with a pair of tiny high-heeled shoes. "See if you can get me twenty-five more outfits just like these—but make the brassieres smaller."

47

KAPOS STEPPED forward and made their reports. The day's dead were being dragged forward through the ranks of rigid prisoners when the ground tremors struck. The movement was brief but distinct. A moment later a thud was heard in the distance, then two more. A few prisoners began to look around. They were brought back to attention by the SS officer. The earth undulated in five rapid spasms. The following explosions were closer and more severe. The SS officer was impervious. He moved forward and began examining the line of ailing prisoners as the next series of bombs struck. The ice crust cracked. Mud, water and dirt geysered from the earth and splattered his uniform. A second series of quakes drenched prisoners and guards alike. Sirens began wailing in the distance.

The prisoners bolted. The officer shouted orders. Guards and Kapos rushed forward with truncheons and rifles. The exterior lights dimmed off. Shots were fired. The panic seemed out of control, then it suddenly ebbed. Both the prisoners and the SS raised their heads skyward. The drone of engines reverberated through the night, and the dark silhouettes of aircraft crept forward just below the cloud cover. Antiaircraft guns could be heard firing from somewhere distant. A solitary prisoner forgot himself and raised a weak voice of approval. All the rest remained inanimate, faces pointed upward, watching, listening.

Tolan darted from the kitchen, grabbed Spangler's arm and dragged him around behind the building. They ducked into the potato shed. Tolan feverishly tore sacks away from the corner and pulled up a wooden trap door. Spangler descended the ladder after him.

The three storm lanterns were lit. Two shelves were spread along one wall of the dirt room. On the top shelf were a few small arms and some ammunition; on the bottom shelf rested three rifles.

Tolan rushed to the table and switched on the radio. Only static came from the speaker. A Kapo technician climbed down into the room and replaced Tolan at the set. Static still prevailed.

"What is it? What's the matter?" Tolan demanded.

"I don't know," the operator replied. "I've been tinkering with it all day, and so far only two wavelengths have come in, Cracow and Prague, and they're very faint."

"Well, get them!"

"I'm trying, but they drift. It's this damned machine. It's built all wrong—put together with spit and manure. Klempf cheated us good on this thing."

The room vibrated violently. Dust and soil showered down. Muffled explosions were heard in the distance.

Spangler looked around. Four locked wooden cabinets leaned against a wall. The names on each were printed in chalk: DER GRONCK, ANVIL, BRILLY, VASSILI.

"Is that my locker?" Spangler asked, pointing to Vassili's cabinet.

"How can you care about that at a time like this?" Tolan snorted.

"If it's mine, I want to see what's in it."

Tolan dug impatiently through his pockets, brought out a ring of keys, slid one off and threw it at Spangler.

Spangler snapped open the lock and pulled back the door. The top shelf was stacked high with bordello passes. A small box at the side contained uncanceled postage stamps. The second shelf was jammed with cut pieces of lead pipe, the kind used in constructing homemade truncheons. Canned foods and sacks of sugar filled the third shelf. Behind them Spangler found a wooden cigar box and flipped open the lid. It contained wristwatches.

Another explosion was heard outside. Minutes later Der Gronck descended the ladder. "Whose planes are they?" he asked.

"We don't know yet," Tolan answered impatiently.

Again the underground room trembled from an explosion.

The speaker crackled. The volume was turned to maximum. ". . . beyond Lomza," was barely audible in Polish.

"It's Cracow," the operator yelled. "We have Cracow!"

"Other elements of the Russian attack have swept south below Warsaw and are reported to have crossed the Vistula at Deblin. To the south, Wehrmacht troops have been routed and the Russians have advanced from Rzeszów to Košice. SS Division Hermann Goering is believed to be moving into the area to lead a counteroffensive. Farther south, Russian units are believed to have circled the town of . . ." The voice faded into static.

The operator turned to the Prague wavelength. The voice was too weak to be audible.

"Get to the underground members," Tolan ordered. "Tell them we must meet immediately. Tell them the Russian offensive has begun."

Der Gronck scrambled out of the bunker. Spangler followed him as far as the barracks.

48

DESPITE THE BLACKOUT the Bourse opened on schedule, with Tolan missing. Suppliers brought their goods, bargained somewhat abstractedly and left. The SS buyers did not appear, but the crowd of Kapos for the open trading was extraordinarily large.

Auctioning had barely begun when Anvil motioned Spangler away from the table and into the kitchen. "The underground is meeting in the back," he whispered as he handed Spangler a Luger. "If any of them makes a move to signal somebody outside the building, shoot." He opened the door and pushed Spangler through.

The cots and bunks had been pushed back to make more room. Tolan and fifteen Kapos whom Spangler had never seen before were speculating on the air attack. One had heard that the English had invaded Germany through Italy, another that the Russians had captured Berlin, yet another that Germany had made a separate armistice with the United States. One rumor claimed that Hitler was dead; a second that it was Stalin who had died. Intelligence about Birkenau itself seemed more reliable. Agents from the smelters reported that the stockpile of precious metals was being prepared for shipment. A field Kapo revealed that an extensive air alarm system was already being installed. An administration Kapo warned that more

245

secret SS detachments were being deployed in a ring around Auschwitz-Birkenau.

Anvil appeared in the door and cautioned that the auction was nearing its end. The underground hastily agreed that no final action could be plotted until more hard information was available. Constant intercompound communication was agreed upon, and one by one the members began to drift back into the Bourse.

Spangler wandered out into the compound, crossed the roll-call area, strolled between the two rows of dark barracks and stopped at the edge of the death ditch just inside the south fence. He lit a cigarette and gazed out into the railroad yard. The SS had just finished inspecting the empty cars of an incoming shipment. Doors were sealed and the SS walked along as the train began backing up the track. As it moved, the ramp beyond became exposed. Only a fraction of the overhead lights were in use; even so, Spangler could see the last of the right-hand line marching off toward the chimneys. Many little girls wearing silk dresses were among the number.

The remaining ramp lights went off. Spangler moved along the edge of the death ditch, staring up at the fence. His eyes strained to follow the conduit from one concrete post to the next. He finally located the transfer box. He traced the feed line back over two insulators and out onto a telephone pole.

The flashlight beam blinded him.

"What are you doing here?" demanded a voice from the darkness beyond the fence.

"Having a cigarette. Want one?" Spangler replied in German.

"Why aren't you in your barracks? Everyone is supposed to be in their barracks."

Spangler could see the rifle nervously pointing at him through the light beam.

"I'm a cook," he explained. "A senior cook." The guard hesitated and lowered his rifle.

"Would you like a cigarette?"

". . . Yes."

Spangler tossed the packet over the ditch and through the wire. The guard glanced right and left, stooped and picked it up. A match flared, momentarily illuminating the face under the steel helmet. The boy was seventeen at the most.

"Thank you," he said, starting to throw back the packet.

"Keep them."

The arm motion stopped. "Thank you."

"Are you new? I don't remember seeing you before."

"I am beginning my sixth night."

"Is this your first camp?"

"Yes."

"You'll get used to it."

". . . I hope so."

Spangler lit another cigarette. "Why are the fence lights off?"

"I think they expect another air attack."

Spangler strolled slowly along the ditch line. The guard kept pace on the other side of the fence. "Do they know who did the bombing earlier tonight?"

"The officers insist it was the Russians."

"But you don't think so?"

". . . No."

"Why not?"

"I saw the silhouettes."

"Didn't the others?"

"Silhouettes are easy to misread in a dark cloudy sky."

"But you read them correctly?"

"I used to build models."

"Whose aircraft do you think they were?"

"Luftwaffe. Junker Eighty-eights. I didn't know we had any left."

Spangler reached the end of the compound, turned and started slowly back. The young guard kept abreast.

"Why would the Luftwaffe bomb us?"

"They didn't. Everything fell half a mile out in the forest."

"Were they off course?"

"I don't think so. They were dropping delayed-action bombs. It's sometimes dangerous to land with them aboard. They were probably returning from an unsuccessful raid and jettisoning extra explosives."

Spangler stopped. "Can I get you anything?"

"Get me anything?"

"From the Bourse. Do you need any merchandise? I understand your kitchen is short of milk. How would you like some fresh milk?"

"I was only drafted six weeks ago. They haven't paid me yet."

"Don't worry, we'll work it out. When are you on again?"

"Tomorrow night."

"I'll bring you fresh milk tomorrow night."

"Thank you."

Early the next morning Spangler took his first shift at the short-wave radio. His instructions were brief. All he had to do was turn on the set every fifteen minutes and dial the two wavelengths, one for Cracow, the other for Prague. He was told that neither station had come on since the previous day. He took this for a good omen—the Russians might already have captured Cracow and Prague. On the other hand, if they *had* taken Cracow, they could arrive at Birkenau any moment—and that wouldn't be so good.

Spangler did not intend to rely on the Russians. He stayed at the set for three hours, formulating escape plans for himself and Jean-Claude. Whether Jean-Claude was at the Bugel or elsewhere was of no particular importance. The bordello passes gave Spangler mobility to search through the camp.

He sketched out a map of the areas to be covered and carefully marked the paths of guard patrols and the distances between manned fence towers. He drew up alternate escape routes and outlined them. Whichever he finally decided upon, two things were certain: first, he would have to find civilian clothing to fit Jean-Claude; second, he would not even attempt to bring Tolan along.

When Spangler returned to the barracks Der Gronck and one of the subcooks were bandaging their hands.

"We have to fight again," Der Gronck told Spangler grimly.

"Just the two of you?" Spangler asked.

"There will be more from other kitchens."

"Good luck."

There was no reply.

Spangler entered the sleeping quarters and started to his bunk. Vassili lunged at him. Spangler sidestepped, and the giant crashed onto the floor. He tried to rise to his knees, but collapsed instead with a gurgle.

"The underground is meeting," Anvil yelled, bursting through the door. "They want you there."

"Why me?"

"Who cares why when the meeting's at the Finishing School!"

49

THE UKRAINIAN SS guard pulled back the gate. Anvil and Spangler entered the sprawling Canada complex and walked briskly up the path. SS sentries were nowhere to be seen as they approached the long, high-roofed building known as the Finishing School.

Anvil and Spangler circled the line of Kapos and "suppliers" presenting their special passes at the entrance and went in through a side door. The main room stretched sixty feet and was forty feet wide. Massive lights and wires dangled from the thirty-foot ceiling. Motion-picture cameras, stanchions, floor lights and other equipment spread across the concrete floor.

"Wait up there until you're called," Anvil said, pointing to a line of chairs against the far wall. Then he disappeared behind a row of packing cases.

Spangler took a seat among the ever-growing audience of privileged prisoners hurrying in from the main entrance. Technicians were adding the final touches to a set depicting a huge and ornate jungle cave with tiers of wide roughhewn steps. Tolan appeared and gave last-minute instructions. Props were realigned and the torches in the cave lit. The powerful stage lights were switched on. A group of large, pug-faced women costumed as bare-breasted Amazons strode onto the set as the prisoner audience cheered and whistled.

"The women guards," a Kapo next to Spangler whispered excitedly with a nudge of the elbow. "That means a Lesbian show. We haven't had one for a long time."

Tolan barked an order and moved behind a big motion-picture camera. The Amazons formed a corridor leading up the cave steps. At the top stood the largest, and conceivably the ugliest, woman Spangler had ever seen. Her powerful legs were bound in Roman sandal straps. A short tunic barely covered her pelvis. The muscular arms were strapped in leather. One masculine fist clenched a whip, the other a steel rod. Link chains were draped around the bull shoulders, partially obscuring the enormous naked bosom. To her side stood a rack, an iron maiden and a glowing oven in which several iron prongs were being heated.

The second cheer from the audience was louder still. As Spangler watched, six girls from sixteen to eighteen years old were being pulled forward by even more Amazons. The girls wore fifteenth-century Spanish finery; all had braided hair.

"Virgins," the Kapo whispered ecstatically to Spangler. "The rumor is they're all virgins this time. That ought to be something."

The Amazon priestess looked over the crop of terrified girls and pointed to one. She was dragged up the steps and forced to kneel. The Amazon lifted her tunic and snapped an order. The girl froze, then suddenly broke away and bolted hysterically through a line of attendants, upsetting torches and collapsing a section of scenery.

"Get me six new ones," Tolan shouted in disgust. "Six new ones who'll do what they're supposed to! And fix the scenery," he shouted, storming off behind the packing cases.

The five remaining girls were stripped of their costumes and hurled into the audience of cheering prisoners.

Anvil returned, drew Spangler from his seat and led him down a hallway and into a room where Kapo leaders sat crowded on benches.

Klempf entered a few moments later, took a rigid stance and hooked a thumb under his belt. "The time for pretense has passed," he began curtly. "I know that you here represent the major force in the camp underground. I have always known it. You have existed only because I chose to let you exist—only because I felt one day your services might be required. I am afraid that day is upon us.

251

"The latest report from the eastern front indicates that the Wehrmacht counterattack has failed to stem the Russian offensive. The Reich's northern defense lines have been annihilated, and the Russians are now swarming down through Poland. Advance units have already crossed the Nida, less than a hundred and forty miles east of here. It is expected that the Russians will be at Cracow within a week and will reach us the following day.

"Needless to say, if the Russians overrun Auschwitz-Birkenau before the installations can be evacuated, if the Russians see what has taken place here—well, that wouldn't be very good for the SS *or* the Kapos, would it?

"I include you Kapos along with the SS for one very simple reason: once the Russians enter Auschwitz-Birkenau and start talking to ordinary prisoners, they will realize that, for all practical purposes, it is *you* who have been running the camp; they will see how *you* have treated your fellow inmates. When that happens you may be even worse off than we SS. Your paltry underground activities will not help you.

"Had Berlin taken any logical action to meet this peril I wouldn't be here talking to you now. Berlin, it appears, has not only ignored our plight, but has openly decided to worsen it. As of four hours ago, transport into Birkenau has been increased. When the commandant protested that the crematoria and the pits can't handle what we have, Berlin was deaf and still insisted on adding eighteen additional trainloads to this week's schedule.

"Berlin's orders to the SS here at Auschwitz-Birkenau were received early this morning. No one is to leave his station. No preparations are to be made for evacuation. To make sure we comply with the orders, Berlin has deployed Waffen-SS troops in the immediate vicinity—but luckily there are not very many of them—so far.

"In a word, Berlin has signed a death warrant for every SS and Kapo at Auschwitz-Birkenau. But that is not the end of it, not for us here in this room. The commandant has no intention of remaining. He and his staff have already made arrangements to flee when the Russians reach Cracow. Mengele and his medical aides have made similar plans. Cars have been requisitioned and prepared.

252

"The commandant and Mengele met secretly several hours ago. They have concocted a plot to shift their guilt to others—to divest themselves of as much responsibility for camp activities as they can before they leave. They have agreed to make it seem that the true persecutors of prisoners at Auschwitz-Birkenau are the Bourse and other exchanges, the bordellos, and so on. To be more precise, they have decided that the men in this room and those connected with us, both Kapo and SS, are to be the sacrificial goats.

"On the commandant's order, SD and Gestapo agents have already opened an investigation and are collecting evidence against us. More agents are on their way. The commandant prefers everything to be legal. If by some miracle the Russians are checked, he can simply put his findings in a drawer and save them until he needs them again. After all, who will run the camp if he does away with us?

"Should the Russian advance continue at its present speed, the commandant will have us arrested, tried and found guilty. Whether he shoots us on the spot or turns us over to the prisoners to hold for the Russians makes very little difference in my eyes.

"So there you have it. Not only must we worry about the Russian advance, we must avoid the SD and Gestapo as well. Under the circumstances, I see no alternative but to emulate the commandant and Mengele: we must escape as soon as possible."

"Where to?" asked one of the Kapos.

"The Russian lines."

"How?"

"I have already worked out the details, but for the sake of security they must remain with me. What I now propose is an alliance between all of you here, as well as those involved with you, and myself and my men. I must insist, however, on having full control of the operation. If you wish to designate one of your number, I will take him as my personal aide and advise him of the details. But only he and I must know the total plan. I will wait outside for your answer," Klempf said, and stepped out the door.

Discussion was brief. Klempf was called back. The Kapos agreed to the alliance and named Tolan as their representative.

"We will go out as prisoners," Klempf said to Tolan, handing him a list. "These are the supplies we need. They can be collected through the exchanges without causing suspicion. The last bit of business for tonight is assigned to you." Klempf added, turning and dropping a thumb at Spangler. "You will kill Vassili."

"Why?" said Spangler.

"We don't question orders here," Tolan snapped.

"Let him ask, let him ask," Klempf said quietly as he studied Spangler. "First of all, Vassili is an SD agent. They planted him here from the beginning. Therefore we must rid ourselves of him. Since you're expected to kill him anyway, no one, especially the SD, will be suspicious when you do. If someone else ended his life, questions might arise.

"Secondly, I don't know anything about you. You just arrived. I haven't had time to check you out. For all we know you may be another one of the undercover men the SD has been trying to send in for the last few weeks. There is no better way of finding out whose side you're on than by letting you take care of Vassili. I doubt whether one SD agent would kill another. You will do the job the day after tomorrow. I don't want it to be connected with our little gathering tonight—just in case someone may be watching. And when you murder him, do it out in the open where you have a good many witnesses."

50

DER GRONCK was not present when the Bourse opened that night. In his place sat a dazed, battered, hulking young man. No one knew the youth's name or where he was from, since his papers had been lost. No one understood the language he spoke. Even so, the Process had to be observed. He had broken Der Gronck's neck fair and square; he was now a senior cook.

Trading hit an all-time high. Three unscheduled trains from Hungary contributed to the activity. The Kapos' cautious purchasing of escape supplies and placing of future orders were also a factor. Goods had never been so plentiful, prices never so right. Spangler's order for women's silk clothing was filled within half an hour. He was able to purchase milk fifteen minutes later.

After the trading he went back to the fence. A train was unloading at the ramp under the emergency lights. Shouting from the other side indicated the progress of the selection. Something else caught Spangler's eye. He looked down at the near spur. Three railroad cars stood in the darkness. They were not freight, but metal passenger cars.

"Sorry to keep you waiting," the guard said from beyond the fence, "but they had me over at the ramp."

"I have the milk."

"Hand it under the wire. It's all right to come forward—the tower guard knows about it. I'm giving him some."

255

Spangler moved across the death ditch and waited as the young guard propped up the bottom wire with his rifle butt. No sparks flew; the fence's electricity was either turned off or kept extremely low during blackouts. This could alter his plan of escape, Spangler realized as he passed the container under; it could alter it greatly. He would even be able to go out at night.

"What's the news?" Spangler asked, stepping back and lighting a cigarette.

"They say the Russians have driven north around Warsaw and are now heading down behind German lines east of Lodz."

"Do you know this for a fact?"

"No. Only rumor. Everything is rumor. They've shut off all our communications. Only a few officers have radios left, and they won't tell us what's happening."

"And what of us? What of the prisoners? Has there been any word on our future?"

"No. They won't tell us anything. My sergeant did say that it wouldn't hurt to start befriending prisoners, though." The guard began walking along to keep up with Spangler. "How do you want me to pay for the milk?"

"See if you can get me some saltpeter."

"Saltpeter?"

"It's difficult for me here. My wife was quite healthy and I am still true to her. I have no stomach for the bordellos."

"I think I understand. But how do I get saltpeter?"

Spangler took a stack of bordello passes from his tunic and tossed them under the fence. "Buy it from the SS cooks, but . . ."

"Yes?"

"I would appreciate your not telling who it's for. If word got out the others might laugh at me."

"I'll do my best—and thank you for the milk."

Spangler turned to go. As he did he saw light along the near spur. He gazed down at the metal railroad coaches. A group of six young girls were being loaded onto the last car by the light of storm lanterns. They were all between sixteen and eighteen. All were blond, with their hair done in braids. All wore white sliplike dresses.

5I

SPANGLER KNEW he was being watched. From the time he left the compound he knew someone was following him at a distance. He didn't bother to turn. Instead he hiked the sack higher on his back and continued along the road. The morning sun was thawing the mud. The breeze carried the scent of forest pine.

He noticed the guard patrols as he walked, and he made a mental note of any deviations from what he had recorded on his map the day before. There were few alterations.

Spangler noticed something else. Prisoners were busy adjusting fence lights in every compound he passed. Every fourth bulb along the strings was being tinted blue. Those between were being loosened. The shielded bulbs along the exterior fence were receiving similar attention. Labor Kommandos stood atop crude stepladders painting some and unscrewing others by half a turn. More prisoners were helping install dull-green sirens.

Spangler was passed through the exterior fence, and he entered the SS billet area. Here too, air defense work was under way. Barracks windows were being covered from the inside. Lights were being painted, sirens attached.

Spangler paused at the bus stop, glanced at the arrival-and-departure schedule and continued on his way.

He undid the bundle and displayed the dresses and toys. The SS sergeant inspected the garments with satisfaction. A trio of wigged,

257

painted Bubels were called into the room. Clothing was thrown at them. They disappeared with drunken glee. They returned begowned and began strutting, hands on hips, about the room. The door burst open and a dozen more Bubels flooded through and swarmed over Spangler and the merchandise. One knelt behind him as others unexpectedly pushed. He tumbled back and fell to the floor as a new wave rushed out and piled on him from another direction. He struggled to break free. The SS sergeant grew hysterical and ordered even more Bubels into the melee. Spangler thrashed furiously, but slowly his arms were drawn behind him as small painted boys darted all about biting his lips, his cheeks, his chin, pinching his nose, tugging at his hair. He tried to roll over, but the weight of two dozen stunted castrated forms kept him from doing so. When he felt his trousers being undone he lurched desperately forward and freed one arm. Again he was swarmed over.

"Erik," a tiny high-pitched voice whispered into his ear.

Spangler jerked his head around. All the faces looked the same. The rouged cheeks, the thick lipstick, the heavy green-mascaraed eyes, the white cracked powdered skin all looked alike.

"Erik," the tiny voice whispered again. "I know you've come to save me, but don't. Please don't. The pain is awful, I could never make it out."

The SS sergeant tired of the sport. He ordered the Bubels to stop. The children paid no heed. They tore at Spangler more energetically than ever.

"Erik," the tiny voice continued, "thank you for coming, but go away. They are waiting for you. They are watching. They think you will raid from the outside. They have questioned me a dozen times, but I have said nothing."

The SS sergeant waded into the pile and began pushing and shoving the Bubels off.

"It is madness here. There is only one man you can trust. He tried to save me. He knows their plans. He will—"

The sergeant caught Spangler by the wrist and pulled him free of the pile. The children scurried from the room.

52

"NOTHING HAS come over. Nothing! Not a single blasted word," Anvil muttered in frustration. He rose to let Spangler begin his shift at the radio. "First the Russians are splashing in our soup, next they're nowhere to be found. What's going on?"

"Here, read this," Spangler said, handing him a mimeographed sheet. "The new air-raid regulations."

"Eh?" the cook muttered as he looked down at the page. "What does it say? I don't read German too well."

"From all I can make out, we have to wear white armbands if we're out at night. They'll tell you the rest back at the barracks."

Spangler waited until Anvil had climbed the ladder, dropped the trapdoor after himself and begun piling potato sacks on top of it, before opening Vassili's locker. Most of the canned goods had been requisitioned by the escape command. Only stamps, sugar, lead piping and a few watches remained. Spangler selected six sections of pipe with pinched ends and brought them back to the radio table. He removed the glass shield from the storm lantern, turned up the blue-white flame and held the pinched end of the first pipe over it. The lead began to soften. Soon the end had melted shut. Two more sections were sealed closed before Spangler had to interrupt his work and snap on the radio.

Nothing came in on the two designated wavelengths. He switched

259

to other bands without success. After five minutes he snapped off the radio and continued the melting.

He scooped out a hole under Vassili's locker, placed the six pipe sections in it and buried them. He took out six of the wristwatches and brought them to the table. He carefully drilled a tiny hole in the center of each crystal with a sharpened fork tine. He reached into his pocket and brought out a handful of metal slivers he had found near the repair shop. From them he fashioned tiny metal poles, which he fitted into the crystal openings until they touched the axis of the watch hands.

Spangler buried the watches with the pipe sections. He returned to the table and glanced at the clock. The scheduled listening time had been missed. He set the alarm for fifteen minutes, took out his map of Birkenau and flipped it over.

He began sketching a ground plan of the Bubel billet. He had seen the first floor, so he had no trouble with it. The second floor had to be calculated from the position of the staircase, the footsteps he had heard overhead and the arrangement of the windows. If his appraisal was correct, the second story was divided into three large rooms and one much smaller. The large room in the middle had dark window shades; this was probably where the SS slept. The rooms to the right and left had lace curtains: this was most likely where Jean-Claude and the other Bubels were kept.

The alarm clock rang. Spangler switched on the radio. Music blared from the speaker. The words were in English.

> *"Mairzy Doats and Dozy Doats and liddle lamzy divey,*
> *A kiddley divey too, wouldn't you? . . ."*

The song faded and a voice in Polish rose above it. ". . . beyond Eblag to the outskirts of Danzig . . ." The music was gone. The voice had risen almost to a thunder. Spangler reduced the volume. "Below Eblag, Russian forces now hold Lubwawa, Brodnica, Sirpo and Plock. The corridor to Warsaw is still open, and a fresh German relief column is speeding in. Farther to the south fierce fighting still continues at Lodz. Kieclec, Tarnow and Grysbow are now in Russian— Hold, hold a moment! This just in: Warsaw has fallen. I repeat, Warsaw has fallen! An estimated one hundred and fifty thousand German troops have been captured. And this too, this too just handed to me," the voice shouted. "Oberkommando Wehrmacht has ordered a general retreat from Plock to Nowy Sacz. The Russian Army now holds one third of Poland and is moving forward almost unopposed . . ."

Spangler turned down the volume, pulled the message rope and began writing as fast he could. The courier leaned into the bunker and was handed the message.

Spangler raised the volume. Warsaw was off the air. He dialed the Prague band. Again he was lucky. Reception was strong and clear.

". . . Had the Wehrmacht been able to hold Warsaw another twenty-four hours," the voice said in Czech, "the northern defense line might have been reinforced and held. Now there is little hope that the half-million troops trapped against the Baltic Sea have any alternative but surrender or total destruction. In central Poland the approaches to Cracow are said . . ."

The voice faded under music and static. Again the lyrics were in English.

> ". . . east, the sun shines west,
> But I know where the sun shines best.
> Oh, Mammy, my liddle Ma-a-ammee,
> I'd walk a million miles
> For one of your smiles,
> My Maaa . . ."

The song drifted into silence. Nothing came over the speaker but gentle static.

A hand reached under Jean-Claude's dress. He spun away coquettishly and fled to the kitchen. The supper dishes hadn't been done. The SS sergeant stumbled into the room after him. Jean-Claude escaped through the parlor. Bubels and SS lay drunk on the floor. Some were embracing, others already passed out. His pursuer tripped over

261

a leg, tumbled forward and landed on a half-sober Bubel. A relationship blossomed.

Jean-Claude climbed the stairs and tiptoed into the SS bedroom. A sergeant lay on his stomach snoring. Jean-Claude quietly closed the door and locked it. He moved silently to the bed, seized the empty whiskey bottle with both hands raised it high and crashed it down onto the German's head. The snoring stopped.

Jean-Claude took apart the emergency lamp and poured the kerosene over the bed and the drapes. He lit a match and threw it. Flames flashed up. He seated himself on the night chair and folded his hands in his lap as the fire began to spread.

53

THICK LAYERS of blankets had been nailed over the inside window so that the Bourse could continue through the semi-blackout. Five unexpected shipments had arrived that day. Trading was heavier and more frantic than the night before.

"By tomorrow," Tolan said, taking Spangler aside.

"What by tomorrow?"

"Vassili. Take care of him before dark tomorrow."

"Why?"

"Because it's an order—and because we may go out tomorrow night. Now go get yourself some sleep."

"I can't. I traded radio shifts with Anvil. I go on after midnight."

"That's your problem."

Spangler wandered into the compound and looked out through the camp. Everything was bathed in soft blue light and shadows. Spangler laughed to himself. There had never been shadows like this before, not at Birkenau. It had always been too well lit to go out at night. Now he could get a truck through and no one would notice. But it was too late. His plan was set.

He walked past the barracks. The sirens began to rise. What dim blue light there was went off. Aircraft engines could be heard in the distance. Then explosions. The raid was brief. The all clear sounded, and the few blue lights were on again.

"I have it" the helmeted form said from beyond the barbed wire. The guard tossed the package through. "Is it enough?"

Spangler examined the saltpeter. "It will do."

"I think I can get you more tomorrow. Shall I get you more tomorrow?"

"All right." Spangler strolled along the fence. The youth paced on the other side. "What are the rumors?"

"They say that Warsaw has fallen. They say the Russians will soon be at Cracow, and then . . ."

"Here at Birkenau?"

There was no reply.

"Is the SS preparing to evacuate?" Spangler asked.

"I don't—I don't think so," the boy said, with a catch in his voice.

"Then what will become of you and your comrades?"

Again there was no answer.

"Why don't you try to get out before it's too late?" Spangler suggested.

"Desert?"

"Call it what you like, it's better than letting the Russians take you, isn't it?"

"We're afraid to try." The boy glanced around furtively. "The SD and the Gestapo are watching us. They won't let us leave." He walked a few more paces, again looked around, then pointed to the near spur. "Do you see those railroad cars down this track?" he said under his breath.

"The three metal passenger coaches?"

"There are only two now, the red one left early this morning. Those two are SD. Secret police. The officers pretend they're not, but we've seen SD come in and out of them. SD are everywhere in the camp. The Gestapo are waiting on the outside. Two men in my barracks were caught trying to get out earlier. So you see there's nothing we can do."

A whistle sounded. A few blue lights went on over the ramp, but they were of little help. The sidings lay in almost total darkness.

Spangler had to strain to see the gates opening under the tower. He didn't realize that SS were walking along the rails until the train had chugged much farther up the track. But he did realize, that the dimly lighted siding yard had become a perfect avenue for escape.

Spangler took his shift at the radio and checked the night schedule. Prague and Cracow came on only at hourly intervals this late. He opened Vassili's locker, brought out a sack of sugar and began measuring it. He filled the cup with one part saltpeter to four parts sugar. Grinding with a knife handle was arduous, but Spangler worked feverishly. By the end of the hour he had pulverized half a paper bag of the mixture.

He could only get Prague. The Russians were reported to be less than fifteen miles from the city. Half of Poland had now been taken, and the Russian advance was gaining momentum.

Spangler went back to his grinding. By the time Prague reported that the Russians had been slowed down twenty-five miles east of Cracow he was already filling the lead pipes with the powder.

The six firing caps he had stolen from the escape-Kommando arsenal were each placed in a pipe and connected with two wires leading out from under the lead plug which sealed each bomb.

The watches were placed on the table and the crystals taken off. The hour hand on each instrument was removed. More steel plugs were added to each face. On two watches he placed them at thirty minutes after the hour; on two more, at forty minutes after; on the last pair, at fifty minutes after. The crystals were measured, drilled and replaced. Two prongs now rose above each of them. Wires were attached to both prongs and led to dry-cell batteries that Spangler took from the radio repair locker. The wires leading from the bombs were also attached to the batteries. The timing mechanism was complete. The circuit was open. When the metal of the minute hand hit against the metal pole on the watch face, the circuit would be closed. The electricity from the batteries would fire the cap and the bomb would explode.

When he got back to the Bourse, the tailors were still fashioning escape uniforms. From the outside they looked like usual inmates' garb, but inside they were triple-lined to provide warmth during the trek to Russian lines. Secret interior pockets would hold the provisions needed.

The other cooks had just wakened and were dressing in the darkness and leaving to prepare the morning meal when Spangler climbed into his bunk and fell asleep.

A huge hand seized him by the neck. Spangler grabbed at fingers. The grip could not be broken. He was dragged slowly to the edge of the bed and his head forced around. He stared helplessly into Vassili's massive face. The flaming eyes bulged. Thick lips moved against Spangler's ear.

"Jean-Claude," came the almost inaudible rasp, "Jean-Claude . . . has . . . killed himself."

Spangler gazed paralyzed at the giant.

Vassili nodded sadly. "Killed himself . . . to protect you, . . . stupid bastard."

The trembling started slowly, then quickly mounted out of control. Tears flooded Spangler's eyes. A deep agonizing moan rose in his throat, but was silenced as Vassili's other hand clamped on his mouth. The giant's grip held tight as Spangler's body heaved and thrashed. It was many minutes before the torment eased.

The powerful hand moved from the mouth, lowered below bunk level, returned a moment later to press a cold gun barrel against Spangler's brow. "Now come, . . . stupid bastard. . . . Time to make you a hero."

"Who are you?" Spangler finally managed to ask.

"Stupid bastard," the laugh-cough spit out sardonically, "I am . . . the one . . . who could have helped you. Now come."

The massive hand tightened around Spangler's neck and jerked forward. Spangler crashed to the floor. He was lifted to his feet by the back of his head. Vassili draped a weakening arm around his shoulder.

"Now . . . walk me . . . walk me out," he rasped, and he slid the gun down under his tunic until it hit Spangler's ribs.

The back door pushed open. Step by step they made their way out

266

into the darkness of the paradeground. The cooks saw them and rushed from the kitchen.

"Tell them . . ." Vassili breathed out, "tell them—go back."

Spangler shouted over his shoulder. The crowd stopped, stepped back a pace or two, then waited.

Spangler walked the listing hulk farther out into the night. The roll-call area lay behind, a fence fifteen paces ahead.

"Far enough," came the rasp.

Spangler stopped.

Vassili pushed himself free, staggered to keep his balance, kept the gun hand in his tunic and raised the other in a fist. "Fight . . . fight me."

"You can't even stand," Spangler objected.

"Stupid . . . stupid bastard—they all watch . . . they all watch us." The body rocked forward slightly. "Now hit . . . hit me."

Vassili lunged ineffectually. Spangler tapped him lightly on the chest. The giant fell past and slammed to the ground. He rolled slowly over, raised himself weakly to all fours and finally back to his feet.

"Stupid bastard . . ." He hissed as he swayed, "they watch. Give them . . . what is wanted. Hit me . . . hard."

Again he reeled forward. Spangler had meant the punch to graze the brow. Vassili had moved his head intentionally. It caught him full face.

"Good. . . . Good. . . ." He struggled and slowly managed to right himself. "Good, stupid bastard. Once again. . . . Again— harder."

Spangler glanced back. The shadowy cluster of cooks stood motionless at the far end of the field. Vassili stumbled into him from the back and spun to the earth. Again he raised himself.

"Stupid bastard—give them . . . their show."

The pathetic ritual continued. Vassili attacked unsteadily. Spangler tried to avoid hurting him. Strength finally gave out. The fading giant could rise no higher than his knees. "Now . . . hit . . . again . . . and drag me . . . over there."

Spangler blanched.

267

"Stupid . . . stupid bastard, . . . don't worry—you murdered me many days ago . . . murdered the only one . . . who could help. Hit—drag me by foot . . ." The gun pointed from under the tunic.

Spangler threw a light punch. Vassili sprawled on the frozen ground. Spangler seized his foot. He pulled him toward the wire. Fence guards who had been watching the fight from a distance moved even farther away. The cooks, however, had moved forward and now formed a ragged line in the middle of the field.

"Sit me . . . sit me up . . . and let me fall against it," Vassili said, bringing out the gun and handing it to Spangler.

"There's no power," Spangler said desperately. "The electricity goes off during the blackout. Come on. I'll take you back. We've given them enough of an exhibition for one night."

"Sit me up against it. I—I can wait."

"No."

"Stupid bastard—would you have me die *their* way?"

Spangler stiffened, then studied the pleading face. He moved forward, raised Vassili to a sitting position and leaned his back against the fence.

Vassili's quaking arm reached out, draped around Spangler's neck and coaxed him forward. "I . . . I am not SD . . . Kuprov—I am Kuprov. . . . Russian . . . espionage. . . . I know who you are. . . . They don't . . . not yet." The former chief of Russian Counterespionage, Second Sector, smiled bitterly and coughed out a laugh. "You . . . you get out of here. . . . Get out on your own. . . . Don't trust—keep away from Klempf escape. . . . Keep away from all of them. . . . Something behind it . . . don't know what . . . but all wrong. . . . Locker—look behind locker in cave. . . . See for self."

Kuprov blinked and tried to focus on Spangler. His eyes were beginning to cross. "Stupid bastard. . . . Do me a favor sometime —pay little Schleebund back for me."

Spangler stood up and glanced to the east. Dawn was near. The black out would soon be ending. Electricity would be restored. He

268

considered momentarily and then moved to shield Kuprov with his body so the others in the distance could not see. His fist shot out. Only the head fell unconscious to the side. Kuprov's massive torso remained sitting upright against the wire.

54

SPANGLER replaced Anvil in the bunker for the afternoon shift. He set the alarm clock and went to Kuprov's locker. A small cubicle had been dug behind it and in it were an SS uniform, a Luger and a long roll of paper tied in red string. Spangler brought out the paper, slid off the binding and spread out the sheets on the table. He knew at a glance that Kuprov had somehow come across official maps of Auschwitz, Birkenau, the Buno camp five miles away and seven smaller subcamps, as well as a chart of the exterior defense lines.

Spangler began studying the Birkenau map. The sheet showed the official guard deployment and schedule for day and night assignments. Kuprov had already begun marking the disparities. Spangler was quick to realize the rest. Almost nothing he had seen in guard numbers and positons since his arrival at Birkenau corresponded to the official arrangement. In the six weeks since this map had been issued, camp security had been reduced by almost a half and the area assignments completely altered. In and around their own compound the guards had been cut to one-fourth the official number.

The alarm clock rang.

". . . after a thirty-six-hour battle," the voice from Prague boomed out, "the German surrender was total and unconditional.

270

Russian officers have already guaranteed that we may continue broadcasting to all of you just as before. We can come out into the sunlight. We are free. Prague is free! Long live Prague!

"On other fronts the Russian advances . . ."

Music began to rise above the announcer's voice. Again the lyrics were in English.

> ". . . *night is clear,*
> *And the bombardier*
> *Drops a bomb that's wired for sound,*
> *How I yearn*
> *To return*
> *With my head in the clouds*
> *To the girl I left on the ground.*"

Spangler quickly switched to the Cracow band.

"Hey there, Tex," a voice said in English, "did you notice anything unusual about that stranger that's been in town the last week or so?"

"Which one?" a second voice asked.

"You know, the fellow with the big white horse? Notice anything queer about him?"

"Nope. Can't say that I did. What's there to notice?"

"Well, he was wearing a mask, that's what."

"Say, you know something? Now that you mention it, he *was!*"

The hoofbeats of a galloping horse were heard in the background. So were strains from the William Tell Overture. The hoofbeats grew softer.

"Come on, Silver," someone in the obvious distance called out with stentorian confidence. "Let's go, big fellow. Hi-ho, Silver! Away!"

The William Tell Overture rose to a finale as Spangler switched back to Prague.

". . . then add the beetroots and let the mixture come to a boil," a familiar woman's voice was saying in German. "If you prefer a darker shade, a teaspoonful of soot can be added. Once the garment is immersed . . ."

Spangler again tried Cracow. Instead he heard:

> *"Who's that little chatterbox?*
> *The one with curly auburn locks?*
> *Whom do you see?*
> *It's Little Orphan Annie!*
> *She and Sandy make a . . ."*

The volume decreased as Spangler heard the noise overhead. He scooped up the maps, returned them to their hiding place and pushed the locker back just as the feet started down the ladder.

"What's the news?" Tolan asked, reaching the floor.

"The Russians have taken Prague."

"What about Cracow?"

"I don't know."

"Can't you get Cracow?"

"I get the wavelength, but something keeps drifting in on it. On Prague as well."

"We have to find out about Cracow," Tolan insisted. "The whole escape depends on that. We plan to go out tomorrow night if the Russians keep their present position or move forward. If they retreat we must go tonight."

"Are we ready to go tonight?"

"Not really. But if the Russians are thrown back we'll have to. The nearer they are to us the better our chances of reaching them."

Tolan fiddled with the radio and turned up the volume. Cracow was off the air. The dial turned to Prague. Prague also was not sending.

"They'll be on again in fifteen minutes," Spangler offered.

"Where were the Russians the last you heard?"

"Anvil said the battle was still raging fifteen miles beyond Cracow, and that's all anyone knew."

Tolan thought. "We can't take chances," he finally concluded. He handed a list to Spangler. "These people will have to be silenced before we leave. Each of us will have to finish five of them. Take your pick."

Spangler read the names. All the Habes were included. So were three apprentice cooks.

"Why?"

"We can take out only a hundred and twenty among all the groups. That means eliminating some of our own. Now pick your five."

"Why am I going out rather than the others?"

"I like you."

"I don't like you."

"Then put it in these terms: if you hadn't beaten Vassili, he would be in charge—and making up that list you're holding. In that case, my name would have been first. So I'm meeting a good turn with a good turn. Pick your five."

"I won't kill anyone."

"We must each pick five. That's an order."

"I took care of Vassili and that's it, order or no order."

Tolan hesitated, then turned and climbed the ladder.

Spangler brought out Kuprov's Birkenau map. He studied the official deployment and schedules of the guards at the railroad sidings and marked in the positions and numbers he had personally witnessed in the last few days. The force he had seen was one-third the indicated requirement. Their stations and patrol routes were nothing like those on the map. Had official specifications been met, escape along the track could not have even been considered. Under present conditions it was the most logical route.

He unrolled the chart of the outer-guard defense positions around Auschwitz-Birkenau as the alarm clock rang.

Spangler switched on the set. Prague was not sending. He moved to the Cracow band.

". . . a third column is believed to have moved up from Nowy Sacz to complete the pincer," the voice said in Polish as heavy fire thundered in the background. "If this should be the case the

Russians would find themselves trapped outside Cracow. German reinforcements and material are moving up quickly for this decisive battle. Whether the Russians will hold their ground and fight or whether they will begin their retreat is still not known. . . ."

55

ALL THROUGH the late afternoon and early evening squadron after squadron of Luftwaffe fighter-bombers roared over Birkenau toward the northeast. The blue dimout was in effect as of sundown. Reports from the radio bunker described the battle of Cracow. German losses were staggering, the destruction was devastating.

Two air alarms were sounded at Birkenau within an hour's time span. On both occasions the camp was pitched into total darkness.

The Bourse began operation at 9 P.M. Forty-five minutes later a subcook burst in from his post at the radio. The German retreat from Cracow had begun.

Kapos began drifting out of the barracks. Tolan ordered the cook back to the radio room and then began organizing his own men. The three apprentice cooks whose names Spangler had seen on the list were told to assemble the Habes in the kitchen. The remaining cooks and the compound Kapos were assigned times to leave for the rendezvous. The subcooks picked up knives, clubs and garroting wire and headed for the kitchen.

Spangler went out alone through the compound gate. The guard stopped him. He had forgotten to wear his armband. He returned to the barracks, tied the white cloth to his upper arm and started out again. He crossed the road, showed his pass at the Canada gate, was passed through and made his way toward the Finishing School.

A line had already formed along a row of tables. Escape uniforms and provisions were being issued. A special table was set aside for the escaping SS. Arms were stretched across and a red-hot iron smoked into the flesh to burn off the double-lightning SS tattoo. Both the Kapos and the SS were changing into escape uniforms. Personal identification papers were thrown into a pile, doused with kerosene and lighted.

Tolan and the subcooks were among the last to arrive. They were processed and changed quickly.

Klempf arrived, and all turned to listen to him.

"In approximately forty-five minutes this building will be raided by members of my Secret Security detachment," he told his audience. "You will be summarily tried, within a matter of minutes, for your various mistreatments of two prisoners, and then marched directly to Crematorium Two."

There was slight murmuring.

"As you all know," Klempf continued, unconcerned, "Crematorium Two is rather defective and is usually breaking down. I made certain that such a breakdown occurred earlier today. The trouble happens to be in the rear of the building—beside the fence. Trucks and repairmen are already there. A great many trucks. This is only natural, since the shipments have been so sharply increased and the crematorium must be repaired as quickly as possible. We have torn down the fence directly behind it so that the trucks can get in. We have even torn a hole in the rear wall inside the gas chamber itself to get to the trouble.

"So you can see, that is our plan. You line up in front of Crematorium Two like any other group of prisoners. You go right in—and then out through the back and onto the trucks. The wall will be quickly repaired, and the next group of prisoners—bona-fide prisoners—will be processed as usual, without anyone realizing what has happened. The trouble will have been corrected and the repair trucks will drive off."

Klempf ordered Spangler and four others to the side.

"To minimize the chance of interference with our schedule," he told the small gathering, "diversionary tactics must be employed.

The air alarm system is our most obvious target. When the sirens sound, the blue lights automatically go off. Processing at the gas chamber, as you know, does not stop. Processing *never* stops, no matter what the circumstances. Therefore," Klempf concluded, "the escape will take place in darkness.

"The air alarm system is comprised of two separate systems, manual and automatic. Manual alerts are controlled from observation points beyond the camp perimeter. The automatic network is set up within the camp and is by far the largest. It works on the premise of interrupted circuits: once a circuit is broken, the alarm sounds."

Each man was given a diversionary assignment. Spangler was given a handwritten chart. He was to strangle the guard at the railroad fence, Klempf instructed—the guard he had become friendly with—then move down the fence and cut the wire leading to alarm sirens in the ramp area. He was to return through the compound to the main road, where he would be "arrested" and brought to the gas chamber.

"How do I get through the electrified wire?" Spangler asked.

"You already know it *isn't* electrified during a semi-blackout," Klempf replied softly. "Or have you forgotten Vassili—and passing milk to the sentry? But that isn't my main concern. The important question is: Will you kill the guard?"

"If you're not certain, send someone else."

"I'm only asking. After all, you refused to get rid of the Habes in your compound."

"They were fellow prisoners, not guards."

"Then you'll take the assignment?"

"Why not?"

Spangler left the building as the SS of the Secret Security unit began leisurely getting off their trucks and strolling inside for the raid.

277

56

SPANGLER SHOWED his pass, and the Ukrainian guard opened the gate. No one was left in the cooks' barracks. He crossed behind the kitchen, entered the potato shed and climbed down the ladder. He pulled Vassili's locker from the wall and stared at the SS uniform, the maps and the Luger. The uniform was slightly too large, but wearable. Kuprov had obviously stolen it for himself, only to find it too small. Spangler took out the gun, replaced the uniform, pushed back the locker and climbed out of the room.

He waited at the back fence, smoking. Another train was being unloaded in the pale-blue light. The two metal passenger cars stood in the darkness down the nearest spur. Spangler studied them carefully as the guard approached.

"What are the rumors?" he asked the boy.

"The Russians have been stopped outside Cracow," the guard said with relief.

"What about the Gestapo and SD?"

"They're still everywhere, but we think they're moving out soon."

"Why?"

"My sergeant says that once the German counteroffensive pushes back the Russians, there's no need for them."

"Do you believe that?"

"Yes."

"Why?"

"See those SD command cars down there?" The boy indicated the pair of metal passenger cars. "Well, an engine is already waiting outside the gate to take them out."

"Are you certain?"

"Yes. My bunkmate is on the detail watching the locomotive. The cars go out later tonight."

"I brought you something," Spangler said, holding out his hand.

"What?"

"Look for yourself."

Spangler moved to the fence. The boy stepped closer on his side.

"I can't see anything."

"Look closer," Spangler suggested, lowering his hand slightly. "It's very small."

The boy leaned down, and Spangler's Luger pressed against his forehead. "Stay exactly as you are and do what I say—and nothing will happen to you, understand?"

The young guard tried to say yes.

"Now ease up the bottom wire with your rifle butt—and remember, my pistol is on you."

The strand was propped up and Spangler slid under on his back. "Now come here."

The boy stepped forward, trembling.

Spangler put a hand on his neck. "Now hold your breath and count to fifty. When you gain consciousness lie as you are for at least half an hour, don't move for half an hour, or I'll come back and kill you. Trust me. I could kill you now, but I'm not going to," he said as two of his fingers began pinching the boy's windpipe. "Start counting, and remember what I told you."

The boy's legs buckled and he fell forward unconscious into Spangler's arms. Spangler laid him on his back and knelt down. The breathing was easy. No damage had been done. The youth would come around shortly.

Spangler moved up the fence, found the lead wire, took out his knife and cut it with one stroke. Sirens began to moan. The yard was plunged into darkness.

He moved back to where the boy lay, started back under the fence, suddenly changed his mind and made for the near railway spur in a crouched run. He reached the first of the two metal railroad cars. A low constant hum was heard from within. The faint odor of burnt rubber was obvious. Spangler moved along to the second car. Like the first, the windows were blacked out. Unlike the first, a strand of telephone cable stretched from its roof to a nearby connection terminal.

There was an explosion in a distant part of the camp, then another. More sirens began wailing. Emergency SS patrols could be seen running along the outer roads. Three more explosions reverberated from distant points. Birkenau was in total darkness.

Spangler moved forward, crossed the tracks, moved between the boxcars and slid under the ramp. He inched forward under the walkway until he had a view of Crematorium Two. A group of new arrivals waited in the darkness at one end. Other new arrivals lined the road leading to the gate.

Tramping was heard and then commands. The column of captured Finishing School Kapos marched up the road under heavy guard and turned into the crematorium compound. He looked for Tolan, but in the darkness it was impossible to single out anyone. He counted the white armbands of the "escapees." Some were missing. Spangler squinted at his watch. They were five minutes ahead of schedule.

An order was shouted. The Kapos, Klempf's SS aides, the guards, the cooks and all the other leaders of the camp's illicit activities formed into two lines.

Spangler knew that the low building along the fence housed the gas chambers and that the large lateral building with the chimney was the crematorium.

Klempf called an order. The four lines merged into one. The single column moved until it was directly in front of the gas chamber. The door was thrown open. On command, the line pressed forward in double time. The column was two-thirds in before the shouting and screaming broke out. The bogus prisoners surged back out of the building; those still outside turned to flee. A wave of hidden SS rushed out from behind the two waiting lines of new arrivals. The flanks of SS merged, formed an arc and slowly and bloodily began forcing the battling men of the illegal industries back into the gas chamber. The arc grew smaller, the number of visible white armbands fewer. The SS gave a final surge and pushed in behind them, kicking and clubbing. A few minutes later the SS came out alone. Then two officers climbed the outside ladder, carrying a canister. They crossed to the center of the roof, pulled up the hatch and carefully poured the Zyklon-B pellets through. There was no hole in the rear of the building, no gap in the fence.

Spangler ripped the white cloth from his sleeve, stuffed it into his pocket and quickly cut back across the railroad yard. He stopped behind the metal passenger cars. A phone was ringing inside as he surveyed the terrain. Lines of SS guards began forming in the area he had just fled. They linked arms and started slowly forward in their search.

Spangler dashed along the fence. The young guard lay motionless in the dark, his knees drawn up under him. Spangler knelt and rolled the boy onto his back. The youth's neck had been broken. Spangler glanced down the track. A dim line of SS could be seen walking forward from the tower at the railroad gate.

He slid under the wire and hurried back into the compound. He was halfway across the roll-call area when the all-clear began to sound. Spangler doubled his pace.

The bunker was dark. He didn't light the lamp. It was twenty minutes before Prague or Cracow would be broadcasting. He pulled Vassili's locker away from the wall so he could crawl in behind if he had to.

Spangler stood in the darkness waiting and thinking. Why had the men of the Bourse and the other exchanges been tricked and murdered? Why had Klempf gone through such acrobatics to do it? Why had they arrived at the gas chamber five minutes ahead of schedule? Everything was worked out to the second; why had they changed the plan? One hundred and twenty men had been assembled at the Finishing School, but he had counted only one hundred and eighteen waiting in line. Who were the men not accounted for? Unless he had been mistaken. Spangler thought he had had a clear view, but maybe he was wrong. Who had killed the fence guard, and why?

The sound of the shifting potato sacks was heard overhead. Spangler squeezed into the hole and pulled the locker back in place.

Footsteps descended the ladder.

"No one's here," he heard Anvil's voice call.

"Is the radio warm? Has it been used recently?" Klempf's voice shouted from above. "Has the lamp been used?"

"No," Anvil announced after a few seconds. "No one's been here."

"Are you sure he came back into the compound? Did you actually *see* him?"

"I saw him come back to the fence. Then he stopped and looked across in my direction. I had to duck so he wouldn't notice me. When I looked up he was gone. He wouldn't have had time to go anywhere else."

"What did you do after killing the boy?"

"I told you—I came through the next compound and waited for him on the road. He never appeared."

"All right, come out of there."

"Shall I bring the radio?"

"No, he may return. Where else can he go? Make sure he isn't scared off. Watch the bunker—from a distance. I'll have the guards sweep the railroad yard just in case he's still out there."

"But we've just searched the yard."

"They may have missed him. Now get a move on."

Spangler heard Anvil climb the ladder and drop the trapdoor after him. He waited a full ten minutes before pushing out the locker and climbing from the cubbyhole. He lit a match and checked his watch. He turned on the radio. Neither Cracow nor Prague was heard from. He waited another hour before trying again. Both cities remained silent.

57

SPANGLER SLEPT in the bunker through most of the day. He did not
expect any air attacks. In the past, they had come at night, around
roll-call time. He checked the early-evening radio schedule. Cracow
and Prague remained silent. Bits of the Lone Ranger and a medley
of Benny Goodman were all that came across.

He opened Vassili's locker and changed into the SS uniform. He
dug up his homemade bombs, stripped the batteries from the short-
wave set and the repair kit and connected the explosives. He took
the trousers of his prisoner uniform, fashioned them into a crude
knapsack and placed the bombs inside.

Spangler gave himself another two hours before he slipped on the
knapsack, climbed the ladder and put his shoulder against the trapdoor. He rose slowly into the potato shed, got to his feet and peered
out. The compound was bathed in dim blue light.

He stepped through the door and out behind the rear of the
kitchen. Two Ukrainian SS guards lolled at the front gate. The usual
road patrol was absent. Spangler moved into the shadows and
waited.

Fifteen minutes passed before he heard a noise. Spangler moved
along the building, silently turned the corner, slipped up behind the
officer, clamped him around the neck and dragged him back into the

darkness. He spun his captive around, shoved him against the wall and pressed the Luger under his chin.

"Anvil, what a pleasant surprise," Spangler said quietly. "It's always a pleasure running into old prison chums unexpectedly. Tell me, which branch of the Secret Police are you with?"

"Spe—Special Security."

"How long have they had you undercover in the compound?"

"Th-three weeks."

"You're answering very well, Anvil. Now let's try a harder question or two. Why were the Finishing School men murdered?"

"I don't know."

"Try to think." He jabbed the Luger deep into Anvil's neck.

"I don't *know* why. I swear it. I didn't even know what was going to happen to them. My orders were only to watch you."

"Watch me do what?"

"Kill the guard and cut the wire. They weren't sure you'd do it. They wanted me to report what you did."

"Who is 'they'?"

"Klempf."

"When you were undercover in the compound what were you supposed to watch for?"

"Anything suspicious, but mostly Tolan and Vassili."

"Why Tolan and Vassili?"

"I don't know. Klempf wanted to know their movements."

"Who is Klempf?"

"You know as well as I do. He's head of Secret Security."

"Anvil," Spangler whispered, as the muzzle pushed deeper under the chin, "I asked you, *who* is Klempf?"

"I don't know for sure. He was here when they sent me in. I think he's with R. S. H. A."

"And what did Klempf ask you about me?"

"Nothing in particular."

"What did you say about me without being asked?"

"That you didn't seem frightened. That nothing seemed to affect you. That's all I told him, except for what you bought and sold on the exchange."

"Why was that important?"

"I don't know, but he wanted to know what each man privately bought and sold on the exchange."

Spangler lowered the pistol slightly. "Anvil, now I want you to think very carefully. Where would you say my best chance of escape would be?"

"Why—why, *anywhere*. The guard detachments are down to almost nothing throughout the camp. Everyone is out looking for you."

"But if you had to pick one particular spot, where would it be?"

"The . . . the railroad yard, that would be best."

"Why?"

"They've taken more guards from there than anywhere else. There are only three to a train now—two on the ramp and one on the track side."

"How do you know?"

"I helped arrange the assignments."

"What about the yard sentries and the guard towers?"

"Only one guard tower is operating, and that's near the gate. It's easier than last night."

"Show me."

Spangler prodded Anvil forward with the Luger. They followed the shadows until they reached the death ditch. A train was almost finished unloading at the ramp under the few scattered blue lights. The rest of the yard lay in darkness. Spangler glanced toward the near spur. The two metal passenger cars could be distinguished in the distance. He searched the area. No guards could be seen.

"Now, precisely how would you go about it?" he asked Anvil.

"Wait for the train to get moving. Then head for the cars near the engine. The doors will be open. There aren't enough men left to seal them. Two more trains are waiting outside, so they must work quickly. The guard is near the end of the train."

"And does the blue light still go off in an air raid?"

"I imagine so, but you don't need to wait for that. You can make it as it is."

"But can both of us make it as it is?"

285

"Both?"

"You're going out with me, Anvil, comrade. You know what's beyond the gate, I don't. Now be a good lad and take off your clothes."

"Take off . . . my clothes?"

"This uniform is too large for me. After all, why should I be the one who's uncomfortable? Change."

They exchanged uniforms in the darkness. The Special Security uniform was also too large for Spangler, but a better fit then Kuprov's. Anvil's new uniform was too small.

"Is the fence electrified?" Spangler asked.

"Not during dimouts. You know that."

"Then let's go through."

They slid under the bottom wire. "Here, you carry this," said Spangler, and hoisted the knapsack filled with time bombs firmly onto Anvil's back.

"Why did you kill the young guard?" he asked, as they waited.

"Klempf's orders."

A whistle blew, signaling that the empty train was ready to move out.

"Eat dirt," Spangler ordered.

"Dirt?"

"Put dirt in your mouth and eat it."

Anvil hesitated. Spangler kicked him in the shin. Anvil dropped to one knee, scooped up a handful of earth, stared at it and began swallowing.

"Faster."

Spangler reached into the knapsack and set four of the time bombs at five-minute delay. The fifth he set for four minutes. He grabbed Anvil's right hand and squeezed. The fingers broke. The dirt-filled throat emitted only a low moan. Then he broke Anvil's other hand and pulled him to his feet. He reached up and cut the overhead wire. Sirens began to wail. The few blue ramp lights went off.

Spangler dragged Anvil down the fence, turned him around, took the four-minute time bomb from the knapsack on his back and placed it at the base of the concrete post holding the main electrical transfer box.

"Now you go across first," Spangler whispered into Anvil's ear. "I'll be right behind."

Anvil took a step forward, but Spangler pulled him back.

"I forgot something," he said, scooping up some dirt and rubbing it in Anvil's face. "And something else." He pulled out a piece of white cloth and tied it around Anvil's arm.

The secret policeman's eyes bulged as he violently shook his head. The train was beginning to move slowly up the track.

"You run toward those cars," Spangler said menacingly. "Run as you wanted *me* to run. Run, or I'll snap your neck in two. I'll snap it forward—*slowly.*"

Anvil stared at Spangler in terror, then dashed awkwardly forward. Spangler darted down the spur. He fell prone when he heard guards shouting in the darkness. He leveled his Luger, fired two shots and moved farther down the spur.

The shouting continued under the noise of the sirens. A rocket flare was suddenly released overhead. Steam shot from the train engine. The drive wheels locked as it screeched to a stop. The platform lights went on, but they were not blue lights—both ramp and siding blazed in the full glare of searchlights as the doors of every boxcar slid open, revealing SS guards with raised machine pistols. Anvil ran frantically, waving his crushed hands in desperation.

Spangler squeezed off two shots. Two SS fell from boxcar doorways. Others began firing in all directions. The ground patrols paused momentarily, then charged forward at Anvil. They had almost reached him when the first explosions went off. The yard plunged into darkness. A minute later the night reverberated with a second explosion, far more prolonged and powerful.

Spangler jumped to his feet and began running down the spur to the metal passenger car, crawled under it, came out the other side and tried the door. It pulled open. He climbed in.

58

SPANGLER STOLE forward between the walls of transformers, eased around the half-open corridor door, moved quietly through the cowled diaphragm and carefully pulled back the door of the second metal railroad car. The corridor was short and carpeted. Spangler walked to the end, slowly slid aside the metal panel and gazed in.

"What do you mean, nothing was left?" Klempf was shouting into the telephone. He was seated in a swivel chair before a control panel, with his back to Spangler. Banks of radio receivers and transmitters stretched along the wall to his left and right. The opposite wall was covered in thick velvet draperies. "Something must have been left of the face! The SS uniform isn't enough. Where's Anvil? How do we know whom we have unless we find him? Continue searching!"

Spangler leveled his Luger. "Tell them to connect the engine."

Klempf's back tensed, then relaxed somewhat. "Engine?" he asked without turning around.

"The engine waiting outside the gate. Tell them to connect it. Tell them that Anvil has just arrived—that the man out there is the one you wanted. Tell them your work is finished."

"Of course," Klempf agreed with a nod, and he picked up the

telephone. "Fergy, have them bring up the locomotive," he said quietly. "It's time for us to leave."

Something inaudible to Spangler emerged from the receiver. "No, Fergy," Klempf replied almost paternally, "our work is finished. Anvil just arrived, so you see we *did* get the right man after all. There's nothing more left here for us. Now do as I ask, Fergy. Call in the locomotive."

Klempf remained facing the control panel as Spangler crossed behind him and moved to the rear door of the compartment. "Who else is in this car?"

"No one to bother you."

"Where's the lock?" Spangler demanded as he inspected the door panel.

"This button here." Klempf pointed to the control panel in front of him. "It locks electrically. Everything is electrical. I designed it myself. Before the war I was a designer of railway equipment. My present position has limited those skills to this car and one other. The one you stand in is an electrical miracle; the other can boast only a steam bath and pornographic films. Shall I lock the door for you?"

"Slowly."

Klempf cautiously pressed a button. Spangler heard the click. He tried the panel. It was locked. On order, Klempf pressed a second button. The door at the opposite end of the compartment clicked shut.

"Now turn off some of the lights," Spangler told him, "but make sure I can still see you."

"Why don't I simply dim them?" Klempf suggested amicably. "I included rheostats in the lighting system. I can lower the lights enough for you to see outside and watch me without danger."

"Lower them."

Klempf carefully turned a wheel, and the lights reduced to a low glow.

"Would you like to handcuff me as well?" he asked Spangler. "Perhaps it would make you feel more at ease? There are handcuffs

289

in the desk to your right. I can still operate the board while wearing them."

Spangler hesitated, then opened the drawer, brought out the handcuffs and studied them.

"They're quite authentic," Klempf assured him, "and I'm no Houdini." He swiveled around toward Spangler and held out his wrists.

The manacles were snapped on and Spangler returned to the opposite wall, pulled back a section of the curtains and looked out. The outlines of helmeted guards could be seen throughout the dark yard, lit by occasional bursts of light from a flashgun.

"I assume it *is* Anvil's remains they are photographing out there?" Klempf asked.

"Assume whatever you like."

"Oh, I have no doubt it's Anvil. You should really thank me for letting you catch him."

"Letting me?"

"I *did* assign Anvil to watch the bunker. And we both know that Anvil isn't—wasn't very bright. I mean, it's hardly very bright to let someone kill you in your own trap, is it? Yes, you should thank me. I had a suspicion you were still in the area."

"And if I hadn't been?"

"Then you would undoubtedly have escaped from the camp already, and I would have been disappointed. When did you know the railway yard was set up as a trap? Was it when Anvil suggested it in his own inimitable fashion, or was it something else—like his not wearing an armband during the blackout?"

Spangler could see the track being cleared. A locomotive was backing toward them under the gate tower.

"And when did you decide that radio Cracow and Prague came from this car?" Klempf continued.

"Did they?" Spangler answered indifferently as he watched a yardman swing his lantern and wave the locomotive onto the spur.

"Oh, of course, you must never give yourself away," Klempf said. "But something must have told you the broadcasts were fakes. Was it when the first few could hardly be heard and we had to move this

290

car right into the camp to provide reception? Or a few little technical slip-ups, like Cracow knowing what was going on in Prague before Prague did?"

"Where are the Russians?" Spangler asked.

"Not yet in Poland. But doubtless it won't be long. Tell me, didn't the radio broadcasts fool you at all?"

"I'm sure they fooled everyone."

"Everyone isn't important. *You* are."

"Why?"

"Because the whole thing was set up just to identify you."

Spangler turned from the window and stared at him.

"Certainly you've been in enough camps to know that there have always been markets, but nothing like the Bourse has ever existed elsewhere. And it was an essential part of von Schleiben's idiotic idea. He put out the bait. He knew you'd be coming for either Jean-Claude or Tolan. That's why he sent them both to this camp seven weeks ago.

"The only problem was that he didn't know what you looked like. He knew nothing about you, except that you were inordinately strong and that you killed in a most specific way. That's why every likely suspect at Birkenau had to fight. If he fought exceptionally well or showed exceptional strength he was immediately made a cook and brought to the Bourse, where he could be watched.

"Every new prospect inherited the Bubel route for a time to see if he'd try to make contact with Jean-Claude. But Jean-Claude outsmarted all of us, didn't he?

"Inside the compound a new cook would always inherit a locker containing the elements to make a bomb—since they were certain you were an explosives expert. I almost caught you on that one, except that I couldn't imagine how you'd get the saltpeter to mix with the sugar. It must have come from that guard, eh?

"Most important, every new candidate was put in a position in which he had to commit murder, so that we could see his method—such as snapping someone's neck. Yes, this was the real test in von Schleiben's mind. Only when he saw you kill in that specific way would he be satisfied. That's why you are still alive. I have been certain of you for some time. I wanted to take you. He wouldn't."

"Do you expect me to believe that the entire air raid and escape scheme was mounted just to see how somebody killed somebody?"

"Oh, other important factors were involved. But you were always a part of them. You're a part of everything von Schleiben does these days. You have become his passion, his obsession, his own private white whale. You fascinate and terrify him. Why should that be? What is it about you that—"

The car lurched as the locomotive was coupled. The telephone rang. Klempf's manacled hands raised the receiver.

"Thank you, Fergy. It was a pleasure working with you as well. Thank all the men for their cooperation."

There was another brief answer.

"Yes, Fergy, the credit is all yours. It was your jurisdiction. I'll take care of it first thing tomorrow. Goodbye, Fergy, perhaps we'll work together again in the future—if there is one. Fergy, you may disconnect now."

Footsteps were heard on the side of the car, then on the roof and then on the side again. Spangler glanced behind the curtain and saw wires fall away.

A string of emergency lights went on beyond the ramp. The Totenkopf guards moved back and formed in columns. A squad began to seal the boxcars.

"Yes, you are von Schleiben's passion," Klempf continued as their train began to creak forward, "but I suspect that comes as no surprise. You see, von Schleiben must prove to himself that he's smarter than you, or should I say smarter than Spangler—though I'm certain you'll never admit to that name."

Spangler watched through the window. The rest of the ramp lights came on. The compounds beyond were also illuminated; the searchlights blazed as they had in the old days. The car began to gain speed.

"Yes, von Schleiben must always prove himself more clever than the next fellow," Klempf said. "He simply is not *original*. He is a copyist, a borrower. His genius lies in bending the ideas of others to his own perverse ends.

"Take the Bourse and the other exchanges at Birkenau. Of course they've been active for some time. The concept of setting up illegal markets within the compounds to use as listening posts on prisoner activities was mine. Von Schleiben let me organize and operate them, but then he added his own embellishments. It was von Schleiben's unoriginal mind which finally grasped that he could make millions of marks off them as well. Part of my function is to act as his collection agent."

The car slowed. They were passing the lines of corpses being lifted onto stretchers.

"With the Russians expected to invade Poland by the end of next month, von Schleiben began to get nervous. He decided that the Bourses and everybody connected with them had better be eliminated —to erase any link to him. So, when we determined there was a strong possibility that you were our man, von Schleiben decided to kill two birds with one stone. Had he been an original thinker, however, he might—"

The car jerked to a stop. Spangler saw lines of SS guards running down the track below his window.

"Why are we stopping?"

"I have no idea," Klempf answered with some concern.

"Find out."

"I can't from inside here. There's only a switch engine pulling us out. The telephone won't be connected until our own engine is put on. I suppose we must remain uninformed, unless you wish me to go outside and see what the trouble is?"

"Come here," Spangler ordered.

Klempf walked to the window. Spangler stepped behind him and pushed the pistol to the back of his neck. "We'll remain uninformed together," he said, pulling the curtains back slightly.

A solid wall of SS guards stood on the roadbed between the empty boxcars and Klempf's radio train. The Totenkopf men froze to attention and turned toward the boxcars. They moved forward.

"What are they up to?" Spangler demanded.

"That's how the searches used to be, before," Klempf replied in relief.

The SS searched in, under and above the transport before sealing the doors and waving the train out.

"Why aren't we going ahead of them?" Spangler asked as the boxcars started moving past.

"There are probably other trains waiting beyond the gate. They have to clear them off the track before we can get out."

Spangler watched closely from the soundproof compartment. The transport moved away and the ramp lay bare. Twice the number of guards and baggage Kommandos he had ever seen there now stood on the long platform. They made no attempt to hide their truncheons. Smoke billowed from the tall chimney of Crematorium Two beyond the ramp. Long columns of new arrivals could be seen waiting their turn at the adjoining chambers.

Minutes passed slowly. A column of SS guards finally marched down the far track before the incoming train. The boxcars rolled to a stop. SS guards stood atop each.

The floor lurched under Spangler's feet. The car began moving forward, the speed increased. The jounce of switching was faintly felt. Spangler studied the towers and the fences of the compounds as they continued through the yard. Patrols were three to four times stronger than before. Every guard tower was manned. Camp routine had returned to the schedule he had seen on Kuprov's chart.

The car rolled through the wooden archway of the gate tower and out into the dark countryside. A fence and a sentry flashed past. They had left the outer guard perimeter. Spangler was free of Birkenau.

59

SPANGLER STOOD at the window watching snowladen black firs flash by. The first traces of a headache began to return. He felt a slight spasm in his left arm. His breathing rate was starting to rise.

"Where are we headed?" he asked, closing the curtains.

"Our clearance is through Cracow and on to Budapest," Klempf replied. "I am expected in Budapest thirty-six hours after leaving Birkenau."

"Turn up the lights."

Klempf obeyed.

Spangler motioned with his Luger. "Let's take a look in back."

The first of the corridor's electrically controlled doors slid back. The galley was constructed of stainless steel. Cooking ranges were electric, as was the refrigerator. The larder was well stocked. An electric coffeepot and an American toaster rested on the counter.

Behind it was an opulent stateroom. The furniture, drapery and carpeting were in various shades of blue. The bureau and the desk were Louis XIV.

The last closed door slid open. Tolan lay struggling on the floor, his mouth gagged, his ankles tied behind his back to his wrists.

"What the hell is he doing here?" Spangler demanded.

"He's our mutual passport to safety."

"Free him!"

"Might I suggest waiting until you hear what I have for you?" Klempf asked politely. "After you've heard, you can do whatever you choose with him."

"Undo his feet," Spangler ordered.

"I am handcuffed," Klempf reminded him, raising his arms.

Spangler severed the rope binding Tolan's ankles to his wrists. He removed the leg binds and pulled Tolan to his feet. He started to untie the gag.

"Couldn't we wait for that? He's rather noisy, you know."

The gag came off.

"*Schwein! Scheiss!*" Tolan screamed, charging at Klempf with his hands still tied behind his back. "Double-crossing swine! Traitor! I'll kill you for this!"

"Shut up!" Spangler commanded, leveling his pistol.

"I *told* you," Klempf said. He led them back to the main compartment.

"You see," Klempf began, "this car was originally designed and built to monitor police and Wehrmacht communications. In a word, von Schleiben was spying on both the military and his own men."

Klempf reached up to a long shelf of phonograph records and brought down two disks. "When von Schleiben learned that Jean-Claude was in Hamburg, this car was moved nearby. In all modesty, the equipment you see before you is the most sophisticated in the world—so we had little trouble pinpointing his sources of radio communication and silencing them.

"We then moved Tolan into the Hamburg area in such a way that even a blind man couldn't miss him. As we had hoped, Jean-Claude spotted him and followed him east to Poland. We made no attempt to stop him from sending out messages by other means—in fact, we counted on it to lure a certain Mr. Spangler out of hiding. We destroyed the radios only to keep him from *receiving* orders which might have recalled him. In fact, once Jean-Claude arrived in the Auschwitz-Birkenau area, we gave him a full week of freedom to make certain he informed the West as to his whereabouts.

"It was during this week of waiting," Klempf went on, "that

something most unusual came across these receivers." He placed the first record on the turntable and flicked the switch.

Spike Jones could be heard singing "In the Fuehrer's Face!" The song ended and the click of a wireless key boomed out over the loudspeaker. The clicking faded into background as a voice spoke out in German.

"Good evening, Mr. and Mrs. Freedom-Loving Germany and all the ships at sea! This is your G. P. G.-of-the-Air Reporter. Let's go to press.

"*Flash:* Father Coughlin has been named special adviser to German Provisional Government's Human Affairs Section.

"*Flash:* Representatives from eighteen leading United States Jewish organizations return from three-week tour of Germany. All have denied rumors of Jewish persecution within the Reich as flagrant and malicious Russian lies. The tour chairman, Rabbi Samuel Cahn of Moline, Illinois, stated that German Jewry has never had it so good.

"*Flash:* Students of eleven U. S. universities have staged massive rallies to protest British bombing of German cities.

"*Flash:* U. S. blood donations for German soldiers have . . ." The voice faded to static and Klempf switched it off.

"Curious, isn't it?" Klempf reflected. "I wonder in which concentration camp Rabbi Cahn found his people 'having it so good'? Anyway, this was my first indication that something slightly insane was afoot. I checked with other listening posts to see if they had run into similar broadcasts. Most had not, but a few, in a small northern sector, reported jamming or faint overplay.

"Once Jean-Claude was taken, I moved the car up north to try to learn more about Father Coughlin's appointment. We quickly determined that these broadcasts were beamed exclusively along a corridor from the Baltic. From all evidence they were test transmissions being relayed by ship. Birkenau was in the direct path for reception.

"Over the next ten days, we picked up twenty or thirty programs ranging from American music and soap operas translated into German to household and cooking advice. But mostly they were newscasts. Outrageous and erroneous newscasts—but they gave me the idea for radio Cracow and Prague. After all, if someone else could create news fantasies, why not I?

"I had already anticipated von Schleiben's decision to destroy the exchanges at Birkenau and elsewhere when I suggested the radiocast experiment to him. Thus the premature Russian invasion of Poland was born."

"What has Tolan to do with all this?" Spangler demanded.

"Everything. He is a witness. He has always been von Schleiben's inside man. He was a prisoner for his own protection; it was easier for von Schleiben to keep him alive inside a camp than on the outside. Tolan and von Schleiben are close friends. They have mutual proclivities. It was only natural for Tolan to become von Schleiben's private agent—as well as a few other things—within the camp. Now times have changed radically, and unfortunately for Tolan he possesses too many details about von Schleiben's activities to suit the *Obergruppenfuehrer*.

"But so do you," Klempf said, smiling at Spangler. "You must realize that we three are the last living persons who know the specific nature of von Schleiben's link to concentration camps above and beyond his official functions. As head of the Council for Extreme Security, of which camps are only a minor category, von Schleiben can always plead ignorance of actual operations—but only if we are out of the way.

"Is it so difficult to understand the implications? Von Schleiben was beginning to fill the Bourse and other exchanges with friend and foe alike. Vassili, for instance, was a high Russian espionage officer by the name of Kuprov, an old adversary—a man who could connect him with many things better forgotten.

"At first I thought von Schleiben was simply doing away with the exchanges as a practical safeguard, as well as setting a trap for you, but when I saw the list for extermination the writing was large on the wall. He was getting rid of everyone with the slightest knowledge of his actitivities. Under these circumstances, how long could I expect to last? You, Tolan—how long do you think *you* would survive?"

Tolan shrugged. "If our places were changed, von Schleiben would already be dead."

"Exactly. So you see my predicament," Klempf continued. "I've known for some weeks that I must leave Germany to stay alive. But where can I go? In a neutral country von Schleiben's agents could reach me. In an Allied country von Schleiben could easily leak my Auschwitz-Birkenau record to the authorities. Would the Allies spare me?

"The solution to the problem came quite unexpectedly," Klempf said, placing the second record on the phonograph. The clicking telegraph key filled the loudspeakers.

"Good evening, Mr. and Mrs. Freedom-Loving Germany and all the ships at sea! Let's go to press!

"*Flash:* A secret meeting of delegates to the German Provisional Government has elected Friedrich Tolan Vice-Chancellor. Tolan is now believed to be leaving his underground activities in Germany to accept the position and join Martin Vetter, Konrad Lottman and Oswald Nebel at G. P. G. secret headquarters to begin formulating . . ."

Klempf turned down the volume as Tolan's eyes widened in disbelief.

"So there you have it: the solution to our mutual predicament," Klempf said.

He turned to Spangler. "They sent you into Birkenau to bring out Tolan for this government in exile of theirs—and I have made sure that you will succeed. Had you come to the gas chamber as instructed, you'd have been taken aside like Tolan and brought right to this car. Since you insisted on running your own course tonight and disappearing, you gave me some trouble. But I did the logical thing: I set the clues—and let you find *me*. You came very close to destroying our chances of survival with your little game.

"Nonetheless, you *are* here. We are all here. I will provide the transportation out of the Reich. For this favor you will guarantee me asylum, as well as immunity from all postwar indictments for war crimes. You see how simple it is?"

"Simple, except for one minor fact," Spangler replied. "I'm not the man you think I am. I didn't come to Birkenau to free anyone. I was arrested and sent there."

"Be whoever you want to be," Klempf countered calmly, "I will get us out of Europe. If luck is with me, you will take it from there. What other choice do I have? Now will you please unlock my handcuffs?"

The train skirted Budapest as Klempf began destroying the phonograph records. Half an hour later it pulled to a stop at a deserted rural depot.

Klempf led Spangler and the handcuffed Tolan to a parked car as the train pulled out. They drove southwest until dusk. Hot meals were waiting at a farmhouse. A second automobile was ready in the barn. In the luggage compartment were business suits and credentials.

60

SPANGLER FELT the gout beginning to throb in his right foot; the headache was becoming unbearable. He clenched his teeth and watched the road through the darkness. They had started the ascent into the Alps. Klempf was driving. Tolan sat manacled in the rear seat.

Another farm provided prearranged food and lodging. All three men slept in the same room. They were up before dawn.

Klempf moved in behind the steering wheel. Tolan was about to duck into the rear door. Suddenly he froze.

"Look!" he shouted to Spangler, gesturing with his bound wrists, "Look on the roof!"

Spangler moved forward and inspected the top of the car. A thick cross of grease was evident.

"They've been following us by airplane," Tolan shouted. "It's been a trap all along!"

Klempf hurried out and stared numbly at the roof. "I don't know where it came from," he stammered.

"It wasn't there when we got out last night," Tolan insisted. "I looked. It wasn't there."

"Maybe someone in the house marked it," Klempf said nervously.

"Who brought us here?" Tolan demanded. "And who was the

only man alone at the car last night? We were inside. You came out for cigarettes, remember? You came out alone."

"I didn't put it there."

"He lies!" Tolan said, spinning toward Spangler. "He almost had me convinced on the train, but now I see what it is."

"Don't listen to him," Klempf implored.

"How stupid I was!" Tolan laughed. "Von Schleiben could never kill Klempf—he'd be lost without him. Klempf has always done the thinking. Klempf's ideas have made von Schleiben successful. Kill him!" he told Spangler.

"You must listen to me," Klempf said, coming around to Spangler. "I know nothing of this. You must take my word."

"Your word?" Tolan scoffed. "The word of a lying butcher?"

"Is it any worse than that of the court pornographer?" Klempf shot back. "The practiced degenerate who trains young girls with animals? Who sent his own daughter into a whorehouse and then shared her with Heydrich and von Schleiben? And when that wasn't enough he used her as a star in his famous movies!"

"It wasn't I who thought of sending Jean-Claude to the Bubel," Tolan replied calmly.

Klempf blanched. "You cannot listen to him," he said, grabbing Spangler's arm. "Do you know who this man is? He's worse than we are. He's worse than any camp guard. He volunteered to spy on his fellow prisoners. He *enjoys* it! He has killed and tortured more inmates than the worst of the green-triangles. He volunteered to make the movies and train the girls. Von Schleiben wanted to put him in a prison where he'd be safer from his old political enemies—but Tolan refused. He loves the brutality of the camps."

"Who put the cross on the car?" Spangler asked, staring at Klempf.

"I didn't, I swear I didn't!"

"Then how did it get there?"

"I—I—"

Spangler motioned with his Luger. "Get going."

"No," Klempf cried, "you must believe me—"

"Start walking."

302

Tolan watched Spangler prod Klempf out into the orchard. The pair vanished below a rise. Several minutes later Spangler returned alone, holding a key. He unlocked Tolan's handcuffs, turned and slipped into the car and started the engine.

"You're not going to leave me here?" Tolan shouted into the window.

"You'll find your way out all right."

"You can't leave me!"

"Why not?"

"Because you need me."

"You're mistaken."

"But you came into the camp to get me."

"No I didn't."

Tolan paled.

Spangler shifted gears and started forward.

"Wait!" Tolan shouted, running after the slowly moving car.

Spangler stepped on the brake and waited.

"All right, I'll tell you," Tolan called, catching up. "It was a trap."

"What was a trap?"

"The escape. The entire escape. I didn't have to be bound or gagged. Klempf and I planned it that way."

"Why?"

"To find out who you were. We thought you'd gain confidence in one or the other of us—that you'd say who you were or where you wanted to go. That was what von Schleiben wanted. He wanted positive identification."

"Then why did you betray Klempf?"

"That was also planned. If you hadn't revealed who you were by the time we arrived here, one of the farmers was to mark the car without Klempf's knowledge, then I was to accuse him of lying to us."

"So I would break his neck?"

"Yes. This place is partially surrounded. They'll wait until we leave, then one of the farmers will check the body. He'll notify the SS up ahead. Then they'll take you. But we can get out of here, avoid them. Turn around and go back the way we came. No one's back there. I'll show you how to get out."

"What makes you change your mind now? Why have you decided to go against von Schleiben?"

"I didn't know what was involved. I hadn't heard those records— no one ever told me about them. I didn't know about the German Provisional Government."

"What difference does that make?"

"I must be part of it."

"Why?"

"Look, my friend, everything Klempf accused me of is true. There is even more that makes less pleasant listening. I admit everything. I deny nothing. I apologize to no one. I am who I am. Von Schleiben kept me alive for his own reasons. For that I am thankful—but there my obligation ends.

"We—the storm troopers—*created* the Reich! Without us it never would have been. And what was our reward? We were murdered, tortured and humiliated, dispersed.

"Himmler and Goering robbed me of my rightful position in Germany. Hitler allowed it to happen. Now I can reclaim that which was mine. I can take that place that was denied me."

"It sounds as if you want to take over the exile government rather than be part of it."

"Who is better qualified? I heard those names: Vetter, Nebel, Zahn. Do you know what they are? Runts. They are nothing to Germany and they mean nothing to Germany. It is I who have a following, the only following that exists in Germany today. There are two and a half million former storm troopers who have not forgotten what was done to them. They will rally to me when the time is right. Yes, that is why I will head the government in exile. That is why they need me so desperately. That is why they sent you for me."

Spangler began to laugh. "Get in," he finally said.

"Then you will take me to them?"

"Why the hell not? You suit one another."

61

VON SCHLEIBEN and his provost moved as quietly as they could down the slope of the mist-choked woods. Tolan was waiting with an armload of logs.

"Where in the name of God have you been?" he whispered to the general.

"Trying to locate you. You didn't follow the agreed route."

"I couldn't. He insisted on driving. We've been riding around in circles. Go down there and take him."

"Has he said who he is?"

"Of course. He's told me everything. Go take him."

"Everything?" von Schleiben questioned. "Why would he tell you everything?"

"Because he trusts me. Because he wants to get it off his chest. He wanted someone to know all the details. Why talk about it now? Don't waste time."

"What do you mean by everything?"

"He admits to being Spangler," Tolan said impatiently. "He told me how it all began—when he and someone named Tramont went to free three priests Gestapo had arrested in France. He claims the reason for all the aliases was because they had originally expected more people to join them—no one did—"

305

"And the murders?" von Schleiben asked quietly. "What did he have to say about the murders?"

"He won't mention them, but what difference does it make? He killed Klempf, so you have what you need."

"He didn't kill Klempf. He only knocked him unconscious."

"Look, I am telling you that we have Erik Spangler down in that cabin."

"And I am telling you we can't be certain until he confesses to the murders—until he describes each one."

"He can do his describing after he's captured. Take him now."

"We can't. The troops aren't here yet."

"How long will they be?"

"Another two to three hours."

"We'll be gone by then. He drives like a madman. If he gets away now and heads further into the mountains you may lose him for good."

Von Schleiben's cheeks puffed out as he thought. "I suppose it is all up to you," he said, pulling his pistol from the holster and handing it to Tolan.

"I'm not going back down there. He's insane. He trembles and shakes. He laughs and cries for no reason at all. I've done what I've said I will do and that's it."

"But what other choice do we have under the circumstances? I can't walk through the snow without his hearing me. If you can delay him until the troops arrive we have no worries. If you can somehow capture him, fire twice. If you find you must kill him, fire three times after the first shot."

"That wasn't our agreement."

"Here," von Schleiben said, holding out a packet of cigarettes, "these will calm your nerves."

Tolan stooped down and gathered up his logs.

"By the way," asked von Schleiben, "did he mention me?"

"Several times."

"And what did he have to say?"

"It was always the same. He thinks you're stupid and predictable," Tolan said descending down the misty path.

306

Von Schleiben flushed and started back through the hillside woods with his provost.

"Are the troops deployed?" he barked at the SS major hurrying to meet them.

"We're having difficulties, Obergruppenfuehrer. This is very difficult terrain. And with the fog and ice it's almost impossible to—"

"Nothing is impossible, Standartenfuehrer."

"But, Obergruppenfuehrer, there's sheer rock face around us and to—"

"Deploy your men and have them move on the cabin now."

The major saluted and hurried off through the woods.

"But aren't we going to see if Tolan can capture him first?" the provost asked as they continued climbing.

"Tolan will be dead in a matter of minutes."

The provost stared at him.

"The trouble with you and the others, my dear Kurt," said von Schleiben, "is that you have never comprehended men like Spangler. These people expect a never-ending game to be played. They anticipate a series of final gambits. When you have finally convinced them that no more maneuvers can be made, they relax. That time has now come."

"I don't understand."

"Spangler has known from the beginning that we were trying to take him. He watched and waited to see how we would go about it. He expected Klempf to lead him into a trap, and now he expects the same of Tolan. That is why he has been circling about. He knew we were out here somewhere, and he wanted to lead us a chase. He also wanted to give Tolan time to betray himself—and now Tolan will do so."

"How?"

"The gun and the cigarettes I gave him. Don't you think Spangler will notice one or the other? He probably already has. Tolan is most likely dead—with a broken neck. So move the troops in on the cabin and then we'll—"

A gunshot was heard. Three others followed.

Von Schleiben stopped in disbelief. "The idiot!" he shouted. Then he spun around and ran down the hillside into the bank of slowly drifting fog.

The provost moved down the hill after him and stopped at the edge of the clearing. He waited several minutes before shouting to von Schleiben. Only the echo replied. He shouted again. Still von Schleiben did not answer. He started to go forward, then thought better of it. He glanced around. Alpine troops were moving gingerly through the mist. He called for them to hurry.

The cabin was finally surrounded. The provost gathered courage, dashed to the door and burst through.

Spangler and Tolan were gone. Von Schleiben's body lay spread on the table, his arms folded on his chest. His decapitated head rested on the mantelpiece.

62

PROPELLER IDLING, the plane stood in the darkness of a pasture.

"You're a fool," Tolan shouted down from the cabin door.

"My own fool," Spangler agreed, standing on the ground, his Luger trained on Tolan.

"Get in here," the German commanded. "You're wasting time."

"You'll be meeting a man named Julian," Spangler told him. "Relay a message. Tell Julian the books are closed. Tell him I am out of it once and for all. Tell him that you and he will understand each other perfectly. And one last thing: Tell him I'm sending you across for only one reason—to let him know exactly what I think of him and all the others like him. Now get inside and close that door, or I'll put a bullet where it really belongs."

Spangler watched the plane bounce down the field, lift off and soar into the low-hanging overcast. He returned to the car and started driving north—nowhere in particular, just north.

By morning the headache was unendurable, the shoulder throbbing convulsively, the hand trembling so that he could hardly hold the wheel. He stopped at the nearest town.

Spangler sat at the restaurant table sipping ersatz coffee and munching a hard roll. He stared numbly out the window at the bomb-torn buildings. Laughter was heard. A group of smocked, laughing children skipped along the rubbled street on their way to school. He followed them with his eyes, paid his check and returned to the car.

He drove northwest through the night. Dawn was breaking as he descended the stone steps. He followed the narrow cobblestoned street to the bakery. The lead-paned windows had been boarded over. There was no smell of fresh bread from behind. He continued on to the square and waited beside the copper statue of Goethe in its center. He watched the uniformed woman pass in front of the single-spired medieval church and enter Forst's columned post office.

"No receipt?" the cherubic postmistress questioned in good spirit.

"I lost it in the east," Spangler replied from the other side of the counter. "At Stalingrad."

"You were at Stalingrad? You were at Stalingrad and you returned?"

"Not many of us did. And those lucky few are not good for too much," Spangler said, slapping a drooped shoulder with a weak hand.

"What did you say the name was on the package?" the woman asked reverently.

"Henri. Ludwig Henri. He was with us at Stalingrad. He was not as lucky as I. I promised to pick up the package and take it to his mother. She used to live near Dobern. Now she has moved to Bitterfeld. She doesn't know about Ludwig yet."

"Of course," the woman said sadly and moved quickly through a side door.

She returned with a dusty suitcase and handed it across without registration.

Spangler's route shifted east. The pain and trembling were worse than ever. Familiar notices began appearing on walls of villages he passed through. He finally stopped to read one, shifted directions and drove faster.

Spangler sat on the bluffside watching the SS marshal civilians toward the railway depot in the evening rain. A new column was converging on the sixteen windowless boxcars from the west. He opened the suitcase and put on the worn suit with the yellow star sewn to its front.

310

Another line of men, women and children appeared at the bend and began passing directly below him. Spangler wrapped a prayer shawl around his shoulders. With a sigh of deliverance he started down to join them.

EPILOGUE

Germany, 1949

A THUNDER of cheers interrupted the speech. Flags and placards waved frantically over the sea of heads jamming the square. Banners hoisted higher as the chant again reverberated.

"Tow-lahn! Tow-lahn! Towlahn!"

Short brassy flourishes blasted from the four bands to call them to order.

"Tow-lahn! Tow-lahn! Tow-lahn!" the crowd screamed.

Special envoy Julian watched through the balcony doors of his hotel suite as Friedrich Tolan stood smiling on the bandstand and finally raised his hands in a bid for quiet.

"Tow-lahn! Tow-lahn! Tow-lahn! Tow-lahn!"

Julian turned back into the room. "What was it you were saying, Mr. Ambassador?" he asked the American ambassador who stood beside him, watching.

"I wasn't saying, Julian, I was asking," the ambassador replied firmly. "I was asking you for the truth."

"The truth about what, Mr. Ambassador?"

"Dammit, Julian, I didn't fly over here to play word games. I want Tolan out of this election. He must withdraw. That can happen only if the truth about him is finally revealed."

"Tow-lahn! Tow-lahn! Tow-lahn! Tow-lahn!"

"Mr. Ambassador, the truth has been revealed. Congress has heard

315

the findings of every denazification organization our country possesses. They have heard my testimony and those of others. Mr. Ambassador, the government has already *passed* him."

"The denazification committee's main source of information was *you!* You were everyone's main source of information!"

"Tow-lahn! Tow-lahn! Tow-lahn!"

"I have told you all I know, Mr. Ambassador."

"Listen, Julian, you realize the implications perfectly well if our government tacitly endorses a man who was part of a conspiracy."

"What conspiracy, Mr. Ambassador?"

"G. P. G."

"G. P. G. was a propaganda operation."

"Tow-lahn! Tow-lahn! Tow-lahn! Tow-lahn! Tow-lahn!"

The ambassador slammed shut the balcony doors. "Do not antagonize me, Julian. I am not a man to be antagonized or trifled with. You and your untouchable organization may intimidate or fool others, but not me. I know the truth. It was you and I who formulated G. P. G., who steered its early course—or have you conveniently forgotten our phone conversations—*Oop?*"

"That was quite some time ago, Mr. Ambassador. Each of us has gone his own way since. Each of us has been busy with his own endeavors. As best I can recall, G. P. G. was simply a propaganda operation."

"It was an illicit government, dammit. And you know better than anyone that Friedrich Tolan never escaped from a camp—you sent for him."

"Where is your proof, Mr. Ambassador?"

"Hidden behind the steel doors of National Security. Under the lids of sealed coffins you filled. In the ashes of burned files . . . but primarily in your own memory."

"My memory, and all the documentation *available,* can only provide what our government already knows: Friedrich Tolan is an extraordinary patriot; he was arrested and imprisoned by the Nazis; he endured incalculable suffering at many concentration camps; he made a spectacular escape from Birkenau on—"

316

"With the aid of one Erik Spangler," the ambassador said firmly. "Erik Spangler—one of your agents."

"Spangler did once operate for me, but he was killed almost two months before Tolan made his heroic escape from Birkenau. I have his death certificate and inquest findings."

"And whatever became of Colonel Lamar B. Kittermaster?"

"Lost in action. On a pre-invasion raid near Calais, I believe. Look it up in the Army records."

"Lies. All bold-faced lies and you know it."

"Then produce one shred of evidence to disprove anything I have said." Julian rounded the couch and turned on the television. "You know something, Mr. Ambassador? You sound very much in tune with propaganda campaigns of certain of Germany's more unfriendly neighbors."

The ambassador pointed toward the window. "That monster out there may damn well win this election—and mainly because of you!"

"I should hope so, sir. I have worked exceedingly hard on his campaign. But if he does lose, there's always next time, isn't there?"

Tolan's face dominated the television screen. ". . . but, alas," he was saying sanctimoniously, "those most responsible for my being here before you today are no longer among us. In memory of their selfless devotion, in the name of their mortal suffering and sacrifice, I shall march forward and bring liberty and justice for all . . ."

The door slammed.

Julian stood for a moment in the empty room, then stepped to the balcony doors and threw them open.

"Tow-lahn! Tow-lahn! Tow-lahn! Tow-lahn! Tow-lahn!"

317